All four of them raised their glasses in a Christmas toast and drank.

The cup was heavy with aromatic fruit juices. It had a wonderful flavor and she looked across at Bruce to congratulate him. Then she felt the words clog the roof of her mouth as she saw the Australian's glass fall to the floor and his face work as though he had been seized by some tremendous force. His right hand, the hand that had held the glass, reached toward his heart, beneath the bright red jacket he was wearing. The distress on his face increased, he was gasping for air, his eyes looking wildly about as his huge figure staggered and then fell to the floor.

Darina was the first to reach his side. She could swear he saw her, that he was trying to say something, but nothing intelligible emerged.

★

"...this epicurean mystery is a sprightly offering, given flavor and dash by its culinary complement."

—*Publishers Weekly*

DEATH
AT THE TABLE

JANET LAURENCE

W🌐RLDWIDE®

TORONTO • NEW YORK • LONDON
AMSTERDAM • PARIS • SYDNEY • HAMBURG
STOCKHOLM • ATHENS • TOKYO • MILAN
MADRID • WARSAW • BUDAPEST • AUCKLAND

If you purchased this book without a cover you should be aware that this book is stolen property. It was reported as "unsold and destroyed" to the publisher, and neither the author nor the publisher has received any payment for this "stripped book."

In memory of Justin

DEATH AT THE TABLE

A Worldwide Mystery/July 1999

First published by St. Martin's Press, Incorporated.

ISBN 0-373-26316-3

Copyright © 1993 by Janet Laurence.
All rights reserved. No part of this book may be reproduced or transmitted in any form or by any means, electronic or mechanical, including photocopying, recording or by any information storage and retrieval system, without permission in writing from the publisher. For information, contact: St. Martin's Press, Incorporated, 175 Fifth Avenue, New York, NY 10010-7848 U.S.A.

All characters in this book are fictitious, and any resemblance to actual persons, living or dead, is purely coincidental.

® and TM are trademarks of Harlequin Enterprises Limited. Trademarks indicated with ® are registered in the United States Patent and Trademark Office, the Canadian Trade Marks Office and in other countries.

Visit us at www.worldwidemystery.com

Printed in U.S.A.

Acknowledgments

I would like to give many thanks to Vicky Loble for providing me with details of the perfect murder weapon and to Dr Audrey Dunlop and Dr James Wright for help on medical details. I am most grateful to Peter Bazalgette and the team of *Food and Drink* for allowing me to attend a recording session and want to assure all readers that the characters and events in the following pages bear absolutely no resemblance at all to any of the personnel or their excellent programme. My sister, Ingrid Duffell, provided much valuable information about the making of television programmes and a splendid lunch with Della and David Robson and guests Helen Thomson and John Davies in the South of France yielded several useful wine details but any errors or misunderstandings are my fault. I also want to thank, as always, my husband for his patience and help. Without him I would never manage to complete a book. None of the characters or events in this book bear any resemblance to any actual event or person except by coincidence.

ONE

'DARINA going on television? That will be the death of your relationship!'

'Ma! How can you say that? It's terrific news! The sales of her books will soar.'

'Well, if that's all you're both worried about, there's nothing more to say.'

Joyce Pigram pointedly turned her attention to the chicken on her plate and started jabbing at the spiced flesh with an angry knife.

Darina Lisle sighed. Inviting her prospective parents-in-law to Sunday lunch had seemed such a good way to tell them she had broken into the television world. She'd thought they would be pleased. The opportunities, William was right, were dazzling. Appearing weekly, even if it wasn't on one of the commercial channels, was going to mean greatly increased book sales and publishers anxious for her to write more, if, that is, she came over successfully. Failure, on the other hand—but she wasn't even going to think about failure.

Joyce did have a point, though; at the moment book sales were the least of her worries. Darina was not at all sure that she wanted to get involved in the hothouse, uncertain world of television.

William Pigram, her fiancé, gave her a reassuring smile. 'I thought you would be as thrilled as I am, Ma. Becoming part of a regular television show means Darina's career is really taking off.'

'It's a most unhealthy atmosphere, quite divorced from reality. You only have to read the newspapers to know what goes on behind the scenes. And what egocentrics! John, do you remember that television producer who had a weekend cottage near us one time who only had two topics of conversation, himself and his programmes?'

Her husband leant across the table and patted her hand. 'He was probably an exception, dear.'

Joyce ignored him. 'And won't it mean Darina spending most of her time in London? While William's working down here in Somerset? You're due to get married in three months, what's going to happen then?'

'The show finishes recording in March, just before the wedding,' Darina said gently. 'I shall have to spend three or four nights a week in London until then but we shall be together at the weekends and William seems to be so busy since he was promoted to inspector he won't have time to miss me.' She hoped that didn't sound aggrieved, she hadn't meant it to. She gave her fiancé a warm smile.

The trouble, of course, was that Darina's prospective mother-in-law didn't think her detective son should have a career wife. Not even one whose profession was cooking. High-flying CID officers should be cosseted and supported in every possible way, not expected to help with household chores. Joyce had expressed her views on this subject before and at that stage Darina had only been involved in writing articles and books. The news that she had been asked to form one of the regular team of presenters on a television food show had been greeted first with shock then outrage.

'Anyway, nobody watches that show,' Joyce continued. 'It's too pretentious for words; a chef you can't understand cooking dishes you don't want to eat and guests who seem determined to make the viewer feel stupid. And if you bought the wines they recommend, you could never afford to eat anyway.'

Table for Four took a different food or drink theme each week, explored its relationship to cookery and wine via two regular experts and invited a suitable guest for a discussion with the third presenter. Each programme started and ended with all four seated around the eponymous table.

'Darina says she's been brought in to make the cookery parts more accessible, isn't that it, darling?' William said.

Food had to be a safer topic of conversation and Darina grabbed at it. 'The chicken you're eating today is one of the dishes I demonstrated at my audition. Very simple, it's just been marinaded in cardamom, coriander and cumin with olive oil, honey and sherry vinegar, but I think the flavour's very good. Anyone like any more?'

'It's not roast beef but I'll eat it any day!' John Pigram passed over his plate for a second helping. 'With food like this I'd say you're going to be a roaring success. You and that Milly girl who does the wine will make the programme really worth watching.'

'I'm afraid she's gone,' Darina said apologetically.

'No! Why?'

Darina shrugged her shoulders. 'I only know they've dropped her as well as the chef.'

'What about the third presenter, Mark somebody or other? Is he going to stay?'

'I quite like him,' Joyce said unexpectedly. 'He's got a nice smile.'

'Mark Taylor, you mean? I don't know. Neil Cantlow, the executive producer, he's the brains behind the programme, just said they were giving the show a new look and thought I could help.'

'I knew that programme wouldn't work,' Joyce said in satisfaction. 'And I don't suppose tinkering about with the presenters is going to make much difference. I shouldn't think you will be appearing for very long,' she said cheerfully to Darina. 'I expect the whole show will vanish quite soon.'

Darina suddenly lost her reservations about entering the television world. 'I sincerely hope not. Anyway, whether short or long, I think my new career is going to be launched in style; I'm to appear with the new chap they've got to do the wine on the Mike Darcy show on Monday week.'

'Really?' Joyce Pigram's voice was suddenly respectful. 'I always watch that.'

NEIL CANTLOW had chosen an Australian wine expert with a vineyard of his own to join the *Table* team of regular presenters. Darina first met Bruce Bennett the following Sunday. Neil had called a production meeting at his Putney house, apologizing to everyone for ruining their Sunday but reminding them how important it was to get down to re-organizing this second series that had gone so badly off beam. It was Neil who had originally conceived the idea of the series and it was his company that was producing it, but it was Bruce who had taken charge as soon as Darina arrived.

'So this is the sheila who's joining the show?' He'd looked Darina up and down in a way that made her feel like a mongrel trying to muscle into a pedigree show.

The Australian was a big man with hazel eyes that glowed like a tiger's but Darina herself was almost six foot tall and heels meant she didn't have to look up to meet his gaze. 'Should I wait for your verdict before I say I'm pleased to meet you?'

The pock-marked face with its broad bones broke into a pleased grin. 'I like 'em feisty,' he said to Neil.

The executive producer looked worried. Neil Cantlow was a head shorter than either of them, a round, bouncy, teddy bear of a man with a well-lived-in face he was always pulling at, dragging the open-pored skin this way and that as though wishing he could change its shape.

'Now, I hope you two are going to be great friends,' he said heartily, twisting hard at an earlobe.

'I'm sure we'll get on fine. Once Darina gives up wearing that drooby gear.'

Darina glanced down at her tailored grey skirt and jacket. She hadn't known what the rig of the day would be, suspected extreme casualness, was too nervous for jeans and a sweat shirt, so had settled for something she felt comfortable in. A mistake, obviously.

'The designer's working on ideas for Darina's wardrobe,' Neil said hastily.

Darina had spent every moment since she'd heard she was to be part of the show practising effective ways of putting over the food she was to demonstrate. That was what she thought was important, not her appearance. Surely all that mattered was that she should look neat and tidy? Television's constant concern with what seemed to her peripheral matters was mysterious and disconcerting.

'Didn't John Franks wear a chef's jacket?' she asked tentatively, thinking its combination of professional authority and anonymity would suit her fine.

The previous cookery presenter of *Table for Four* had been known for complicated recipes executed with rapid professionalism and a mind-blowing sleight of hand that reduced advanced techniques to a play school activity, his secrets unrevealed by a series of brief explanatory statements delivered in thick Yorkshire.

'Forget chef's jackets,' ordered Bruce. 'You need style! Those clothes are as effective as a screen door on a submarine. You suffer from the same fault I used to, a refusal to stand out from the landscape.' Darina took a look at the vivid red and orange patterned sweat shirt topping the designer jeans and cream loafers he wore and found it impossible to accept a vision of a quietly dressed Bruce Bennett. 'When you're the size we are,' he continued, 'you have to face the fact you can't merge into the background, so you might as well make your mark.' He stood surveying her for a long moment. 'Let's see how much hair you've got there.' A large hand reached out and flicked at her french pleat, then swiftly plucked out anchoring pins like a yachtsman releasing a sail.

Darina gave a squawk of protest that went unheeded as straight cream-coloured hair fell down past her shoulders. 'That's more like it! Get that fixed by someone who knows what they're doing, choose you some clothes that are a little less crook and we could be in business! What do you say, cobber?'

Neil Cantlow gave an exaggerated sigh. 'Bruce, what is left for me to say?'

Bruce threw himself into a chair. 'Now, mate, don't be like that, I'm not taking over as producer, it's just that I have a bit of an eye when it comes to the sheilas.'

'I'll say!' Neil spoke from the heart, his expression grim.

'You're not cutting my hair,' Darina broke in on the male camaraderie bit. 'My fiancé would have a fit.'

As she had known it would, that brought Bruce's head up. 'Fiancé, is it?' He ran a considering eye once again over her figure. 'Can't have the poor bod upset now, can we? You leave it all to little Bruce, darling, and he'll be as happy as—'

'Just so long as Darina looks good for the chat show tomorrow evening,' broke in Neil hurriedly and he took them both through to his garden room where the rest of the production team were waiting to start the meeting.

NEIL HAD FINALLY managed to impose his authority over the meeting but Bruce insisted on taking charge of his fellow presenter's appearance the following day.

First stop was a top London hairdresser. Three hours later Darina looked at the tumbling mass of her hair and hardly recognized herself. This was a sexpot, not a sensible cook.

Bruce collected her and gave a satisfied grin. 'Little beauty, ain't she?'

'Hardly little,' murmured the stylist, dwarfed by Darina's generous form.

'Now for some clothes.'

He hustled her into a taxi then gathered up a handful of the waving hair and buried his nose in it. 'Fair dinkum, that is! Smells as great as grape flowers in spring. Ever stood in a vineyard in flower? Drinking in the aroma? I tell you, nothing like it.' He dropped the hair and sat back against the seat, watching Darina struggle to fasten her safety belt.

'Bother with those things, do you?'

'It's the law, you have to wear them these days.'

'Great little doer of what should be done, aren't you? We'll have to break you of that.'

Darina looked at him for a moment and thought of the astute comments he had made during the production meeting the day before. 'You're a sham, Bruce, you know that?'

For a moment he looked genuinely startled. 'A sham, *moi?*'

'It's all an act, the rude, rough Aussie who doesn't know how to behave, has no education,' she said severely, beginning to enjoy herself. 'I bet you've been to university, speak perfect French and German and can keep your end up in the most intellectual of company.'

'You've been checking me out,' he said sorrowfully.

'I do have a good library of wine and food cuttings,' she acknowledged. 'I had a very interesting time with several on you when I got back last night.'

'I'm touched.'

'Degree in chemistry from Melbourne, degree from Montpellier Viticulture Centre, two years spent working with various French and German vinters, then back to Aussieland to work with your father and a French viticulturist, managing to raise the standard of Yarramarra wines to the point where they received international recognition, at the same time establishing yourself as an international wine judge. Not to mention masterminding the marketing of your wines. Quite a record for a simple Aussie dag. Have I got the term right?'

'Depends on what you think it means,' he said straight-faced.

'According to an article I read once, it's a bit of a wally.'

'It's actually that matted mixture of wool and old excreta sheep carry around on their backsides. By a simple process of Aussie logic, yes, it means a bit of a wally, but one you're fond of.' He gave her the open grin of a simple Aussie wally.

'Are you sure you know anything about female fashion?' she asked doubtfully. Today Bruce was dressed in a pair of jeans an incredible shade of deep violet, a white polo neck that showed off his tan and a caramel-coloured leather jacket with odd pleats back and front that added extra width to his already generous breadth of shoulder.

His grin widened. 'Wine wasn't the only thing I learned about in France. You can't get together with the native sheilas there without learning a little about female chic.' He glanced down at his outfit. 'This clobber is all part of the act. It's like I was telling you, you've got to have an angle. I'm the simple Australian backwoodsman who just happens to have a perfect palate and to know more than most about wine. If I dressed like that poncey journalist who's our fellow presenter, spoke like Cambridge educated Neil, who'd remember anything about me? I'd have to work three times as hard at making my name. This way no one can forget me!'

That was indisputable. 'And what sort of an angle have you in mind for me?'

He gave another grin and patted her hand. 'Trust your old cobber!'

Trust was not a quality Darina found herself able to associate with Bruce. Her press cuttings had included mention of marriage to an attractive Australian food writer but there was nothing of the uxurious husband about him. His eyes told her she was attractive, his hands as he bestowed a careless caress or helped her into a cab had an incipient possessiveness that was unsettling. And that chameleon ability to move between simple Aussie lad and sophisticated man of the world was not one she could feel comfortable with.

Darina made up her mind that her cleavage was not going to be revealed, her skirts were going to remain long and nothing was going to be too tight around her hips.

Bruce once again surprised her.

They finished their shopping with a clutch of carrier bags holding a collection of tops in singing colours. Beautifully cut, with subtle detail, easy to wear and move in, they flattered her figure and emphasized her good bones. To go with the tops he had selected a couple of simple skirts in crepe wool that minimized the size of her hips.

'I love them all but I don't see that they're going to help me cook better,' objected Darina as she turned in front of the mirror, trying to see her back view.

'Television is all about looking at things. Viewers have to look at you before they see what you're cooking. It's the same effect as the aroma of coffee has, makes the mouth water before you've got your taste buds near the stuff. If you hadn't been very attractive to start with, I'd've suggested we went for something pretty wacky to deflect attention from your looks, give you an angle of eccentricity.'

'Like you,' stated Darina unfairly.

'Right!' he said without rancour. 'Now, we need to choose you an outfit that will knock 'em in the aisles this evening.'

As Bruce started examining outfits with expensive designer labels, Darina wondered briefly about the cost of her new wardrobe. He dismissed her concerns with a casual, 'All part of the production expenses. Neil's company will be picking up the tab for everything.' He wielded a credit card with careless authority. It wasn't possible to argue with Bruce and when she had seen herself in what he chose, Darina had no inclination to try.

THE TELEVISION LIGHTS were blinding. Darina stood waiting to be sent into their remorseless blaze not knowing whether she was ready to be fed to the lions.

Bruce was on stage, leaning comfortably back in his chair and talking to Mike Darcy as easily as though the chat-show host was an old friend. His large figure dressed in leather trousers, a white silk shirt and some sort of buckskin jerkin complete with fringes, he appeared to feel as at home in front of the cameras and the large studio audience as in the Australian bush that he claimed was his natural habitat. He was swapping jokes with Mike at the same time as managing to give a vivid account of his vineyard. The broad Australian accent compelled attention and the graphically down-to-earth vocabulary nudged crudity without ever becoming a bedfellow.

There was a mesmerizing quality about Bruce Bennett that refused to let you be shocked by anything he said. His craggy face was alight with enthusiasm, the bright hazel eyes, overshadowed by heavy lids and bushy eyebrows, glowed with enthusiasm as he described his new sparkling red Shiraz, the latest addition to Yarramarra's collection of internationally acclaimed wines.

'Wait till you taste it, Mike.' Bruce reached down beside his chair, brought up a bottle of wine and started unwrapping the foil from the cork. 'Makes champagne seem like a drink for *Neighbours!* It's got guts, flavour and a sparkle like a virgin on her first date. How about something to drink out of, think your channel can run to that?' Bruce started unwinding the cork's securing wire.

His host whipped out a tray of glasses, placed it on top of a small table, and rose. 'Stay your hand with that cork for a moment, Bruce, while I introduce my next guest. I know you have a lot in common and maybe she can provide something to go with the wine.'

A gentle prod and an encouraging look sent Darina along what seemed an endless walk into the spotlights.

'Darina Lisle, cook, writer and now television demonstrator, welcome to the show,' Mike Darcy said as Bruce gave her a big, welcoming grin.

As she sat down, Darina set a plate of small eats on the table beside the glasses. *Amuses gueules* they would call them in smart restaurants, little bites of something to titillate the taste buds, get the salivary juices running before the serious stuff arrived. There were smoked mussels wrapped in fine overcoats of organic streaky bacon; tiny pastry cases filled with small prawns in a red pepper sauce; little rounds of bread stroked with olive oil, baked to crispness and topped with a paste of black olives, anchovy and garlic; more topped with whipped salmon and cream; and cubes of goat's cheese speared with medlar cheese. Darina looked at the toothsome bites and wondered if the television camera could pick up the detail—then wondered if it mattered. What had possessed her to agree to this ordeal?

Darina had been introduced to Mike Darcy before the show. The creamy Irish charm had been as devastating in person as it appeared on the screen, the voice teasing and tantalizing with its suggestion of immediate intimacy, giving the impression there was an unspecified joke existing just between the two of them. Then the charm had quelled her misgivings, now they were back in full force.

'Being a man who loves his food, it's a double pleasure to have you here tonight, Darina,' Mike was saying, the voice beginning once again to exercise its calming spell. 'Because not only are you a beautiful woman, and everyone knows how much I like beautiful women, but you are also a great cook.' His gaze fell towards the plate of canapés. 'Those look good enough to eat.' His hand almost picked one up then Mike smacked himself. 'Down boy, those come later! But, Darina, isn't it right that you are going to be giving poor souls like me who struggle to boil an egg all the secrets of *haute cuisine?*' Before Darina could say anything, he continued, 'In fact, both of you are joining that most esoteric of food shows, *Table for Four,* on the other channel.' His voice dropped to a stage whisper and he gave a big wink to the camera. 'But I'm willing to bet that once Bruce here is aboard with the lovely Darina it's not going to be quite so esoteric?'

Bruce picked up the cue. 'You can bet your balls on that, Mike! Between us Darina and I are bringing back good honest taste. None of your arty-farty nouvelle cuisine or cat's piss wines for us. We're into bonzer food and honest descriptions of enjoyable swills.'

Mike raised an eyebrow ever so slightly. 'Is that really what you'll be into?' he asked Darina.

She took a deep breath and gave him a radiant smile. 'Food doesn't need to be complicated to taste wonderful,' she started. 'I don't have Bruce's colourful way of expressing things—'

'Being a nicely brought-up English girl?' Mike broke in, his voice dulcet and laughing. 'Forgive me for saying so, but you don't look a nicely brought-up English girl! And that's a compliment, in case you were in any doubt.'

Darina was all too well aware of how she looked and that it was all Bruce Bennett's fault. She sat in front of the cameras wearing a Giorgio Armani set of pantaloons, vest top and long jacket in a soft, creamy material, the sexy waves of her new hairdo teased back into place by the make-up girl, her eyes subtly emphasized, her mouth glossy with coral lipstick. She tossed back a chunk of cream-coloured hair with a casual gesture. Suddenly she felt in command. 'I want to show people just how easy it can be to cook really delicious food. Give them confidence in their ability to come up with something that tastes really good. We'll be taking a new look at classic dishes and showing what can be done with some of the exotic ingredients that are now available everywhere. Good cooking is just a matter of confidence.'

'And I can see you've got all the confidence in the world, hasn't she, Bruce?'

The Australian leaned forward and placed a big hand on her thigh, where it sat warm and heavy. 'Darina's a ripper of a cook, I shall be learning along with the viewers, no doubt about that.' He gave her thigh a possessive little squeeze.

'But Darina has another talent I think the viewers would like to hear something about,' pursued Mike Darcy. 'Don't I understand that not only are you engaged to a detective, you are something of a whizz at detecting yourself?'

This angle had definitely not been introduced into the discussion she had had with Mike's researcher. Darina gave what she hoped looked a sphinx-like smile and said nothing.

'Haven't you just solved a murder mystery in the West Country, and not the first by all accounts?'

Darina gave another toss to her waving hair; if she kept this up, starlets could be queuing for lessons. 'Sheer luck, nothing else,' she stated with a modest smile. 'William is the real detective, he's the one solving crimes.'

'I'm sure he'd be the first to admit you give him some competition in that area,' Mike persisted and proved the efficiency of his research team by producing details of some of the murder cases Darina had found herself involved with.

'You make it sound as though dead bodies appear wherever I go,' she protested. 'Don't start suggesting people should be wary before eating my food!'

Mike gave a laugh that sounded genuine. 'Any time you ask me to dinner, you can be sure I'll be there. It'd be a pleasure to die at your table! No, forget I said that, but to prove the quality of your cooking, I'll start in on these delicious looking goodies. Bruce, you open that wine and I'll bring on the last of my guests to share all this bounty.'

A film star joined them and Darina and Bruce took back seats while he plugged his latest movie, absentmindedly grazing amongst the plate of eats and sipping at the wine while managing to avoid mentioning either.

'LET'S GO ON somewhere,' said Bruce after Mike had closed the show, complimented his guests on their performances and dissolved away.

Darina, on a high, William down in Somerset, only her empty Chelsea house to go back to, agreed. Just before they left the studio, someone produced a video of the show that Bruce had apparently asked for. He popped it without comment into the large pocket of a trench coat that looked a parody of that worn by every Hollywood newspaperman.

They went to a newly opened restaurant that was crowded,

even on a Monday, with London's elite. Somehow Bruce managed to get them a table. He ordered drinks then gave only the most cursory of glances to the menu before dropping it on the table. The previous day he had spurned the delicious cassoulet Neil's wife had cooked for the *Table for Four* production team and produced a plastic box of grated vegetables instead.

'Don't you like food?' Darina asked him now.

'You bet! It's all part of the taste experience and when I'm at home I love preparing dishes, I can guarantee the quality then.' For once he sounded perfectly serious. 'How many people really care about what goes into their meals? Most people don't even taste what they're eating. Take this bread.' He lifted a piece of baguette from the basket that had been placed on their table. 'It's literally the staff of life, you could live on bread alone, yet how often does anyone actually *taste* it?' He tossed the piece on to his plate. 'Have you ever chewed grains of hard wheat, chewed until it becomes a soft pulp?'

Darina shook her head.

'Do it sometime and note the different flavours that are released. Then start tasting breads made from other grains. Savour the heavy sour flavour of rye, the sweet softness of oat, the idiosyncratic taste of corn. You can spend days assessing the flavour of bread. But what do most people do? Smother it with butter and eat it without thinking.'

Darina picked up the menu and found its dishes offered an explosion of taste flavours that now seemed crude and obvious.

'*Garçon!*' Bruce attracted the attention of one of the French waiters that staffed the restaurant. '*Excusez moi, un moment, s'il vous plaît.*' There followed an exchange too rapid for Darina to follow. A moment later Bruce had disappeared into the nether regions of the restaurant, telling Darina to order what she wanted. He returned to his place as her food arrived. With it came a simple omelette that was placed before him.

'All you could trust the chef to produce?' Darina asked pointedly.

Bruce gave her one of his wide grins. 'Need to keep my fighting weight. Don't know why it is but on anything but the simplest of diets I put on weight like a Strasburg goose raised for foie gras.'

'You won't be trying my dishes then? I noticed you didn't eat anything on the programme this evening.'

'Might just try something some time, if it looks particularly good.'

'Pig! I bet you eat your wife's cooking.'

Darina had made the remark without thinking but instantly knew she'd hit a nerve. Bruce closed up like a sea anemone that had been brushed by a shark. His good humour vanished as his eyes narrowed and his face went blank. Then he laughed, made some joking remark and moved the conversation on to the popularity of the new restaurant.

Darina followed his lead until coffee arrived, when she asked, 'What brought you over to England? From what I read last night, you seem to have a lot going for you in Australia, plus a healthy business to look after.'

'I've got good chaps in place there and my sister keeps an eye on things. That's who the video was for, by the way, she'd never forgive me if I didn't keep her up to date with what I'm doing, she likes to keep tabs on her little brother.' He leaned back in his chair and looked at Darina, his humour back in place again, his big body relaxed. 'Why did I come over here? Well, we Aussie backwoods types can't get rid of a sneaking feeling that Europe is where wine is at, that until you've made it big over here as a wine buff you haven't really made it. I suppose you could say it was ambition.'

IT WAS NEARLY midnight by the time Darina got back to her house after a fight with Bruce over sharing the bill that she had finally managed to win. She had also managed to insist he had no need to get out of the taxi to see her to her door.

She had no intention of asking him in and it was only the fact that he had rented a flat in a block not far from her house that had made it impossible to insist she took her own taxi. She had enjoyed her evening but she didn't want Bruce getting any of the wrong ideas.

'I read every day what goes on in your London streets to unwary birds,' he said, once again sounding serious.

'This bird isn't unwary,' Darina said firmly and got out of the cab.

The taxi, though, remained stationary while she sorted out her key, aware for once of how quiet and unpopulated her street was at that hour, how inadequate the lighting. Next door's cat appeared from nowhere, winding its sinuous body round her legs, the unexpected contact of its soft fur making her flesh contract and shiver. She hastily opened her front door, turned to give a reassuring wave at Bruce then watched the cab's rear lights as it drove off leaving dark shadows invading the suddenly empty space. She closed and locked the door quickly and ran upstairs.

She was undressing as the telephone rang. It was William.

'Where have you been?' he demanded. 'I've been worried out of my mind.' She stood clutching the receiver, her tights half off. 'I've been ringing and ringing, why didn't you call back when you got in?'

Darina hadn't given a thought to checking her answering machine. 'I'm sorry,' she apologized. 'I've only just got home, we went for a meal after the show.'

'We? Who's we?'

'Bruce and I.'

'That brash Australian?'

She was shocked by the cold anger in his voice. 'Darling, we're going to be working together, we have to get on. Anyway, I like him.' It was the wrong thing to have said.

'I could see you did and so could a million other people. What on earth were you playing at. He almost had it off with you on camera? And what the hell have you done with your hair?' Dismay filled Darina; where had her rational, understanding, reliable fiancé gone? Possible ways of defusing the potentially damaging situation rapidly deployed themselves through her brain but, before she could clutch at any of them, her rational, understanding, reliable fiancé added, 'You might have warned me, I didn't know what to say when Ma rang!'

TWO

DARINA had expected recording her first *Table for Four* show to be stressful and she wasn't disappointed.

Not that everyone wasn't most helpful.

Neil had already made sure she was happy with all the stages of the demonstration they had worked out together and was endlessly encouraging.

Mark Taylor, the only survivor from the three original presenters of *Table,* as the show was known, had welcomed Darina to the team as soon as he met her at the first production meeting she attended and showed a heart-warming appreciation of her food.

Darina liked his dry sense of humour and self-deprecating charm. A food journalist who had carved a niche for himself on television, Mark was tall with dark hair that tended to flop over his brow, needing to be constantly swept back by a well-shaped hand. Soulful brown eyes enlivened a face a touch too ordinary to be termed handsome but his trim figure wore well-cut clothes that unostentatiously breathed Savile Row and provided a nice contrast to Bruce's exuberant wardrobe.

Then there was the home economist, Lynn Winters. It was luxury for Darina to have someone to order and prepare all the food, including enough for back-up supplies if it was necessary to reshoot part of the demonstration, enabling Darina herself to concentrate on her presentation. A thin girl with a frizz of fair hair and blazing blue eyes, Lynn had already spent some time preparing food before Darina arrived at the studio. She had nevertheless managed reassuring comments while continuing to prepare a half-done version of the pasta dish of penne with a prosciutto and chicken sauce that Darina was to demonstrate.

'Just keep the food out of Mark's reach,' Lynn said, lightly smacking the presenter's hand as he tried to dig a spoon into the penne and sauce. 'You're such a greedy so and so.'

'It's your fault,' he said, 'it's all so delicious. I didn't have any breakfast and you always do such masses.' Darina watched, amused despite her nerves, as he pounced on some stray bits of prosciutto, popped them into his mouth with little noises of appreciation then moved on to sample some wonderful looking black olives.

'Mark, those are for the table, stop it!'

He grinned at the girl and ran an exploratory hand over the short leather skirt that topped long legs encased in opaque tights. Lynn's behind gave a quick wriggle and she swatted him off like a horse swishing off a fly. Then Mark's glance fell on a huge hunk of Parmesan cheese sitting beside the olives. A piece had already been hacked off its rough surface but it had been no more than the tip of a hefty iceberg. Mark's eyes gleamed greedily. 'Oh, super! Bags I the rest.' He suddenly turned to Darina with a sweet smile. 'Unless, of course, you want some as well?'

Before Darina could answer, Neil announced they were to rehearse her spot and she went to her kitchen area, her nerves jangling.

Nor was she the only one. Bruce arrived on the set a little later and she watched his natural ebullience seep away as the same small section of his wine spot had to be recorded over and over again. 'Sorry,' Neil had apologized when it was all safely over. 'Jan wanted to get the light coming through that wine glass just right.'

Jan Parker was the studio director. A quiet woman in her late thirties, usually dressed in well-cut slacks and designer sweaters, her comments at meetings were infrequent but always to the point. During recording she ruled the proceedings from the gallery high above the studio floor.

'Our bold Aussie is beginning to discover that television isn't just about the projection of personality,' said Mark, appearing beside Darina where she stood quietly watching the proceedings from the sidelines. She gave him a quick look, wondering exactly what lay behind the remark, but his face was bland.

'How do you think he comes over?' she asked.

'He'll soon be dominating the camera just the way he did on the Mike Darcy show,' he said. Now she was sure there was a definite edge to his voice.

'Losing Milly must be difficult for you,' Darina suggested.

He gave her a sharp look, seemed about to say something, then changed his mind and shrugged his shoulders instead.

'What made Neil decide to change the format like that?' All that Darina knew about *Table* so far was that, after a successful start to the first series, the show's audience ratings had plummeted.

Neil gave another little shrug to his shoulders. 'He had to do something and firing that chef was a natural. Then, in a way, Milly had become a bit of a parody of herself. All those adjectives, you know? God, she'd kill me if she heard this. No one has a more sensitive palate or a more encyclopaedic taste memory. Once Milly's tasted a wine she's got its name, provenance and vintage locked up in her brain for instant recall. You wouldn't believe what she can do.'

His enthusiasm was impressive. Darina wondered if their partnership had been personal as well as professional.

'It's curious how many female wine experts one sees on television these days,' she commented. 'And interesting Neil has chosen Bruce as a replacement rather than another woman.'

Mark gave a dry laugh. 'Neil's always one to buck a trend. I think the fashion for female masters of wine started as a revolt against the tradition that said it was a masculine preserve. It's probably time now, though, to give the old pendulum a push the other way. Choosing an Australian is clever, too. Australian wines are all the rage and Bruce's approach is undoubtedly fresh. No one could call him precious!'

Darina laughed but watched thoughtfully as Mark went forward to greet that week's guest, Theresa Mancusa, an Italian cookery expert.

After the introductions, Neil rehearsed then recorded the programme's opening shots round the table. Here Mark proved really helpful. Somehow, by a mixture of charm and authority he managed to calm the nerves of the other three, set the right atmosphere of conviviality and get them talking about Italian food and wine. Darina particularly admired the way he allowed Theresa Mancusa to air her superior knowledge so that she relaxed and, with graceful gestures of her small, pudgy hands, talked in a grating voice that minted vivid phrases.

Then the lunch break was announced and the production team went over to the hospitality room across the corridor from the studio.

'Thought we managed a more than creditable performance there,' said Bruce as he stood beside Darina while they waited to help themselves to food from the buffet table.

'It was quite scary without an autocue, even though we'd discussed more or less what we could all say beforehand,' said Darina.

'Gets the adrenalin going, doesn't it?' Bruce's bounce and innate confidence had reappeared. 'What happened to the hair?' he asked, his eyes surveying the way it had been piled on top of her head in a pillowy effect, softened by a few artfully loose tendrils.

'It's better for cooking like this, I don't think it looks good if hair's floating around everywhere, do you?'

Bruce looked as though he would have preferred it down but any comment he might have made was arrested by the appearance of David Bartholomew, the Nigerian production manager. When Darina had first met him she had been struck by the severely beautiful lines of his face, he looked like a classical statue carved out of ebony. Now he seemed worried and harassed.

'Darina, can I have a word, please?' He drew her off into a corner and pulled out a slew of bills from a laden clipboard he was clutching. She caught the name of one of the dress shops Bruce had taken her to and felt a shiver of unease.

'I don't understand these,' David said, waving them at her. 'We didn't authorize any of this expenditure, your wardrobe is organized by our designer.'

Darina had already had to battle with the wardrobe girl to be allowed to wear one of the new outfits. Eventually Neil had arrived and agreed that it was in order. Now here was more trouble.

'And these amounts are way over budget in any case.' David was consulting a sheet of figures, his brown eyes concerned, his voice fretful.

Darina gathered her forces but suddenly Bruce was there; his big hand grabbed David round the back of the neck, his tall figure dominating the medium-height production manager, and the broad Aussie accent rose above the hubbub in the room. 'Stop browbeating the little girl, Dave. I chose her outfits and you can stuff your budget up your ass, Neil's perfectly happy, aren't you, Neil?'

David Bartholomew angrily released himself as the executive producer hurried over. The room had gone quiet, everyone's concentration fixed on the little group in the corner.

'I'm quite capable of fighting my own battles, thank you, Bruce,' said Darina, furious at his treatment of the production manager. 'If the clothes are too expensive, I'm happy to contribute to the cost, I think they'll be an excellent addition to my wardrobe.'

David began to look more cheerful.

'No question of that,' Neil stated crisply.

David looked at the producer, shock freezing his features for a moment. 'Am I or am I not in charge of budgets?' he demanded. 'I thought you relied on me to see to the financial side of things. If I can't control expenditure, I can't answer for the consequences.'

'David, you do a fantastic job,' started Neil.

'This is a piss in a pond!' Bruce grabbed David's clipboard, took out a pen, altered some figures and gave it back to him. 'Now, work to that and everyone will be happy. After all, chic is the second name of this programme, right?'

'You can't do that,' David spluttered. 'Who do you think you are!'

Bruce's eyes narrowed and he poked a giant finger into David's chest. 'Listen, where I come from, Abo's don't tell me what can and can't be done.' He increased the pressure of his finger and the Nigerian staggered back, his patrician features apoplectic.

There was a gasp from the assembled company and Neil said, 'Hey, Bruce, don't you think you should apologize?'

But the Australian had strolled away to the back of the room, picked up an attaché case, got out a plastic box, found a fork from the buffet table and started munching on one of the grated vegetable salads he seemed addicted to.

The texture of David's skin had altered, it was as if anger had caused the blood to stop flowing. Darina thought he was going to explode.

The situation was defused by Theresa Mancusa, who came up and slipped an arm through the production manager's. 'David, *cara*, how nice to see you again. Still chasing the girls?' she said with an arch look towards Darina. 'I was so busy in Italy, I had too little time to talk to you. Come and tell me how you liked your trip.'

She led the production manager off, laughing and talking in strongly accented English, and gradually the room returned to normal.

Theresa Mancusa had recently opened a school outside Milan for well-heeled cooks interested in expanding their knowledge of Italian cuisine. There had been a special session laid on for the press to generate publicity for the new courses and Neil had decided to capitalize on the popularity of Italian food by designing a programme around it. Jan Parker had led a small team sent out to do some filming. With her and the technical staff had gone Mark to interview some of those attending the course. David Bartholomew had been organizer and budget controller.

Judging by the film that had been shown to the production team, the trip must have been a delightful experience; Darina wished she could have been there. The school was housed in a palatial Italian villa amongst magnificent scenery, the course had looked fascinating and everyone had seemed to enjoy themselves.

The big surprise at the showing, though, had been Bruce's roar of amazement. 'I'll be damned if it isn't the little woman!' he exclaimed as an attractive dark-haired girl with creamy skin was shown rolling out pasta, her face a study in concentration, the tip of her little red tongue caught between her teeth. 'She never told me she'd got involved with *Table for Four* on that Italian press trip. But, then,' he added with throwaway confidence, 'she'd have had no idea I'd be meeting up with you lot.' For the briefest of moments, though, Darina had seen something unsettling lurking in the Australian's eyes.

'But that's Shelley del Lucca!' Mark had cried, glaring suspiciously at the other man.

'Her maiden name, Mark. What is it? Didn't you know she was married?' Bruce had seemed to enjoy the other man's discomfiture.

'Of course I did, I just didn't know it was to you!' Mark had retorted.

WHEN RECORDING STARTED after the lunch interval, Neil assembled Mark, Theresa, Bruce and Darina around the table again to record the ending of the programme. Everyone was more relaxed now and Mark had no trouble making sure each of the other participants contributed to a valedictory signing off on Italian food. Then Darina started ladling out portions of her penne dish and they discussed the versatility of pasta, providing a background over which the closing credits would eventually roll. After they had the all clear on the recording, Neil told Bruce and Darina they could leave. With a sigh of relief, Darina gathered together her things for the long drive back to Somerset, leaving Mark to interview Theresa Mancusa.

THREE

DARINA finished her demonstration of a classic *coq au vin*, the sauce, lightly thickened with a *beurre manié*, dark and glossy, the aroma so captivating the entire studio crew were salivating as a man. Jan had wanted the whole spot shot in one take so she now placed the casserole on one side, pulled forward a bowl of pears and moved smoothly into the business of poaching them in a white wine syrup.

After four programmes, Darina thought she might be over the worst of her nerves. She had absorbed the rhythm of each programme's gestation and completion, knew how to work on her part of each show and was beginning to be aware of what came over on camera. The greatest difficulty was managing to project her enthusiasm for each dish without appearing pretentious or artificial. She was conscious all the time of criticisms she had heard levelled at other television cooks. So and so was affected, another never explained directions properly, yet another never seemed to understand basic cookery principles, then there was the one who was too pedestrian, the other who looked a dog, not to mention several who strove so hard to make the whole thing fun the viewer was too exhausted to contemplate cooking. It was, she discovered, easy to criticize and much more difficult to avoid all the pitfalls oneself. She had been grateful to Neil for his unflustered way of taking her through the rehearsal for each of her spots and sorting out problems of presentation.

Never before had it been necessary for Darina to concentrate on the look of her food to the exclusion of flavour. Television was visual and aural. It could show how delicious something could appear, even convey the sizzle of the cooking, but there was no way the viewer could taste the result.

Darina made it a personal aim to have each dish produced for the camera tasting as good as one cooked in her kitchen. For at the end of each programme that week's guest was shown sampling the result. Afterwards the crew usually descended on what was left. It had become something of a joke with viewers that Bruce and Mark were never shown trying the dish as well and Neil was currently torn between bowing to demands for the presenters to eat on screen and wanting to keep what was now a signature note. Darina wondered what Bruce would do if he found himself compelled to try her food. Unlike Neil, who was always picking at this and that, and the rest of the team, who loved an opportunity to sample the dishes, he never ate a thing.

When she became a little more confident, Darina determined to see if there wasn't some way of tempting him, it was starting to become something of a personal challenge. But there was still too much to think about at present to worry about tempting Bruce Bennett.

Darina explained to the viewers who would later watch the programme, 'I'm doing these pears in white wine but you could use red instead. Let them cook in the syrup like this with the liquid hardly moving. That's poaching, the gentlest form of cooking. It'll take some twenty-five minutes for the syrup to seep through the fruit so you need to start with firm pears. If it doesn't penetrate to the centre, they can turn a little brown inside. There, we'll leave them cooking and I'll show you some prepared yesterday in red wine then you can appreciate the colour.'

Darina turned to the side of the demonstration area and reached for the glass bowl of pears cooked in red wine Lynn had prepared for the show. It wasn't there.

For a moment she wondered whether to fudge the omission and continue with the recording but she knew the hesitation had been fatal. Already the cameras had been cut and the floor manager was listening through her headphones for more orders from the gallery.

A mortified Lynn appeared in front of the demonstration unit holding the missing pears. 'Christ, I'm sorry, Darina! I don't know what happened, I thought I'd checked everything!'

Darina looked at her assistant. It wasn't the first time in the last couple of programmes Lynn had failed to prove as efficient as her reputation.

Darina stood back and allowed the resetting of her demonstration area for the pear item to be reshot. Neil wouldn't get the whole demonstration in one take now but editing would be able to make it seem as though it flowed unchecked. The break was a pity when she had been going so well but that was television, it wasn't only one's own performance that dictated the success of the programme. She watched Lynn.

The girl was pale, her only colour a nasty bruise on her cheek, the result, she'd explained, of a fall downstairs. Earlier in the week it had been an angry purple-red, now unpleasant tinges of green and yellow were calming down the colour.

The fall had obviously shaken her, at the production meeting she had had trouble keeping her attention on the details being discussed. Neil had even suggested she go home and look after herself. Lynn had said that wasn't necessary. If the suggestion had been a threat, it had worked for a time, Lynn had pulled herself together and returned to her previous efficiency.

But the trouble had started before the fall. Loin of pork had arrived last week instead of tenderloin and the sweet red peppers that should have been delivered from the greengrocer had turned out to be chilli peppers. Lynn had got on the telephone and found somebody to rectify the errors but precious time had been lost. Neil had not been pleased.

'Are you all right, Lynn?' asked Darina as her assistant finished bringing over and arranging another set of food.

'I'm fine,' the girl said, glancing around to make sure nothing else had been forgotten. Then her voice was raised in a screech of rage. 'Mark, put that chicken down!' She darted over to the preparation table and yanked a leg of *coq au vin* out of the presenter's hand. 'How many times have I told you, *Don't touch the food!*'

Mark's pleasant features turned resentful and his lips drew back in what looked remarkably like a snarl. Lynn took an involuntary step backwards. Then Alison, the floor manager, was asking if Darina was ready to go again with the pears. Mark stalked away from the preparation table, Darina nodded and Alison called for quiet in the studio, they were going for a take.

Darina wiped her mind of everything but poaching pears and picked up the first bowl of fruit again.

A few minutes later she was on her close. 'Pears in wine freeze beautifully and they are very versatile, you can serve them by themselves, on a gateau, like this,' she picked up an almond cake that stood ready, its top covered with drained pears and decorated with whipped cream. 'Or as the base of a fruit salad,' she brought in another bowl that held the pears mixed with segments of oranges and fresh grapes, 'or for that famous dish, Poire Belle Hélène.' Darina poured chocolate sauce over pears and meringues. 'The recipe for the chocolate sauce is on the fact sheet you can apply for, details at the end of the programme. But remember, for the pears as for the chicken, the better the wine the better the flavour. Use some from a good bottle and you will notice the difference. If we can persuade Bruce not to finish the ones he's chosen for today's programme, I might be able to save some for cooking. How about it, cobber?'

She looked to her right as she spoke. It was the cue that took the camera from her demonstration area to Bruce's part of the studio and brought him in for his spot on the pro-gramme. But Bruce's comfortable chair was empty, his con-tribution would be brought together with Darina's in the ed-iting process and now the studio waited quietly for word to come down from the gallery on whether another take was needed.

'I'm sorry, Darina,' said Alison. 'The editor found a glitch on the tape, we'll have to record again.'

Darina groaned. What she found more difficult than anything else was maintaining the spontaneity of her delivery in take after take, often caused by something that was no fault of hers.

Once again her work area was reset. Once again she demonstrated poaching pears and this time, it seemed, the take was in order.

Normally Neil would now record Bruce's contribution but today it had been decided to go for the opening of the programme next, with everyone sitting round the table.

Neil had announced this at the production meeting. 'And so as it will obviously be better if Bruce and Mark interview Jean-Pierre Prudhomme together...' Neil's voice was lost as Bruce broke into one of his Aussie roars: 'Jean-Pierre Prudhomme? I thought we were going to have that Napa Valley fellow?'

'We were,' Neil replied impatiently. 'But he's had to cut his visit to England short. Mark was in the office when he rang and said he knew a French vintner was over here and why didn't we ask him. Didn't he tell you?'

'It's your fucking job to keep me informed and who's the bloody wine expert on this show anyway, Mark or me?'

The meeting waited expectantly for the executive producer to annihilate Bruce, normally he had little patience with members of the team who came the prima donna.

Neil shifted uncomfortably in his chair. 'Bruce, let me remind you we're leading up to Christmas and the theme of this particular programme is the versatility of wine. You're going to be looking at wine cups, Darina's using it in cooking and all we need our guest for is some background on what affects the flavour of wine. I thought any grower would do, as long as he comes over well.'

'I don't give a fuck for what you thought! The wine part of the show is mine! I should have been consulted!'

Darina had never seen Bruce so angry. There had been bust-ups before but the Australian had always maintained a sense of humour in putting over his point of view. Suddenly a different side of him was revealed. Just as it had been when he'd been so unforgivably rude to David Bartholomew. In vain did Neil emphasize the reputation of the Prudhomme wines and the excellent English of Jean-Pierre, Bruce continued to rage his opposition to the Frenchman appearing without Neil consulting him beforehand. At last Mark, who'd said nothing during the argument, just doodled on his pad with an odd little smile playing around his mouth, asked, 'Just what is it you've got against Jean-Pierre, Bruce? Methinks you protest too much here over a measly point of principle.' He looked sweetly at the Australian.

Bruce caught himself and looked carefully back at Mark, who returned his stare guilelessly. 'No point of principle can be called measly,' the Australian said at last.

Neil grabbed at the brief pause in hostilities. 'Right,' he said warmly. 'Right, but I don't think this is one to go to the guillotine for, Bruce. I hear what you're saying and next time of course you'll be consulted. That I promise!' The tone was confident but Neil failed to look the Australian in the eye. 'Now, can we get on? We've got an awful lot to get through. First, though, I do want to say thank you to everyone for the enormous effort you've all been putting into *Table*.' His voice strengthened. 'As you know, the viewing figures are improving, we're gaining audience with each show.' He seemed happy in the belief he'd steered the meeting away from any further confrontation over the wine issue and Bruce didn't refer to it again.

Darina wondered whether Bruce's success on *Table* was going to make him unbearable. There was no doubt that he was a success, he had far more mail than anyone else, newspapers and magazines were queuing for interviews and he was being approached for promotional appearances by representatives for anything from a supermarket opening to a church fête.

At the end of the meeting Bruce went up to Neil. 'We need to talk.'

The voice wasn't loud but there was no mistaking the authority behind the words.

Neil frowned and took a quick look at his watch. 'My office in half an hour,' he said.

What went on at the meeting Darina had no idea but when recording day arrived and Jean-Pierre Prudhomme was brought on to the set, Bruce gave him a big smile.

'Jean-Pierre, you old rogue, good to see you again!'

The Frenchman, a thin, middle-aged, middle-height figure with a face of wrinkled charm, shook his head. 'Bruce, it is always an experience to meet you.' His lightly accented English was careful but confident.

Neil got the scene set. With the trouble over Darina's demonstration, they were now running behind schedule.

All went well with the opening shots. Then Bruce's spot was recorded and they broke for a late lunch at the point where Neil was supposed to bring over Jean-Pierre for the joint interview.

After lunch Neil announced they would carry on from that point, leaving the closing session round the table to be recorded last. 'There may be something in the interview we can pick up on for the wrap-up,' he said.

Normally Darina would have been dismayed at having her drive back to Somerset delayed in this way but this week they were recording another show the following day before the team broke for a two-week holiday over Christmas.

While the cameras were reset round Bruce's wine area, Darina climbed the stairs to the gallery. It was fun to sit in up there and watch the pressured order of the calling of the camera shots that implemented the director's script.

All was quiet and subdued in the gallery, even the lighting. All the attention of Jan, the studio director, and her semicircle

of assistants was fixed on the control panels in front of them
and the bank of screens on the wall facing them.

There Darina could see close-ups of the three men now
settled into Bruce's wine area, the low side table by his chair
holding the special wine drinks he had prepared for Christmas: Buck's Fizz, Kirs, champagne cocktails and mulled
wine. Bruce was offering Mark and Jean-Pierre tastings while
instructions from the gallery moved the cameras until Jan was
pleased with the positioning.

The only view of the studio floor from the gallery was
through the cameras. Though there were huge windows over-
looking a catwalk high above the studio, black curtains hung
from the ceiling to the dusty floor and obscured everything.

'OK, Alison,' said Jan through her microphone. 'Let's see
if we can do this in one.'

The item started well enough with Mark producing a nice
segue from wine's ability to combine with other ingredients
to the effect of outside influences on the making of wine.

Jean-Pierre Prudhomme proved interesting on soil composition and climate and the skills of the French vintners that
were responsible for the subtlety of French wines.

'What about the fashion for Australian wines?' asked Mark
with a sly look to Bruce. 'Aren't their sales to the UK growing
by leaps and bounds and those in France falling away?'

Jean-Pierre was unimpressed. 'Pouf! It's something small,
nothing more. Some three and a 'alf million cases from Australia compared with over twenty-two million from France.'

'Admit it, Jean-Pierre,' Bruce leaned forward, 'Australian
wines are big news these days. We produce gutsy flavour the
public likes. Quality wines everyone can afford. Italian, Bul-
garian, Hungarian wines are all looking to Australia in the
way their wines are being made.'

'It's, what is it you say, a fad? Yes, you abandon subtlety,
the art of mixing grapes and producing a distinctive result for
something that is ordinary and undistinguished.'

'Sour grapes, Jean-Pierre! You won't accept that we've overtaken your technology.'

'Stolen it, you mean,' Jean-Pierre said quietly.

The camera shot chosen for transmission was a close-up of the Frenchman's face but one of the standby screens showed Bruce, his face suddenly wary, like a dog that senses the presence of a rival.

'That's pretty strong, Jean-Pierre,' said Mark and a barely controlled excitement in his voice came through to the gallery.

'Something's happening,' breathed Rita, the production assistant, and Jan sat a little straighter, her attention riveted to the screens.

'These Australians, they zink they are so clevair. Take Bruce 'ere'—a quick cut to another camera substituted Bruce's look of guarded caution for Jean-Pierre's one of contempt. 'Bruce, 'e work at my vineyard, learn my arts, 'ow we make the wine, yes?' Strong emotion was playing havoc with the Frenchman's command of English. 'Zen 'e disappear, with some of my precious yeast, what I spend years cultivating, and my master vintner. Zen 'e 'as ze gall to say 'is technology is superior! I tell you, wizzout me, 'e could nevair 'ave made success of Yarramarra.' He sat back in his seat.

A quick change of camera shot captured Bruce's contemptuous response. 'You can't patent yeast, it's absurd to say I stole it.'

'And the master vintner?' Mark asked eagerly.

'People change jobs all the time,' Bruce said dismissively.

'Cut to camera two,' said Jan and the central screen showed Jean-Pierre with narrowed eyes looking at Bruce with disgust. 'You bribed 'im, a man 'oo worked wiz me for years,' he hissed.

'Bruce made him an offer he couldn't refuse?' suggested Mark, smiling smugly.

'Keep going,' said Jan in an undertone. 'We won't be able to use any of this but it's great stuff.'

But already Neil had strode in and ordered the item stopped.

'I thought that was going really well, Neil,' Jan said through her microphone.

But Neil wasn't listening to his headphones, he was addressing Mark. 'I've told you before, we are not in the business of sleaze here, Mark. Jean-Pierre, I'm sorry, whatever quarrel you have with Bruce will have to wait until after the recording. Now, can we please get back on track?'

He strode out of the camera shot.

Mark leapt to his feet. With a quick glance at Jean-Pierre he appealed to the executive producer. 'Neil, we can't leave this, don't the viewers have the right to know what a shit Bruce actually is?'

Neil came back into camera shot. Small, bouncy, irate, he walked up to the presenter. 'Mark, unless you sit down, shut up and get on with the job, you won't have one.'

Bruce was sitting back casually. 'I'm sure Jean-Pierre doesn't want a case of slander thrown at him, Mark,' he said. 'And I promise you that is what will happen if the accusation of theft is repeated.'

For a moment Mark appeared incredulous. 'Neil, you can't let him get away with this!'

Jean-Pierre said nothing, his face now a mask of polite interest surveying Bruce and Mark; his bitterness seemed to have been replaced with a philosophical detachment.

Jan was attempting to get back in control. 'Alison, tell Mark to ask Jean-Pierre to offer viewers some advice on what to serve with the turkey then suggest they all go back to the main table for Darina's food.'

As Alison started relaying the director's orders, the vision mixer in the gallery remarked, 'Proper little stirrer Mark's turning into these days. What's his game?'

Darina knew they were all remembering his interviewing of Theresa Mancusa, the Italian cook.

He had led her into a paean of praise for simple Italian

home cooking then turned the tables on her by asking just why her courses were so expensive and without allowing her to respond had wound up the interview.

Theresa Mancusa had insisted on seeing a rerun of the item and then on its being re-recorded. Neil had refused. She had then stormed off threatening legal action if the item was broadcast.

Neil had hauled Mark off for what was obviously to be a dressing-down and their talk had obviously had some effect. Mark had contained his investigative instincts—until today.

'Somebody's nose has been put out of joint by the success of our big, bad Aussie,' said the production assistant with a knowing curl of her lip.

On the studio floor Alison called for quiet and the cameras started recording. Mark hesitated a long moment. In the gallery they waited, Jan's hand poised over a microphone switch. Then the presenter looked across at Jean-Pierre and asked for suggestions of wine to drink with the turkey and Bruce ended the spot by explaining to viewers that in the next programme he would be dealing with non-alcoholic drinks for the festive season.

Darina slipped out of the gallery and went back to the studio floor where the make-up girl was hovering to check her hair before the last section of the programme was shot. Her heart was thudding and her throat was dry. She couldn't see how they were going to achieve the usual atmosphere of camaraderie around the table for the final session.

Nor was it easy. Comments between Jean-Pierre and Bruce were barbed and Mark appeared to be controlling some deep-seated emotion. Darina chattered on, asking Jean-Pierre's advice on cooking with wine, reminding Bruce to pour the burgundy he'd chosen to accompany her *coq au vin* and begging the remainder of the bottle from him for her next cooking session. She felt like a husky with an overloaded sledge, trying to drag the others into a never-never land of festive warmth. It was a relief when Neil finally announced he was satisfied.

THE ATMOSPHERE in the studio the following day was still charged with tension.

It was as if everyone was waiting to see what Mark would try to pin on Bruce this time. There was no sense of end-of-term frivolity and the silver tinsel someone had wrapped round one of the camera cranes seemed an inappropriate touch.

As guest for the last programme before Christmas Neil had invited a director from a high-class provisions company. Darina's spot was to cover toothsome little extras, preserves, small eats, etc., that could either be used to add a touch of class to the festivities or given away as presents; the table itself was laden with what the commercial world was offering along the same lines for the show's presenters to pass judgement on.

The guest from the provisions company was a sophisticated middle-aged man with an engaging way of expressing himself. Normally Darina would have responded to his charm and enjoyed herself. Today she found herself braced for more unpleasantness.

The morning's recording ended with Bruce's spot. On his own, the Australian recovered much of his usual good humour as he mixed together various fruit juices, topped up the result with sparkling mineral water, added some diced dried apricot and slices of orange and lemon, sipped the result and nodded to the camera. 'A real bonzer drink. Even hardened liquor drinkers may appreciate its simple charms and it won't give anyone a hangover or trouble with the breathalyser.' He gave one of his infectious grins. 'I'll take it over to the table and see what the rest of them think.' He moved away, out of camera shot, and the recording came to an end.

After the usual anxious wait, Alison announced everyone was happy with the recording.

Bruce put the jug of fruit drink back on his side table and stretched his big frame. 'Can't wait to get this over,' he said. 'That Aussie sun seems more attractive every minute.' He was spending the two-week break filming various down-under vineyards, including a few in New Zealand, that would be featured in later programmes.

The opening scene round the table was set up and recorded without a hitch, then Alison announced they were to break for lunch.

People began to move in the direction of the hospitality room and Bruce strolled over to the preparation table where Lynn was packing away stuff not needed that afternoon. He laid a big hand on one of her shoulders.

Darina saw the girl jerk away from him and start to fling food and utensils into cardboard boxes with unnecessary force, at the same time spitting words in a hissed undertone that failed to carry beyond the two of them. Bruce looked discomforted, flung some sort of retort at her then strode off out of the studio.

Darina looked at Lynn, noted the keep off signals and decided to leave her to sort out whatever her problem was herself.

Over lunch a holiday atmosphere began to pervade the company at last. There was champagne provided by Neil and a Christmas cake baked by Anthea, his wife. Mark produced a large box of Belgian chocolates and handed them around and then, suddenly, Jean-Pierre Prudhomme was there. 'I've brought you all wine for the turkey,' he said as Neil greeted him in surprise.

He dragged in a small trolley laden with gaily wrapped parcels and proceeded to hand them around to cries of appreciation. When he got to Bruce, Jean-Pierre said, 'We bury all axes, yes?'

'Not such a dork after all, are you?' the Australian boomed, his hand closing round the package the Frenchman held out.

Darina cradled her gift and wondered if yesterday's bad

feeling could be so easily forgotten. Nobody else seemed to have similar reservations.

The afternoon started badly when Neil announced they would record first Mark's interview with the provisions merchant, leaving the final session round the table to the end of the day.

'Neil, you can't do that!' insisted Bruce. 'I'm flying to Australia tomorrow! I was counting on getting off mid-afternoon, my car is here already.'

'Sorry, Bruce, it's going to be done my way,' Neil said cheerfully, giving a little bounce on his toes.

'Neil,' the Australian started.

'Bruce, I haven't forgotten yesterday.'

'Yesterday was not *my* fucking fault! If you hadn't insisted on going along with Mark and Jean-Pierre's little plot...'

'Come on, Bruce, what's happened to your sense of humour!'

For a moment Bruce towered over the much smaller producer and the studio waited expectantly; Darina could imagine what the atmosphere in the gallery was like. Neil calmly faced his wine expert and suddenly Bruce shrugged his shoulders. 'OK, Neil, if that's the way you want it.' Darina would have liked the Australian to have got his way, it would have meant an earlier start for her back to Somerset, but she wasn't sorry to see Neil asserting his authority. It was time he showed Bruce just who was boss.

Mark's interview with the provisions merchant went well. Yesterday's confrontation appeared to have done Mark nothing but good, he was charm itself with the guest and the two produced a sequence sparkling with Christmas fun.

Eventually the cameras were set up for the final part of this last programme before Christmas and an air of relaxation began to creep over the studio. Even Lynn looked a little more cheerful.

Darina sat herself down at the table with Mark and the suave provisions merchant in front of a plate of her goodies and waited for Bruce to fill their glasses with his drink. Then Neil spotted a badly washed glass and called for clean ones. Lynn brought them over and they were placed carefully on the table. Finally Alison called for silence in the studio and recording started.

Bruce poured the fruit cup with some quip of sending himself out of business as a wine producer and all four of them raised their glasses in a Christmas toast and drank.

The cup was heavy with aromatic fruit juices. Darina hadn't been paying full attention when it had been composed but she could recognize apricot, passion fruit, mango and orange spiked with fresh lemon. It had a wonderful flavour and she looked across at Bruce to congratulate him. Then she felt the words clog the roof of her mouth as she saw the Australian's glass fall to the floor and his face work as though he had been seized by some tremendous force. His right hand, the hand that had held the glass, reached towards his heart, beneath the bright red jacket he was wearing. The distress on his face increased, he was gasping for air, his eyes looking wildly about as his huge figure staggered and then fell to the floor.

Darina was the first to reach his side. She could swear he saw her, that he was trying to say something but nothing intelligible emerged.

'He's having a heart attack,' she heard someone say. 'Get him sitting upright, that's the best thing.'

'Send for a doctor,' said Neil's voice. 'No, dial 999 and ask for an ambulance, say we think it's cardiac arrest.'

Bruce's eyes seemed to be pleading. Darina grasped his hand. 'Don't worry, everything's going to be all right,' she tried to soothe him. His hand gripped hers, the pressure urgent. His wide mouth was open, gasping for breath. Hands were under his huge chest now, dragging him into a sitting position, Darina helping, propping him up against the dresser that was at the back of the set.

A few moments later he seemed to slip into unconsciousness.

'Where the hell's that ambulance?' Neil shouted.

'Jan says it's on its way,' said someone else; Darina thought it was David Bartholomew.

The entire studio was now gathered around Bruce. The studio nurse appeared and asked everyone to move back and give the man more air. She took his pulse, raised his eyelids and inspected his pupils. Her starched professionalism seemed to harbour unease.

Jan materialized, her face worried. She looked at the unconscious man and the nurse beside him. 'I rang through for an ambulance as soon as he collapsed,' she said. 'It must be here soon. He looks dreadful.' She turned and surveyed the waiting technicians and production team. 'Take a tea break,' she ordered. Slowly one or two people started to drift away then more followed as two ambulancemen arrived with a stretcher. Neil explained Bruce had seemed to suffer a heart attack; they exchanged words with the nurse, performed their own examination of the Australian then one of them opened a medical bag and gave him an injection.

For a moment Darina expected Bruce to respond and open his eyes, but nothing happened, his figure remained as inert and lifeless as before. With swift expertise the ambulancemen manoeuvred the heavy body on to the stretcher and bore it away. The nurse disappeared.

Neil looked at the table, at the glasses standing still filled with fruit cup. Those left in the studio followed his gaze. 'What's going to happen to the programme?' Mark asked.

FOUR

DARINA never knew how she managed the journey back to Somerset that afternoon.

All during the drive through the cold drizzle that licked the motorway and veiled the windscreen, squeaking the wipers, she was haunted by an image of Bruce fighting for life on the studio floor. Then by the news of his death, announced by David Bartholomew after the tea break. His call to the hospital had received the information Bruce had been pronounced dead on arrival.

None of them could believe the big Australian's life could have been snuffed out so quickly. One moment he had been vital, dominating, contentious, the next helpless. Had he, Darina wondered as the rain increased and she switched the windscreen wipers on to full, had a weak heart? The very idea seemed laughable yet why else would he have succumbed so quickly?

It seemed to take even longer than usual to get to the cottage.

When she finally arrived, she switched off the engine and sat in the car looking at the squares of light that said William was home. She didn't want to analyse her reluctance to go in.

He came out and opened the driver's door, his tall frame bending down to peer in at her. 'Darling, what are you doing, sitting in the rain? Let me help you with your stuff.'

Darina got out and opened the rear of the car. After a quick glance at her face, William made no further comment but picked up a bundle of papers, added them to the top of a large box of food and carried everything into the cottage. She hefted a small case and her laptop computer and followed him inside.

In the kitchen she blurted out the news and then stood in

the circle of William's comforting arms, shivering, waves of released tension shaking her frame as tiredness and grief overwhelmed her.

After letting her cry for a little, he sat her down in a chair and got her a brandy. He seemed as shocked as she by the sudden death of her colleague. But, as she continued to weep, unable to articulate the depth of her distress, she could sense strain building behind his sympathy.

She felt abandoned, lost. She wanted him to be strong for her, to give her nothing less than total understanding. To be sufficiently confident in her love for him to allow her to show the extent of her grief for another man. It was too much to ask of anyone, certainly of a fiancé whose self-esteem seemed to have been dented by the advent of television and a certain large Australian into her life. She could just manage to understand that he needed some sign from her that he was still the most important person in her life but she was unable to control herself sufficiently to give him one and that hurt as well.

Wearily, scrubbing away tears with what was left of her handkerchief, she got up and started to unpack the box of food, trying to find the dish of *coq au vin* she'd brought home for their supper. As she sniffed away her tears and forced her body to stop shaking, Darina could feel William's smothered resentment at the depths of her response to Bruce's death coming at her in waves and she felt frightened at the fissures that had appeared in their relationship over the last few weeks.

DARINA FOUND the *coq au vin* and put it in the microwave for a reheat. William gave a deep sigh and looked into the bottom of his empty glass. 'The worst of it is,' he said slowly, 'that though I'm shocked at the news, really deeply shocked, part of me is pleased you no longer have to work with Bruce Bennett.' His eyes, dark and troubled, met hers. 'There, I've said it. I'm ashamed, truly ashamed, but it's the truth.'

She was grateful for his honesty. It cut through the dan-

gerous emotions that were swirling about her and took her
straight into his arms. 'Oh, darling, I'm sorry! You never had
to worry about Bruce. I liked him a lot but it's you I love!'

Even while he kissed her and she felt her body dissolve
against his, a little voice inside Darina said she had been less
honest than William. There had been something dangerously
compelling about Bruce. The electrical strength of his personality, his unconventionality, his sense of humour, even the
capacity for violence that seemed to exist not far below the
surface of his volatile temperament, made other men seem
pallid by comparison.

Over supper she got William talking about his week. More
relaxed now, he told her about the crop of small-time villain-
ies Somerset and Avon had produced, the tedium of dealing
with unsolvable minor incidents and the sad tale of a confidence trickster preying on elderly ladies. 'Two widows have
been done out of a large portion of their savings for phoney
insurance policies that were supposed to protect their futures.
We've issued details to the local press and they've all printed
stories but I fully expect to hear more of the man. Why can't
people look below the surface? Why do they always believe
what they want to believe?' Then his face softened as he
looked at her. 'I suppose that goes for me too, though I've
been believing what I didn't want to believe. Poor love,
you've had a hell of an experience. Do you want to tell me
about it properly?'

Slowly at first, then more confidently, Darina told him
about Bruce's collapse and the consternation it had caused.

'Neil was the only one who kept his head, he was amaz-
ingly quick to react. Within minutes he persuaded Mark to
record a tribute to Bruce that could be broadcast at the start
of next week's programme. He said that way it could be seen
as a sort of valediction.'

'You mean they're actually going to use the programme? I
don't believe it!'

Darina found herself apologetic. 'Neil hasn't decided yet,

he wanted to have it as an option, I think. He's got to discuss it all with the channel chiefs.'

'But he organized this tribute, you did say it was a tribute, didn't you? Well, you said he organized that the moment he heard Bruce was actually dead?'

Darina nodded. 'He wanted me to take part as well but I couldn't.'

'I should think not! But this Mark fellow had no such sensibilities?'

'Well, he is a professional, he's been at it for ages.' Even to William Darina couldn't admit that she had found Mark's ability to produce an eminently well judged and graceful short eulogy to his former co-presenter slightly chilling.

'Well, at least Bruce Bennett wasn't murdered!'

Darina looked up, startled. 'I hadn't even thought it might be murder!' Speculation began to fill her grey eyes.

'Now don't start imagining things, didn't you tell me he had a heart attack?'

'It certainly looked like it. Though,' she added thoughtfully, 'I've never actually seen anyone with a heart attack. But he did look as though he was having a seizure of some sort, he was in great distress, unable to breathe.' She looked more and more thoughtful. 'As you know, I liked Bruce but there were certainly one or two others who could well have harboured murderous thoughts towards him. David Bartholomew, the production manager, couldn't stand him and Mark didn't seem too keen, either.'

'He didn't give that impression on the programme.'

'You haven't seen the one we recorded yesterday. He more or less engineered a confrontation between Bruce and a French wine man. Jean-Pierre Prudhomme actually accused Bruce of founding his success on the double theft of yeast and a master vintner from himself.'

'Hardly sounds a motive for murder!'

'If you'd seen them together, you might have second

thoughts! Either seemed capable of killing the other at that point.'

'Shall we see all this tomorrow night?'

'No, Neil stopped the recording and then got Jean-Pierre to produce some wine suggestions for Christmas instead. But it certainly showed another side to Bruce.'

'But you can't really be suggesting that he was poisoned?' William sounded incredulous. 'You're beginning to see murder at every turn, my girl.'

Darina found herself able to laugh. 'You're right, I'm being ridiculous, Bruce couldn't possibly have been poisoned. Anything that could act as dramatically as that would have had to have been in the fruit cup and Mark, Jean-Pierre and I all drank it as well as Bruce. If he had been poisoned, so should we all.' She stretched out her arms. 'Do I look dead to you?'

William smiled and shook his head.

'Anyway, the hospital will undoubtedly have to do an autopsy after a sudden death like that. They should be able to confirm it was a heart attack.'

'What's going to happen to the *Table* series?' he asked.

'I don't know.' Darina tried not to sound worried. 'But I think finding a suitable replacement for Bruce could mean another upheaval to the programme. Neil could go back to having a female wine expert and swap me for a male cook. I could well find myself out of a job.'

'Surely not, you're doing so well!' he said gamely but Darina could tell the thought didn't appal him the way it did her.

She gave him a slightly forced smile. 'Thank you for that, darling, and there could be a case for saying Neil will keep the show much as it is. But it won't be easy to find someone to take Bruce's place, he was not only brilliant on wine but he was also such a personality.'

William banged wine glasses on to the table. 'Personally I thought he was brash and a bit of a pseud.'

Darina fought a spurt of temper. 'Well, there were millions of viewers who didn't agree with you.'

William winced. 'I'm sorry, I shouldn't have said that. My trouble is, much as I enjoy seeing you on television, I enjoy seeing you here more.'

'And you think if I was no longer part of the show or if it folded, we'd have more time together?'

He said nothing, just looked at her warily.

'How much were we seeing of each other before I started doing *Table?* You spend most of your time these days hunting down criminals. Even at weekends you're not around home much.'

'It's only temporary,' he said hastily. 'We'll soon have things under control and you wouldn't know I wasn't in the most regulated of nine to five jobs.'

'When have you ever had that sort of life? No, what it is is that you want to know exactly where I am all of the time, just in case you might be able to get off for an early night once in a while.'

'Not to mention the free days I manage to squeeze in every now and again to make up for all the overtime. But I honestly would prefer it if your television career did keep on developing successfully.'

All at once she felt herself relax and be able to grin affectionately at him. 'Liar!'

'When will you know what's happening with the show?' he asked.

She shrugged her shoulders. 'No idea. As you know, we've all got a two-week break. I imagine that between now and Christmas Neil will be working out what his options are. I should think he'll ring when he knows what's to happen.'

'Anything you can do to help protect yourself?'

'Can't think of a thing,' she said cheerfully, getting up to make some coffee. 'I shall just get on with finishing that book and looking after my neglected man.'

'How about putting your neglected man first?' His tone was cheerful but there was an undercurrent of real feeling. 'Shall we have coffee with the news in the other room?' He went through to the living-room.

Darina was left grinding coffee beans, waiting for the kettle to boil and feeling stricken. She realized she was by no means innocent in the deterioration of the state of affairs between them. William was straightforward and caring, she remembered his pleasure and pride when she had landed the television job, the way he had stuck up for her against his mother. He was intelligent and imaginative. If he seemed to have lost his sense of humour for the moment, it wasn't too difficult to understand why. And she loved him, even when he was being prickly and resentful. No big, charismatic Australian was going to come between them, particularly now he was dead.

For a vertiginous moment Darina wondered what might have happened if Bruce hadn't succumbed to his heart attack. She put any such speculation firmly behind her. She had never really known Bruce. It was, though, damning to realize just how careful she had been *not* to get to know him, how, after that first dinner together, she had held back from entering into even the most casual of friendships outside the business of putting on the programme.

Perhaps it would have been better not to have remained so aloof. First Bruce's rudeness to David Bartholomew and then that business about Jean-Pierre, his yeast and the master vintner had been a shock, had suggested a less than pleasant side to him. He had threatened a lawsuit if Jean-Pierre persisted in his allegation but he hadn't denied the basic facts. Darina tried to imagine William behaving in that way and failed. But she couldn't, either, see him taking her over the way Bruce had and transforming her appearance.

It came to Darina that Bruce had used his charm to coat a basic ruthlessness. She recognized that what had motivated Bruce was self-centred ambition. *Table* was his bid for international television recognition. Everything that affected the success of that programme mattered to him and that included Darina's appearance. Once that had been sorted out, Darina saw that his interest in her had not been great enough to make it worth his while overcoming her reluctance to become involved. Had he, indeed, even really considered a relationship with her? Had she been worrying about nothing? Quite suddenly Darina remembered the way Lynn had snapped at Bruce the previous day, the look of frustrated anger on his face.

What exactly had been going on between them?

'Am I getting any coffee?' William called plaintively from the living-room.

Darina picked up the coffee tray. She would forget Bruce Bennett, at least for this evening.

FIVE

NEIL CANTLOW stretched himself. 'Whisky?' he suggested to David Bartholomew, his production manager. He walked over to the drinks tray that stood in one corner of the large and comfortable room he used as his study, poured out two generous glasses, added splashes of soda water and gave one to the other man. He took his own towards the large windows that looked out on to a small garden, winter-bare and tossed with wind, dead leaves blowing into drifts.

'So, scrub the amount earmarked for the down-under filming trip but keep in the figure for other filming,' he said with his back to the room.

David Bartholomew checked his notes and nodded. He set down his drink and looked again at the budgets that were scattered across the coffee table in front of him.

'Have you decided yet on Bruce's replacement?'

Neil shook his head but didn't look round.

'What about bringing Milly back?'

At that Neil did turn. 'Have you lost all sense of reason, David?'

'It isn't quite such a mad idea, Neil. She had a following, she knows her stuff and she's available.'

'Seen her, have you, David? She gone running to you to ask if you could weasel her back into the programme? I didn't think you were one of her fans.' Neil left the window and threw himself into his large leather chair.

'I'm not, as you well know, but there is all that film we shot in the autumn with her.'

Neil grimaced. 'I told you when we changed presenters that we had to write most of that off, that we could only think of using some of the establishing shots.'

'You really can't consider Milly, then?'

Neil put down his drink. 'Look, David, we've just got the ratings for *Table* looking respectable again. You know it was almost disappearing down the plughole in October. I know John Franks was the main disaster but Milly didn't exactly help.'

'But wasn't the trouble really that the whole thrust of the show was wrong?'

'The first six we made last year were what got us the second series,' Neil pointed out, not for the first time.

'But the viewing figures had already dropped drastically by the time the last programme was shown.'

'We were up against stiff competition by then, scheduled opposite that new sit-com and a scandal-packed investigation into the Common Market.' Neil pulled his stubby hand down his face, dragging the skin away from his eyes. 'I thought the show just needed to settle down. It takes time to establish a steady audience. Everyone was talking about *Table* after the first programme went out.'

'You mean someone mentioned it in your local?'

'And the proposal for a second thirteen-week series was accepted.'

'Some of the channel programming decisions are hard to explain.' David's tone was heavy with irony.

Neil flushed. 'I didn't hear any complaints from you about the show's format then!'

'Would you have listened? Have you forgotten the way you went on about how *Table* was raising public consciousness on taste, *haute cuisine,* wines that were really worth drinking, the fostering of small producers?'

'It's all still valid,' protested Neil.

'Come off it, boss. What we've got now is solid, middle of the road stuff that everyone can relate to.'

'The *standards* are still there!'

'OK, I'm not arguing about that.'

'And the show has worked. Since Bruce and Darina joined

us, we've started to look viable.' Neil rubbed his face with his hand. 'We've sold it to Australia as well as Canada, it looks as though Zimbabwe could be interested and yesterday we had approaches from a German channel. That's why Bruce is going to be so difficult to replace and why Milly is not an option. We can't go back.'

David looked at him for a moment then said, in a different tone of voice, 'Neil, you know I've mentioned I've got a new programme idea? Well, can I talk to you about my outline?'

'David, I've enough on my plate at the moment without having to listen to another of your cock-a-mamie ideas.'

Resentment lit the production manager's eyes and Neil realized he'd better backtrack a little. 'Look, David, you're a great organizer and number cruncher, right? And one of these days I'm going to give you a chance, let you act as a creative producer. But not yet, you're not ready. Just trust me.'

David opened his mouth but before he could say anything Anthea Cantlow popped her head round the study door. 'Staying to lunch, David?'

The production manager started shuffling together his papers. 'Thanks, Anthea, but no thanks. I have a date in town.'

She came into the room. 'That's a shame, we haven't seen you properly for some time. Come round over Christmas.' She didn't look at Neil.

'You mean this catastrophe has called off your holiday?' David sounded unsurprised.

'What with everything, Neil's decided the Caribbean has to manage without me.' Anthea tried for a brave smile but gave up half-way, her mouth settling back into discontent. 'The children are devastated and I'm scampering around like a demented shrike trying to get the festive food together.'

'You have my deepest sympathy and I'd love to come round sometime,' David said, closing his attaché case and getting up from his chair. His white teeth gleamed as he gave her a wide smile.

'We'll have to get together again anyway over the new arrangements.' Neil got up as well. 'I'll be in touch, right?'

He saw David out and went back into the study, where Anthea was collecting together the debris of their meeting.

'You got the boy back, then?'

She nodded.

Neil watched the way her hands impatiently slapped empty coffee-cups on to the tray, the line of her back a reproach. 'How did he take it?'

Anthea added overflowing ashtrays with a bang that dislodged half their contents on to the tray. She stood and faced him. 'How do you think? It was incredibly mean of you to make me go and collect him. As I arrived, he was boasting to all his chums about Christmas in the Caribbean. You know what little snobs they all are at that place.'

'It's got a good academic record,' Neil said absently.

'I waited until we got to Guildford before telling him, I judged that left just about enough of the journey for him to get rid of the worst of his temper.'

'Did you tell him about the mountain bike?'

'Don't think that's going to get you out of trouble.' Anthea collected the whisky glasses and banged them down on the tray. 'He reckoned that was coming for Christmas in any case.'

'What!'

She nodded grimly. 'Don't you remember mentioning it last Easter?'

With dismay a few casual words came back to Neil. Something about mountain bikes possibly featuring on the Father Christmas sack list. 'But that was before we decided to go away.'

'No connection in an eleven-year-old's mind between the two; you didn't get the programming right.' She bent to pick up the tray, hesitated, then collapsed in a chair instead. The dark shoulder-length hair, worn pushed back by a black velvet hair band, fell forward as she buried her face in her hands.

'God, I'm exhausted and I haven't even started Christmas yet.' She looked up at her husband. 'You have no idea what I've got in front of me—and I thought it was going to be lying on a beach in the sun with someone else to do all the work!'

Anthea's fragile face and dark hair had once made her the prettiest undergraduate at Cambridge. A girl avidly pursued by men, the most determined, relentless and finally successful being Neil.

Fifteen years on the fine skin was showing signs of wear and she refused to do anything about the grey hairs that were more and more noticeable. 'I earned those,' she said after the first few appeared. 'They're my badges of courage. Two children, a husband in television and a hard-won job in publishing aren't achieved without scars.' Anthea was fiction editor and a director with a medium-sized publishing company. She said the balancing act required to buttress the avant-garde critical successes that made her name with the commercial successes that guaranteed the company remained financially viable was excellent practice for dealing with the demands of her family. Neil said she used the constant pile of manuscripts to be read as excuses for not coping with his shirts, the family's meals and the children's chauffeuring requirements.

These were dealt with by a daily housekeeper and an au pair with a driving licence.

When Gavin went to prep school, Neil assumed the chauffeuring, not to mention the housekeeping, would be reduced, perhaps to the point where the au pair could go, but Sarah's social and education schedule seemed to have escalated on the Parkinson principle and Anthea said one less at home hardly made any difference to the household budget. The prep school fees certainly made a difference to Neil's pocket.

He looked at his wife's tired face and his expression softened. 'You haven't managed to persuade Muriel and Gretel to cancel their Christmas plans and stay with us?'

'Not a chance!' She closed her eyes and leaned back in the

chair. 'God, Christmas without our housekeeper or the au pair!' Slow tears began to ooze down her face.

Neil couldn't bear it. 'Buy all the stuff, can't you? Pam in the office can tell you all the best places to go, everyone's been sending us details of their special offers for weeks now. And how about trying for some help from one of the agencies?' To hell with the cost, he told himself, it would be peanuts beside what the Caribbean holiday would have cost them, even after the cancellation charges.

Tears continued to roll down Anthea's face.

Neil stood awkwardly in front of her, knowing with sick certainty the real cause of her distress and wondering how best to handle the situation.

After a moment she wiped her eyes with the back of her hand, leaving dark smudges of mascara that emphasized the drained quality of her face. 'I still can't believe he's dead,' she said.

Neil held himself very still. 'I know, sweetheart, I know,' his voice soothing.

'It was so sudden, so unexpected. We were all enjoying ourselves over lunch and he was making a date to take us out to dinner. Then no sooner do I get home than I hear he's dead!' Her face grew even paler, the soft, brown eyes were drowned in tears.

Neil squatted down in front of her, took her hands in his. 'Darling, he's gone. Even his body now, back to Australia.'

At least she didn't pull her hands away. 'I don't see why he couldn't have been buried here, so ridiculous sending the coffin all the way to the other side of the world.'

'It's what his sister wanted. His widow, too, I expect. At least, I don't suppose his sister could have organized it all if it hadn't been Shelley Bennett's idea as well.' He felt Anthea's hands grip his and was grateful she seemed to think he could give her some support.

'And the hospital didn't object, even though his seizure wasn't a heart attack or a stroke? Didn't they think that strange?' Gone was all her sophistication, her intelligence, her ability to turn life her way. Childlike, she looked into his eyes asking for answers he didn't have.

'As I told you, they didn't know what caused his death but they found no evidence it was unnatural.'

Anthea sat slumped in the chair. She seemed to have lost all ability to get some sort of hold on the situation. Neil's heart bled for her. She was all the world to him and he'd do anything for her, anything. He cast caution to the winds. 'Look, shall we see if we can book into a nice hotel over Christmas? You deserve something better than killing yourself over the turkey.'

A rehearsal for a smile touched her face, she bent and lightly kissed his mouth. 'You're a love and I'm a spoiled bitch. Of course we won't go to a hotel, we haven't avoided one lot of bills we can't afford to incur another set.' Gently she released her hands and rose. 'Lunch will be ready; brace yourself for dealing with Gavin. Perhaps you can take him somewhere this afternoon, how about Christmas shopping?'

He got up, finding his knees stiff and creaking, he didn't take enough exercise these days. 'Sorry, I've got to work, we'll go out to dinner and the flicks tonight instead.'

Suddenly her temper broke and the tragic queen image vanished. 'Sorry! Sorry! You owe me more than sorry, Neil! Don't you have any idea what I'm going through? I had to drive and fetch that wretched boy this morning and deal with his tantrums, I've got Christmas to arrange without any help, five more manuscripts arrived this morning with no time even to look at them and all you can say when I ask you for a *little* help is sorry?' She cast him a look of contempt. 'Just don't ask me to do anything else. Bring those with you.' She swept out of the room without a backward glance.

Neil stood and looked at the loaded tray. The dirty crockery failed to register. He ignored it and went upstairs.

SIX

IT WAS two days before Christmas. The bar was full of happy office workers celebrating before going home to families and loved ones, or just families.

David Bartholomew held two whiskies high above his head and worked a safe passage to the table in the corner where Mark Taylor was waiting. The pages he'd given him to read whilst he fetched more drinks were sitting on the small table in front of him.

David handed over one of the whiskies and sat down. 'Well, what do you think?'

'Do you really think you can set up on your own?' Mark sounded incredulous.

David's eyes narrowed. 'Don't you think I can do it?'

Mark lowered his drink. 'Now don't get touchy, it's just that I didn't know you could manage the finance.'

'I'm not setting up my own production company, Mark, I'm providing the idea and the expertise. Someone else can put up the money.' He sat back in his chair and watched the presenter of *Table*. Long ago David had learned the value of knowing when to open his mouth and when to keep it shut.

Mark gave the sheets of paper a little push. 'Have you shown this to anyone?'

David shook his head. 'I want to have a complete package to present. If you agree to come in, that will give the proposal real weight.' He could see something was worrying Mark and he didn't think it was the outline he'd been reading.

'Why me, David? We've never got on particularly well, what makes you think we could work together?'

'Because you're good. You know that and I know that. And we're honest with each other. You think I'm a pushy black bastard and I think you're a small-minded woman chaser, OK? But you know your job. You know how to interview people, you know the food world, you know television. You come over well, you can let confident personalities shine and bring out the shy ones. And you're really interested in the issues I think we can bring out in this series.' He tapped the outline.

What David hadn't said was that if he could have thought of anyone else who met the criteria he'd just mentioned and would be likely to listen to him, he wouldn't be sitting with Mark in this pub. But you had to hand it to the man, he was everything David had said. If Mark agreed to front the programme, David believed he might really be in with a chance.

'What about Neil, have you mentioned it to him?'

David laughed. 'Man, are you crazy? Do you think I want him pinching my ideas?'

'But he's got a production company, he's known for food programmes, surely he's your best bet?'

'I joined Neil because he promised me I'd have a chance to produce my own ideas but he won't let me near the creative side, nor is he interested in listening to any of my proposals. This isn't the first of them by any means.' He indicated the outline sitting on the table. 'He keeps me chained to administration and the budgets by handing out the odd promise of some chance in the future. Well, I'm fed up with it. I may be the only person in the company who can add but I have more to offer. It's time I produced my own programmes but Neil won't hear of it. Anyway, Cantlow Productions is on the way out.'

'But surely the audience figures for *Table* are looking so much better now!'

'That was before the brilliant new wine presenter copped it in front of the cameras.'

'At least it wasn't live! And Neil did a marvellous job with that last programme and my piece saying what a fantastic chap Bruce was, how we were all going to miss him but he would have wanted the last show to be transmitted as a tribute to his contributions. I bet the shares in Kleenex will be up today, there must have been empty boxes all over the land last night.'

'Mark, you were a real trouper.' David's voice was dry. 'Not a viewer in the country would have twigged what a shit you really thought him.'

Mark shifted uncomfortably in his chair. 'Ill of the dead and all that, David.'

'You really are one of the world's arse-lickers, aren't you, Mark? The man was a shit of the purest sort, the only people in that studio sorry to see Bruce Bennett expire were the women. For some unfathomable reason he really knew how to come on to them. For the rest of us it was one of those times that make you believe in a higher justice.'

'Come on, the man suffered a heart attack!'

'Not what the hospital said. According to them he just upped and died. If it had happened in my country, we'd have said the witch doctor had been paid to see him off. And I don't want any jokes about native superstitions and black naïvety, Mark. I tell you some of the things that happen there are beyond scientific explanation.'

'Come off it, David, you told me you hadn't been back to Nigeria since you were a child. Eton surely knocked all that out of you!'

'Sound as scornful as you like, Mark, but there was a hale and hearty man in the prime of life who suddenly, before our very eyes, had a seizure and died. And, according to the medics, it wasn't a heart attack or a stroke.'

Mark stared at him. 'David, if you insist on pushing this line, I shall think seriously about the advisability of going along with your proposal.'

David pushed away his deep unease and recovered his poise, alienating Mark was no part of his plan. He seized on the implication behind the presenter's words. 'Then you agree the outline has possibilities?'

'A crusading programme, fearlessly investigating areas of

concern in the production of the nation's food? With me doing the interviewing? Yes, of course I do. As you know, it's something after my own heart. And I'm not afraid of contention, I would like to see more of it on *Table*, it's all too cosy for my taste.'

David felt a surge of excitement. 'Mark, that's great!'

'Don't assume too much. My agent will have to approve terms and conditions and, remember, I've an exclusive contract with Neil for this series plus an option for another. That could mean I couldn't contract for another show for a year or so.'

David wasn't worried. '*Table* isn't going to last this series, let alone another, not without Bruce. With his personality, shit that he was, it had a chance. Without him,' he shook his head, 'no way!'

'I thought Neil was talking about increasing the cookery emphasis with Darina and shortening the wine section.'

David thought of the tall blonde cook. 'It might work, given time. She's good, has a knack of making classic recipes interesting, she doesn't talk down to the viewer and has a nice style that makes you feel you can do whatever it is she's demonstrating. But it will take time for her to build a real following and Neil doesn't have time. He's changed the format once already.'

'I'm trying to get him to ask Milly back,' Mark said.

David shook his head. 'I pushed that as well. But, quite apart from the fact that Neil wants to keep Darina and he doesn't think he can go with two women presenters, he's determined not to turn the clock back. I'm sorry, Mark.'

The other man shrugged his shoulders. 'We're finished, anyway, Milly made that quite clear when Neil dumped her.'

'Why blame you? Didn't you tell her Neil was convinced Bruce was going to save the show?'

'You can't reason with Milly.' Mark raised his glass and changed the subject. 'So, do you know if Neil's come to any sort of a decision on Bruce's replacement?'

'Jean-Pierre Prudhomme.'

'The Frenchman?' Mark thought about it for a moment. 'Could work. He's got charm, all the expertise and that accent is a wow with the women. Clever old Neil! Will Jean-Pierre do it?'

'Apparently, yes. He thinks it will increase the market for his wines over here. And he's hoping the sale of the programme to Australia will continue so he can increase his exposure over there as well. If you ask me, he sees himself as a one-man crusade for French wines over the Australian invasion.'

'He might just come over as well as Bruce,' said Mark thoughtfully.

'You think so? Well, Neil had better keep Anthea away from the programme, then.'

Mark's interest sharpened. 'Anthea? You mean it?'

'Didn't you ever see the way she looked at Bruce? Neil was beside himself!'

'Nonsense,' said Mark. 'Anthea's the last person to go for a backwoods hunk like that.'

David let it go. Despite the way he pursued them, Mark never did understand the ways of women. David flattered himself that he did.

He was also convinced he could be on to a winner with his programme idea. Now that Mark had more or less agreed to come on board, he was ready to approach the channel programmers and a production company.

Briefly David wondered if he shouldn't abandon the idea of pushing himself as a creative producer and just settle for getting the whole idea off the ground and running. Perhaps if Neil had been more forthcoming, David would have proposed that to him, it would have been very useful for the series to find a production company willing to take it on and Neil had good contacts amongst the programme planners. And he must be desperate for good ideas. Perhaps David had been a little too autocratic in his dealings with him?

Then he rejected the thought. First off, Neil would probably think the new idea a rival for *Table*. Secondly, David knew he'd dreamed for too long of being able to control the creative thrust of a programme. He watched images on the screen and itched for them to have been realized *his* way. At university, studying English but fascinated by current affairs, politics and the dynamics of modern life, he'd toyed with the idea of journalism but he'd known all along that it was the visual approach that really interested him. Words were all very well but it was pictures that stayed with people. It was being able to *show* people the truth of a story that counted. And in order to do that exactly as you wanted, you had to be in control of the creative side.

Control, that was what everything was about. A speaker could control his words but found his eyes and mouth more difficult. David loved watching politicians on the screen, they were more careful with their faces than actors but even they sometimes found it impossible to control their body language.

David remembered the way Bruce had shifted in his seat as Jean-Pierre had lashed into him that time. The Frenchman had really reached him! The production manager wondered whether there was more to their dispute than yeast and a lost master vintner. Both men were professional charmers and both, for an instant, had allowed raw dislike to strip away the swagger they showed the world.

'Sorry, Mark, what did you say?' Belatedly David realized the other man was speaking.

'I just asked if you'd like another drink? I think we ought to toast our new partnership, don't you? It'll be one in the eye for Neil if he does go under.' Mark sounded almost excited by the prospect.

SEVEN

THE LETTER lay on top of a small pile on Pam's desk. It was an air-letter card that someone had opened none too gently, the edges were torn and one-third hung by the slightest of connections to the rest.

'These are yours,' said Pam after Darina had shed her coat and asked how Christmas had gone for the production secretary.

Darina took the mail with some words of thanks and continued on her way into Neil's office, glancing at the one on top as the production team settled around Neil's desk, exchanging Christmas news while waiting for a couple of researchers to arrive.

It was from Australia; 'Yarramarra' said the return address. The typed contents were quite brief. They informed Darina that the writer had seen the Mike Darcy video of Bruce and Darina, that she was coming over to England and wanted to meet her because she thought there was something Darina could help her with. Would she please ring her hotel in the afternoon of the 7th January so they could make an appointment. The letter was signed Kate Bennett.

Darina's first thought was that the letter must be from Bruce's widow. Then she remembered that Bruce had been married to an Australian food writer called Shelley. Kate, then, must be his sister.

The day of Kate Bennett's arrival was recording day for the next *Table*. Well, it would be easy enough to find time to make a telephone call. Darina folded up the letter, then noticed that it was marked *Personal and Confidential*.

The meeting still hadn't started. Darina slipped out to

Pam's office and asked the secretary if she knew when the letter had arrived and why it had been opened.

'I'm sorry, I really don't know,' the girl apologized. 'At the last minute Neil said I needn't come in between Christmas and New Year, he'd look after the office. Was it something private? Neil never looks at envelopes before ripping them open. I haven't read your letters, I promise. All the mail was sitting in piles when I got here this morning.'

The missing researchers arrived and the meeting started.

MOST OF THAT WEEK'S programme was already set up. The director of a health farm, a lithe and sparkling lady whose looks belied her age, had agreed to come on the programme several weeks earlier. Darina had worked out some attractive slimming recipes and Bruce had been supposed to talk about alcohol-free wines. Jean-Pierre Prudhomme had agreed to take on his mantle for four programmes at least. The Frenchman was at the meeting, welcomed by Neil. But he insisted on abandoning the non-alcohol approach. 'There is no such wine worthy of the name,' he announced. Instead, he would consider some sparkling white wines that could add interest and not too many calories to the New Year health conscious approach to the table.

Neil turned back to Darina. 'Tomorrow I want film of you taking an exercise class at the health farm and talking to the chef.'

Mark interrupted. 'Neil, if there's any interviewing to be done, that's my job.'

'This is something for Darina,' the executive producer said impatiently.

'But surely...' Mark started.

'Shut up, Mark.' Neil's voice was weary.

Mark shot him a furious look that burned with malice and reluctantly subsided.

Neil continued, 'Jan, can you direct? Peter rang last night, he's broken a leg skiing and I can't find anyone else.'

Jan Parker, the studio director, remained composed. 'If the meeting finishes in time for me to get the revised camera script done today, yes. I suppose the cameraman will be Dick?'

'Do you have a problem with that?'

Jan shook her head. 'The problem is all his, Neil. One of these days he's going to have to wake up to the fact that females have been directing for some time now.'

THE FOLLOWING DAY Darina was collected from her Chelsea home early in the morning. Already in the mini van were Jan, her production assistant, a girl called Fiona, Dick, the cameraman, Tarquin, the sound recordist, Kevin, the electrician, referred to as Sparks, and a collection of dimpled metal boxes.

Darina was eyed up and down as the driver helped her into the van. Her greetings were acknowledged by the men who then lit up cigarettes and started discussing between themselves their personal Christmas disaster stories. The vehicle filled with smoke.

As they drove into Surrey, Jan said, 'I'm sorry but can you cut the cigarettes until you get outside?'

The men exchanged glances that spoke volumes about interfering females but fags were stubbed out. A little later Dick addressed himself to Darina. 'This your first filming experience, then?'

She nodded. 'It's quite exciting getting out of the studio.'

He broke into a smile, his solid, taciturn face suddenly looking more approachable. 'Stick with us, you'll be all right. Bit of an élite, we are. Your chaps back in the studio don't know night from day, we're the real experts.' Then he added, 'And we don't have to be saddled with nannies.'

Jan ignored his remark.

At their destination, they all piled out of the van and stood for a moment looking at the classical portico of the stately home that had been transformed into a temple of good health.

'Right, Dick,' said Jan briskly. 'While we make our number

inside, can you get us forty seconds of establishing shots here?' With a pleasant nod in his direction, she led the way in, leaving Dick and Tarquin happily assessing angles.

'Christ,' she exploded as they entered the hall. 'If I could only once, just once, tell that chauvinist pig what I think of him! Nannies indeed! If only he wasn't exactly what he thinks he is, a bloody good cameraman! I don't have to waste time holding his hand over what's wanted out there, he'll give me exactly what we need as an establishing shot.'

A ravishing-looking girl in a pretty overall came up and whisked them off to see Helen Donovan, the health farm's director. Slim, vital, perfectly groomed with short, dark hair and a vivid red mouth, wearing a red jersey suit with black braid and brass buttons, she was full of enthusiasm for the filming.

'We'll show Darina where to change in a minute, the regular class is just coming to an end but I've got some volunteers to stay on for your filming. Then I thought you might like to get some shots of some of the equipment such as the langlauf and rowing machines, the weights, that sort of thing. Followed by a massage session and a mud bath. And how about ending up in the beauty salon?'

'We really need to concentrate on your food.' Jan appeared slightly taken aback by the whirl of activity Helen Donovan created around her. 'Your chef is going to be available, isn't he?'

'Of course, he's very publicity conscious and I'm sure he'll come over well, he loves talking about his work. We have a marvellous lunch-time buffet plus, of course, personally plated diet meals. Some time before twelve would be best, before the vultures descend, there's no way we can hold them back. Would you like me to ask Chef to be available then?'

In no time it was all organized.

Darina hoped she wouldn't have to spend too much time leaping about. Displaying her thunder thighs in the turquoise leotard and brilliant blue tights that wardrobe had produced for her was a daunting prospect. With immense tact, though, Helen Donovan seemed to have managed to find several figures which exceeded hers, as well as a number of slender souls who would be excellent publicity for the health farm. As was the lithe instructor who led the little group through a series of body-stretching movements gradually leading into more strenuous activity that left Darina temporarily exhausted before Jan and Dick were satisfied they had what they wanted.

Much to her surprise, however, by the time Darina had attacked the exercise machines, showered, switched to a swimsuit, been shot in the whirlpool, then dressed in a track suit ready for interviewing the chef, she discovered she felt marvellous, full of energy and with her mind crystal clear.

The buffet lunch looked mouthwatering: a hot clear vegetable soup that smelt wonderful, colourful salads concocted from various fresh fruits and vegetables, fatless fish and poultry presented in imaginative ways, and a huge bowl of out-of-season fresh strawberries.

Nature's excesses had been outlawed, only the purest impulses of the taste buds were allowed to be indulged.

Darina looked at the strawberries, flown in from Heaven knew where.

'No cream, I see,' she joked to Francis, the chef, a Viking of a man, his fresh skin glowing with vitality, the blond hair tied back in an exuberant pony-tail.

'Lemon juice and a little black pepper is all you need,' he shot her a smiling glance.

'Black pepper?'

'It's a great taste enhancer, we use it a lot. All the dressings are low in fat, all are full of flavour and freshness, a delight for the taste buds. And look at these Mediterranean prawns, pure, tender, succulent and so good for you! Isn't this indulgence of the purest sort?' His clean-cut features defied her to admit anything else.

Darina thought of the marvellous marriage those prawns could make with an aïoli mayonnaise made with garlic, egg yolks and the best olive oil. She forced herself to reject the image.

'Of course, we also cater for clients' special needs.' Francis became confiding, here was a man totally dedicated to his job, burning with missionary fire. 'Some of our guests have medical conditions that necessitate strict attention to their food. It makes one realize what a delicate instrument the body is.'

'Do you see yourself, perhaps, as a scientist designing fuel for a Rolls-Royce engine?' asked Darina.

'Oh, yes, that's a *wonderful* way of putting it. For everything we eat has two functions, the first is to provide an enjoyable experience but the second, and it has to be the more important, is to enable our bodies to perform at maximum efficiency.'

'Do you have trouble with getting that over to some of your guests, or are they all willing victims?' Darina caught back her words as the hint of a frown appeared on the classic forehead. 'I mean, of course, disciples?'

Francis smiled gently. 'Our clients pay large sums of money to have bad habits corrected and the physical results of their dissipation repaired. It would be foolish for them to cheat at the table but, I have to say, some of them do.' His fine features became sorrowful. 'You wouldn't believe what arrives in suitcases, or the way some guests sneak out to gorge themselves on fatty horrors outside our gates.' His voice dripped with disgust. 'Mind you, there are also those who make a fetish of fads. The demands some of them make as to what should and shouldn't go into the food they're served!'

'But you pander to them?'

'Of course, as long as they conform to our nutritional principles. It's not always a whim, though. As I said, there are people with certain conditions that mean a strict diet is vital.'

'I think we're ready to start recording,' Jan said from across the room. Dick had set up his camera, lights had been organized, sound had been checked. 'Darina, get Francis to show you the display and explain what they are aiming for and how

they compensate for the lack of cream, butter and other goodies. Just what you've been talking about, in fact. OK?'

LATER, over an after-lunch tisane, when Dick and Tarquin
and the driver had disappeared outside for a smoke and Fiona
was checking out various details, Darina said to Jan, 'Bruce
would have appreciated this food. Remember how he always
took his grated vegetable salads everywhere? He was always
on about the purity of taste, the importance of eating the right
thing.' Darina paused then added, 'I still find it incredible to
realize he's dead, he seemed so vital, so *alive*.'

Jan drank some of her mint tea. 'I'm afraid I was never
one of the Bruce Bennett fan club,' she said. 'To me there
was something bogus about the man. I'm sorry but that out-
back act of his really turned me off.'

This was the first female Darina had come across immune
to the Bennett charm. Darina inspected the series director
more closely. Jan's appearance was as disciplined as her professionalism; fair hair with sparkling highlights was cut short,
providing a splendid helmet for her strong face with its
straight nose, severe mouth and eyes the colour of a sea-
washed pebble. As usual, the director was dressed in elegant
slacks which today were topped with a heavy silk sweater
worn over a silk shirt, all in shades of cinnamon. She took as
much trouble with her appearance as with her programmes
and had a reputation for perfectionism.

'How did you think Bruce came over as the *Table* wine
expert?' Darina asked curiously.

'Extremely well,' Jan said crisply. 'I certainly admired the
way he handled his spot. His death is a catastrophe for us.
His personality, the atmosphere you had created between the
three of you, all breathed success. The show could have gone
on to be one of the classics, with series after series commis-
sioned. And I could have made my reputation with it,' she
added ruefully.

'Is it that hard to get jobs as a director?'

Jan's pleasant face grew set. 'When I started, as a researcher fifteen years ago, women directors were a rarity, they weren't supposed to make it beyond production assistant. I've had to fight every inch of the way. Many's the filming trip I've been on with cameramen like Dick who've assumed that I was the production assistant and looked around for the director.' She paused, gazing beyond Darina through the window to the bare landscape outside.

'So much has changed today. There are many more women around but the careful training I went through has all disappeared. Take Neil, now don't get me wrong, I'm very grateful to him for giving me my chance to direct *Table* but he's never directed himself in his life. He joined a regional station after university, became a dogsbody, said all the right things at the right time and worked his way up the production side without even having drawn up a camera script. The industry is full of men like him these days, who don't really appreciate what the director's job is. Would you believe I don't have anything to do with the editing of the programmes? At the end of recording that's my job finished. In the old days, the director was in charge of the whole process and I'd have had my say as to how the final programme was put together. Now idiots like David Bartholomew with no technical experience think they could write a shooting script and direct.'

'You mean he wants to be a director?'

'He wants it so much you can smell it. He thinks Neil should get rid of me and appoint him instead.' Jan gave a short bark of a laugh. 'Well, I don't suppose soon there'll be a programme for him to direct.'

'Are you saying that without Bruce we haven't got a chance?' Darina demanded.

'I'm sorry, I didn't mean to put it like that.' Jan put down her cup with a little bang. 'It must have sounded totally crass and insensitive. You are coming over well and Neil is quite right to give you more air time. But having to change the format yet again, losing someone the public had instantly

taken to, well, it's not easy. We were only just pulling ourselves out of a position of instant blackout. Viewing figures
are the bottom line in commercial television these days. Not
only commercial,' she added. 'All the channel controllers eat
the ratings for breakfast. Indigestion can call for rescheduling,
heartburn means goodbye.'

'And you think without Bruce we are heartburn?'

Jan started gathering together her things. 'I'm very much
afraid so.'

For no very good reason she could immediately identify,
Darina remembered the letter from Bruce's sister. Why was
she coming over to England? What exactly was it she wanted
to discuss? And why with Darina?

EIGHT

DURING THE LUNCH BREAK on recording day, Darina used the public telephone in the hospitality room. She closed her ears to the hubbub around her and got through to the hotel that Kate Bennett had given in her letter, only to find that Bruce's sister hadn't yet checked in. She tried again later that afternoon, when the quiet was only broken by David Bartholomew and one of the researchers talking over some detail of a future programme in a back corner.

This time Kate Bennett was there.

'Honey, it's so good of you to ring, I'm just desperate to get together with you, you're the reason for this trip, but I'm bushed after that flight. Could we meet tomorrow?' The voice was flat with tiredness.

Tomorrow would mean delaying her return to Somerset. Darina asked exactly what it was that was so important.

There was a long pause then Kate Bennett said, 'On that video Bruce sent me it said you had solved several murders. That was true, wasn't it?'

Darina murmured something about being in the right place at the right time.

'Well, I don't believe my brother died a natural death, I think he was murdered.'

'Murdered? What makes you think that?'

There was a long pause. 'Look, I don't want to discuss this on the telephone and, like I said, I'm just bushed by the flight. I was hoping you could come round tomorrow, say in the morning, so I could tell you exactly why I am certain Bruce's death wasn't natural and we could discuss how you could help.' The suggestion was bizarre, but there was no touch of hysteria in Kate Bennett's voice; she sounded matter of fact and eminently sensible.

'What about the police?' Darina asked. 'Surely you should be talking to them?'

There was a pause. 'It's difficult, when I explain you'll understand. Is it impossible for you to come here tomorrow? Would it be easier if I came to you?'

Darina found herself saying she would go to the hotel, made a date for eleven o'clock and replaced the receiver, her mind spinning.

WILLIAM WAS NOT sympathetic when, after several abortive earlier attempts that evening, Darina finally managed to get hold of him to explain that she wouldn't be down until the next day at the earliest.

'What the hell do you mean, Bruce Bennett may have been murdered? Are you sure you're not getting a complex about sudden death?'

Darina once again went through her conversation with Kate Bennett.

'She must be out of her mind. Saying she can't go to the police and running half-way round the world to talk to you, what on earth does she think you can do?'

'That's what I have to find out.'

'If there'd been anything suspicious about his death, the autopsy would have found it.'

'Don't you think it could be suspicious that they didn't find anything? Neil says the pathologist reported there was no evidence that the death was anything but natural but that he didn't die from a heart attack or a stroke. Well, something must have caused that seizure.'

But she was talking to a hardened professional, one who dealt with the importance of evidence every working day of his life. 'You're beginning to sound like Sherlock Holmes.'

'The dog that didn't bark, you mean?'

All at once his attitude softened. 'I miss you,' he said quietly.

'And I you, darling.' Darina hesitated then said, 'This mayn't be going on much longer, people are talking about the programme not lasting now that Bruce has gone.'

'You're not serious?' William's incredulity warmed Darina's soul.

'The studio director seems to think the channel could pull the plug on us.'

'I'm sorry, darling.' She could hear the effort he was putting into sounding sincere, how his relief battled with what he knew would be crushing disappointment for her.

'But don't you see, if that really is so, someone could have had a motive for getting rid of Bruce?' It seemed so obvious to Darina, she couldn't understand how the implication could have passed Detective Inspector Pigram by.

There was a long pause at the other end of the phone.

'Are you really sure the show is likely to be cancelled?' There was a sharpness in William's voice that had been missing before, the professional had been brought into play.

'No,' admitted Darina. 'Neil acts as though the improvement in *Table*'s audience figures can be sustained, that real success is just round the corner.'

'Sounds a dodgy motive for murder, then.'

'But he would have to act like that, wouldn't he? He couldn't afford to sound anything but confident.'

Another pause. 'Darina, darling, don't let your imagination run away with you. We'll talk about this tomorrow.'

'By then I'll know what it is Kate Bennett thinks is so suspicious.'

Darina could hear the effort William put into not saying that it was unlikely that could alter anything.

DARINA presented herself the following morning at Kate Bennett's hotel just before eleven o'clock. She had deliberately forced any further speculation about Bruce Bennett's death from her mind. Much better to come fresh to what his sister had to say. Any temptation to mull over the little she knew and to spin together some theory from the hints, gossip and her observations around the production team was avoided by working hard on her contribution to the *Table* book, now, thank heavens, nearly finished.

As she walked towards the hotel, though, Darina could no longer restrain her curiosity over Kate Bennett's visit and theories, each wilder than the last, rose like sugar-paste castles.

The hotel was one of London's modern boxes, towering up towards the sky not far from Hyde Park. Just why, Darina wondered as she entered the busy reception area, were people so keen to stay in places that offered such anonymous atmosphere? Why not a hotel that said something about the place you had just arrived in? Was the unfamiliar too unsettling?

She asked the quietly efficient young man behind the enquiry desk for Kate Bennett's room number, explaining she had an appointment.

He consulted a computer terminal. For an instant the pleasant, professional smile disappeared. 'Would you mind waiting a moment?' he asked Darina, then disappeared into some nether region.

She remained where she was. After a couple of minutes an older man lacking the polished smile appeared. Darina took one look at the keen eyes and closed mouth and alarm bells began to ring.

The newcomer, followed by a younger man, took Darina into a small office furnished with the same low key slickness as the outer hall and gestured towards a chair. The older man sat himself behind the desk and pulled out a notebook, placing it on the blotter that sat on the shiny expanse with a telephone and a computer video unit. Nothing else sullied the polished surface.

'I am Detective Chief Inspector Gatting,' he said. 'Are you a friend of Miss Bennett's?'

'What has happened to her?' Darina asked.

The chief inspector's gaze never wavered but he brought his hands up and clasped them on the blotter. Inconsequentially, Darina wondered what its function was. Surely no one here would use an actual fountain pen with real ink? The absorbent surface was spotless, yielded nothing for a detective to work on.

'I'm afraid there's been an accident.'

Slivers of ice formed inside Darina's gut. She felt a profound reluctance to take this conversation any further and sat quite still, her face a mask of polite enquiry.

'I am sorry to have to tell you that Miss Bennett is dead.'

The shock had already been delivered, the bare statement merely confirmed it.

'What sort of accident?'

His eyes were very steady, studying her reaction with clinical detachment. 'Last night she fell from her window. Her room was on the twelfth floor.'

Darina closed her eyes briefly against the image of Kate Bennett's body tumbling down the outside of the hotel on to hard London pavement.

'I understand you said you had an appointment with Miss Bennett?'

Darina nodded.

Unnoticed, the younger policeman had left the office. He now reappeared with a tray of tea. He poured out a cup, added sugar without asking if that was what she preferred and handed it to Darina. She took it gratefully and found the unaccustomed sweetness refreshing. Energy against shock. She waited for the chief inspector's next question.

'What was the purpose of your meeting?'

Slowly Darina started to recount Bruce Bennett's death, his sister's letter and the brief telephone conversation she had had with her the previous day. Even to her ears it sounded an odd story and for the first time she began to understand William's reaction the previous evening.

'So Kate Bennett's brother died over here just before

Christmas?' The chief inspector scribbled something in his notebook. 'And you are suggesting her fall is somehow connected with his death.' The detective's voice revealed nothing but his eyes watched her with the sharpness of an Alsation guard dog.

'I'm not suggesting anything,' Darina said with asperity. 'You asked me why Kate Bennett wanted to see me and I'm telling you.'

'Do you have Miss Bennett's letter to you?'

Darina dug into her large handbag and retrieved the air-letter card that had been waiting for her at Cantlow productions. She passed it over and gave the inspector its history.

Handling the letter carefully by the corners, he laid it on the blotter and started to read.

It didn't take him long. 'It says nothing about her brother's death being suspicious.'

'No, that was what she told me on the telephone yesterday afternoon.'

'Tell me again exactly what she said.'

Darina repeated the conversation as well as she could remember it.

The inspector leant back in his chair and eyed her coldly. 'So for some reason she didn't explain she couldn't come to the police and preferred instead to talk to you as you have some sort of reputation as an amateur detective. Is that it?'

Darina wished she hadn't stuck quite so rigidly to the truth. 'Look, I don't see myself as any sort of detective. I'm only telling you what Kate Bennett apparently believed. Why do you find that so difficult to accept? And don't you think it's odd that someone who said she believed her brother had been murdered has died before she can explain why?' Darina sat back in her chair.

'People can react in strange ways to the death of a loved one,' Chief Inspector Gatting said quietly. 'For some it's impossible to accept that natural forces have operated. They believe they've been robbed by something or someone unknown. They make wild accusations and sometimes find it impossible to continue living themselves.'

'Are you suggesting that Kate Bennett came all the way from Australia to London to throw herself out of a window because she couldn't stand life without her brother?'

'As I said, Miss Lisle, death affects people in strange ways. However, I don't want you to think we shan't investigate the circumstances of Bruce Bennett's death. We have to follow up every lead.' His tone was courteous but promised little in the way of an open mind as far as his 'investigation' was concerned. 'May we please have your name and address?'

Darina gave him the Chelsea details, reluctant to complicate the picture by informing him she lived in Somerset as well. She thought it was unlikely he'd want to contact her again.

She, though, could certainly want to contact him. She asked for the details of his station and made a note of them in her little expenses notebook.

Then he asked, 'Can I just confirm that you never met Miss Bennett?'

'As I said, her letter came out of the blue.'

'Do you know if she had any friends over here?'

'I'm afraid I don't know.'

'Pity, there's the matter of identification, you see. Well,' he rose, 'we shall be in touch with Australia and her relations there. It's possible they may know something about the state of her mind and why she came to London.'

No doubt he wasn't being deliberately obtuse, he couldn't afford to accept the obvious, Darina thought, then a question occurred to her. 'Her brother was a very large man, was Miss Bennett also tall and strong?'

For a moment the chief inspector was startled but he recovered almost instantly. 'The body is small, about five foot four inches, looks to be under eight stone in weight.'

'How old?'

'Around the middle fifties, maybe a little older. Now, if you have no more questions, Miss Lisle, I would like to continue my investigation. Thank you for your help.' The courteous voice was heavily ironic.

It had little effect on Darina, who thanked him and walked out of the hotel with one thought in her mind. Kate Bennett seemed unlikely to have been able to offer much resistance to someone determined to push her out of a twelfth-floor window.

NINE

WILLIAM was being maddeningly calm and patient.

'Why is it you police won't see what's in front of your noses?'

Darina asked in exasperation. It was Sunday and she still hadn't convinced him there was a case to be investigated.

'Look,' he said with tedious forbearance, 'let's approach it from the other direction. Can you suggest how Bruce Bennett could have been killed without leaving any identifiable trace?'

Darina got up and walked quickly from one end of their small living-room to the other. She wanted to howl with frustration. 'I don't know! As I keep saying, that was what Kate Bennett was going to tell me!'

'Exactly, you don't know. You're building a whole case for a possible murder inquiry on the word of an unknown woman in her mid-fifties.'

Darina could see exactly how his mind was working. A frustrated spinster with a mind no doubt warped by the menopause and finally sent off-beam by the death of a beloved brother.

She was about to explode at the crassness of his attitude when she suddenly collapsed into a chair. What if he was right? What if she was being as blinkered and dogmatic as she was accusing Chief Inspector Gatting and him of being?

What proof, after all, was there that Kate Bennett had any idea how her brother had died? Wasn't it more likely that, as Gatting had suggested, she was unable to accept the fact Bruce was no longer alive, especially since he'd been on the other side of the world from her at the time of his death?

Yet her voice on the telephone had sounded exhausted but

sane, rational and as unemotional as the situation allowed.
Could Darina have been mistaken?

What motive could there be? At the moment all Darina
could think of was that without Bruce Bennett *Table for Four*
just *might* fold. William was right, it sounded too dodgy as a
mainspring for murder.

Then Darina remembered Jean-Pierre Prudhomme and his
allegation that Bruce had stolen both his yeast and master
vintner. On the surface that didn't sound a particularly strong
motive for murder either but perhaps there had been something else going on there as well? Jean-Pierre had certainly
sounded very bitter.

Then she wondered who else Bruce might have upset. What
was it she had said to William the other week, a man who
could arouse strong emotions?

She looked at her tired but eminently rational fiancé,
slumped in his chair, his Sunday lunch sitting heavily in his
stomach.

'Well, if I think about it, you and Gatting could be right,'
Darina said quietly. Then, before he could get too excited at
having proved some sort of point, she added: 'I need to look
at the situation much more carefully.' As doubt and horror
grew on his face she continued, 'Who knows, I may yet un-
mask another murderer!'

Before he could say anything, she left the room, found the
secateurs and her gum boots, put on a warm anorak and went
out into the cold, grey January afternoon to clear away dead
growth with ruthless efficiency, feeling she had at last given
William some thing to think about.

DARINA had no real intention of starting an investigation but
she thought a chat with Mark could well be interesting. He
was the one who had suggested Jean-Pierre be invited on the
programme and had obviously known of the animosity between him and Bruce. He was the one who had raised the
popularity of Australian wines in the UK *versus* the French

and it was he who had kept the argument going until the allegation of theft emerged. And he had kept it going in a way that revealed all his latent hostility to Bruce and stripped the *bonhomie* and warm comradeship from the relationship he had created between them for the camera, revealing it for the sham it was. If anybody knew the dark side of Bruce Bennett, it was Mark Taylor. She decided to ask him to lunch with the ostensible purpose of discussing how he saw Jean-Pierre fitting into the team.

Darina caught up with Mark at the end of that Monday's production meeting and issued her invitation. The presenter seemed hugely flattered. He produced a computer notebook, flashed up his diary for the week and announced that Wednesday was free.

'Splendid, shall we say the Capital Hotel at twelve thirty?' The food at the Capital was famously good and the small dining-room offered comfort, a deliciously pretty ambience and a certain amount of privacy, all ideal attributes for Darina's purposes.

Mark arrived at 12.35, dressed in a dark suit, a red shirt with dark grey stripes and a dark grey silk tie decorated with capsicums. 'Like it?' he grinned as Darina couldn't resist commenting on the glowing green, red and yellow peppers that seemed to float on the heavy silk. 'Bought it in France last year, during a filming trip on truffle hunting. Pity, you just missed that programme. We had something like a thousand pounds' worth of truffles in the studio and John Franks demonstrated pigeons with a truffle sauce and then an omelette with shavings of truffles. The smell was indescribably wonderful!'

'Did you hope to get people truffle hunting in Britain? Apparently there's a chap making quite a business out of it in Scotland and I know they've been found in Sussex.'

Mark shrugged his shoulders. 'We were just looking at what a gastronomic jewel the truffle is.'

Darina was conscious she hadn't produced quite the reaction he'd been looking for and hastily ordered drinks then got him talking about how he began his career as a food journalist.

'In the early eighties I was a news reporter; I'd just got my start in Fleet Street when I was made redundant. I didn't want to go back to the provinces and couldn't find another job, it was hard times in those days, almost as bad as what we've just been going through, so I decided to try and make it as a freelance.' Mark accepted his gin and tonic and toasted his hostess before continuing. 'Somehow I kept finding myself coming across food stories. We were all so unaware in those days. It was sheer luck that I stumbled over a battery chicken farm and saw what appalling conditions they were kept in. Well, I knew it was a marvellous story, that the public couldn't fail to respond. Then I came across details suggesting vested interests were suppressing nutritional reports recommending we reduce animal fats in our diets. Another gift to an investigative journalist. And there were other stories. Soon I didn't have to look for them, people were begging me to take a look at this or that.' He sat back, satisfaction oozing from every pore of his body.

'I think it was when I started broadcasting for *Woman's Hour* that I began making a popular name for myself. My pieces stimulated a heavy response and I gradually became something of a regular feature. Then I got a chance at television. I was lucky, I was in the right place at the right time, available just as people developed a tremendous interest in food.'

'Interest which you and people like you have helped to foster and educate.'

Mark gave a quizzical smile. 'You're too kind but my part has been tiny, it's really been a case of many forces coming together. But do keep on thinking that way.' Darina's interest in Mark grew, he was more intelligent and more aware than she'd given him credit for. Then she kicked herself, of course he had to have had more than a smooth appearance and cocky manner to have got where he had.

Darina now found it quite natural to bring up the future of *Table for Four* and get Mark going on what he saw as the difficulties ahead.

'Of course, one realized that Neil was quite out of touch with what the public wanted. How many can afford truffles? And John Franks' dishes were, frankly'—he smiled at his pun—'frankly, beyond most home cooks. But he had presence and was a tremendous stylist despite that "ee by goom" accent.'

'That had an attraction of its own,' Darina suggested.

'Quite, and that's what Neil was aiming for. Cashing in on the market for something out of the ordinary. He designed a programme with appeal for those tired of what one might call the housewife school of food presentation, that and the travelogue approach. What *Table* was supposed to cook together was a winning combination of great style, expertise and an insider's view of what is, after all, one of the most important aspects of modern life.'

'But it didn't seem to work?'

'Not after the first half-dozen or so programmes, no,' admitted Mark.

'I thought Bruce was a marvellous breath of fresh air, didn't you?' Darina commented ingenuously.

'Well...' Mark paused for a moment as if assessing the wisdom of what he wanted to say, then plunged. 'I thought he was very effective in his way but, really, I did question what Neil was trying to achieve by including his backwoods approach.'

'There appears to be a school of thought that holds the programme can't survive without him.'

Darina watched, fascinated, as Mark's eyes bulged from their sockets. 'Who the hell has been saying that?'

'Then you don't think it's true?'

'*Table* is more than one man; after a few weeks, no one will remember Bruce Bennett was ever part of it.'

The waiter arrived with their food and Mark looked with

enthusiasm at an airy cushion of mushroom-laden hot mousse. He picked up his fork and wielded it with eager attack.

'I'm so pleased to hear you say that,' Darina said demurely. 'I'd hate it if the programme came to an end. I should think Neil would be pretty devastated too.' She looked at Mark with what she hoped came over as a pretty air of enquiry.

'The end of *Table* would be the end of Neil and his company,' obliged Mark, almost licking his lips as he ate his starter. Darina was savouring its exceptional flavours, Mark was putting it away like a schoolboy faced with his favourite beans on toast after a hard rugger match.

'So Bruce's death would have really come as a blow to him?'

Mark looked irritated. 'I've already said that *Table*'s success doesn't depend on one bumptious Australian.'

'And with Jean-Pierre Prudhomme we can go on improving our audience figures?'

'I think we're in with more than a chance. You're getting a good response, I'm well established,' no mock modesty here, 'and Jean-Pierre's Gallic charm should go down a treat.'

'I was staggered by the way you got him to accuse Bruce of stealing his yeast and master vintner, did that really happen and how did you find out about it?'

'Ah! Now that really is a story. Jean-Pierre told me all about it a long time ago, when I visited his vineyard on a story. His place is heavenly; marvellous old château that's been in the family for aeons and a vineyard that goes back to the time Henry V was stomping around France. He's done the most enormous amount to modernize all the production, of course, that's what the story I was working on was about.'

'Just like Bruce and Yarramarra,' put in Darina.

'Quite!' said Mark, looking at her sideways. 'And as if that wasn't enough for one man, his wife was the most gorgeous-looking thing, full of French chic, quite irresistible! Anyway, enough of that. I didn't know Bruce at that time, of course, and Jean-Pierre didn't tell me his name. It all came out in the

evening after we'd had the most wonderful meal with stag-
gering wines. We were both a bit in our cups by then, I can
tell you, and Jean-Pierre suddenly tells me this story about an
Australian who worked with him and, well, you heard all
about it on the programme. I never forget a detail on a story,
certainly not one like that, he was so virulent, it was as though
it had happened yesterday, not several years back. No wonder
Marie left the room as soon as he started on it, I wouldn't
want to keep on hearing the language Jean-Pierre produced!'

'So when did you put two and two together?'

'Oh, shortly after Bruce joined *Table*, when he was telling
me how he'd worked in France, learning some of their wine-
making secrets, and I realized he fitted every detail of the
story Jean-Pierre had told me. And when he made such a song
and dance about Jean-Pierre coming on the programme, I
knew I'd got it right.' Mark's satisfaction shone about him
like light from a Christmas candle.

'You mean he really did steal the yeast *and* the master
vintner?'

'From what Jean-Pierre said, Bruce wouldn't stop at anything that would help Yarramarra. He was ruthless, single-
minded and amoral.'

'Was there anything else between them?'

Mark stared at her. 'What do you mean?'

'Nothing, just that I got an idea there was something that
wasn't coming out.'

Mark shook his head. 'Nothing that I know about. It was
enough, I thought, to prove what a shit Bruce was.'

Darina said nothing but her face must have been expressive
for Mark took a quick gulp of wine and said, 'Come on,
Darina, you can't be that surprised! He must have made a
pass at you?'

She gave a noncommittal little shrug of her own shoulders,
wondering, not for the first time, if Bruce had or hadn't. If
she hadn't choked him off quite so comprehensively that first

evening they'd spent together, would he have taken matters further?

'Did Neil understand what sort of a man he was?'

Mark pushed out a sulky lip. 'For some reason I could never understand, Bruce could do no wrong in Neil's eyes. I told Neil that the programme would be completely unbalanced by his approach but Bruce Bennett was going to save the show in Neil's book and that was that.'

'Did you really expect that row to be broadcast? Wouldn't it have been bad publicity for the programme?'

A knowledgeable smile lit Mark's pleasant features. 'I knew Neil would never allow it to go out. I expected the recording to be stopped and my wrist to be slapped.'

'But it was worth it just to see Bruce upset?'

'It was worth it to expose him to the rest of you.' There was a vicious edge to Mark's tone. Darina realized he had enjoyed engineering the little scene in the television studio.

'He really got under your skin, didn't he?'

Mark flushed slightly, his confident attitude slipping a little. 'I dislike being made a fool of.'

'And Bruce made a fool of you?'

He was surprised. 'Didn't you see? Didn't you see what he was doing with every programme? Putting me down, making me seem ridiculous?'

Darina was genuinely puzzled. 'But it didn't come over like that at all, Mark. You seemed to have a good relationship on the screen.'

'That was only because I refused to rise to his snide little remarks. Because I worked so hard at defusing his little bomb blasts. You have another look at those programmes, you'll see what I mean.'

Darina regarded Mark thoughtfully. He returned her look with quiet composure.

'Do you have any other stories about Bruce like Jean-Pierre's yeast and master vintner?'

Mark shook his head. 'But that's not to say there aren't

others around, just that I haven't managed to come across them.' He gave a laugh that was almost a giggle, high-pitched and childish.

'You should have seen Jean-Pierre's face when I brought up Bruce's name after I ran into him in London, I thought he was going to have apoplexy!' Darina would have bet a sizeable sum that that was when Mark had put two and two together.

'Yet Jean-Pierre agreed to come on the programme?'

'Oh, he knew it would be good publicity for him.'

'I think I can understand how Jean-Pierre felt,' said Darina carefully. 'He must have looked on it as a bitter betrayal by Bruce, especially if he had actually been an apprentice there.'

The waiter cleared away their first course. After his departure, Darina asked, 'Would you have preferred Milly back on the programme rather than Jean-Pierre?'

Mark played with the stem of his wine glass and avoided meeting Darina's eyes. 'I won't deny it would have been nice. We,' he hesitated for a moment then said, 'we were an item, Milly and I, and she blamed me for Neil getting rid of her.'

'Surely not?'

He shrugged his shoulders. 'When your pride's hurt, you'll hit out at anyone, particularly someone you're close to. Perhaps I didn't give her the support she really needed. Relationships are a two-way business.'

Darina could endorse that.

'Is she going to blame you now for Jean-Pierre being taken on in Bruce's place?'

'Who knows? Anyway, that's history. Remember, if Milly came back, you'd probably have to go!'

'I would?'

'Two females and a male wouldn't be a good recipe, not when so many of the guests are female as well.'

'Not to mention the audience?'

'Don't you know most women would rather watch men than their own sex?'

It wasn't a view Darina had much time for but she held her tongue.

Mark gave her a genuine smile of encouragement. 'Cheer up, Milly isn't coming back, you're being retained and are really doing very well. If, though, I could make a suggestion…' he paused delicately.

'Do, that's one of the reasons I asked you to lunch today.'

He allowed their main courses to be placed in front of them then said, 'Don't be afraid to let go. I feel you're holding yourself back, being very controlled. Relax, let it all bubble out.' He looked across the table at her, mischief in his face. 'Know what I play to? Imagine what the camera is?'

'Your aunt in Basildon?'

He shook his head. 'Never admit to an aunt in Basildon! No, a naked girl I'm about to make love to.' He looked at her with an air of expectancy.

Darina laughed then realized he was being serious. 'You mean that's what gives you that air of intimacy and relaxation?'

He smiled like a pleased professor. 'And, I hope, a bit of a sparkle! You've got a fiancé, haven't you?' His glance rested on the diamond engagement ring. 'Well, forget everyone else but him.'

'I don't think he's really interested in the programme,' Darina said slowly.

'No? Then make him!'

Darina laughed. 'Easy enough for you to say!'

'He's a policeman, isn't he? I knew a policeman once, he was interested in everything. He never knew when odd bits of information might come in useful with his job.'

'William's rather like that, he's always absorbing facts, studying people and their attitude to life, picking up bits of expertise, how things tick, that sort of thing.' Darina hesitated for a moment then decided that if she expected confidences from Mark she had to offer something in exchange. 'I have a nasty feeling sometimes, though, that William thinks all the time, effort and a lot of the money that we put into food would be better spent on something more worthwhile.'

'More worthwhile? What could be more worthwhile than food? It's what keeps us alive after all.'

'Isn't that different from food as an art form, an indulgence, an extravagance?' Darina looked down at the meal she had been so enjoying eating, a perfectly cooked piece of succulent cod arranged on a bed of delicate-tasting threads of courgette.

'Ah! So the worthy detective is a puritan?'

'A little of one, yes, I think so.'

'Then convert him, seduce him, suborn him.'

'For a moment, there, you sounded just like Bruce!'

'You've got to be joking!'

'No, it was just the sort of thing he would have said.' Darina finished her dish and set knife and fork neatly together. 'You know, Mark, I think Bruce came over very differently to women from the way he affected men.'

His look was jaundiced. 'I found his success with women quite impossible to understand.'

'Was he really something of a stud? Judging by that film you made in Italy his wife looked very attractive.'

'A gâteau in the fridge doesn't stop you glancing in the pastry shop,' said Mark coarsely. 'You only had to see the way he looked at women. I came across Bruce and Anthea in a quiet little restaurant just after he joined us. He wasn't fazed but Anthea looked pretty sick.' He grinned mischievously. 'I promised her I wouldn't breathe a word to Neil and she looked even sicker. She obviously wanted to deny anything was going on but didn't dare even to raise the issue. What she could see in him buggered me, such an intelligent, educated, socially, well, what shall we say, privileged woman? You know her father is loaded, one of England's top industrialists? She's attractive as well and she falls for this rude, crude Australian!'

'Anthea?' Darina had met Neil's wife a couple of times, including at the Christmas lunch on the fatal day Bruce's last programme was recorded. She remembered a contained, fine-drawn figure, mixing easily with the production team, having a word with every one, including chatting with herself about cookery books, doing the chairman's wife bit, in fact. No sign that she might be smitten with Bruce, they'd hardly exchanged more than the odd word or two. Darina suddenly remembered the Australian putting his arm around Anthea's shoulders for a moment as she was taking her Christmas cake round. But there was nothing odd in that, Bruce was always finding reasons to be in contact with women, it was something you accepted about him. Remembering Shelley Bennett's appearance in the Italian film, though, Darina thought she could see why Bruce might have been attracted to Neil's wife.

'Anthea looks rather like Shelley, doesn't she? Dark hair, slim figure, small face with wistful eyes, rather older of course.'

'Like Shelley? Did you think so?' Mark gave the idea some thought. 'Physically, perhaps, but nothing more. Shelley is more yielding, much softer. Nothing like Anthea's education, of course, but with a real understanding and genuine love of food.'

'You must have got to know her quite well during that trip,' Darina suggested.

Mark looked at her with amusement tinged with regret. 'My dear, if I'd been able to tell Bruce he was a cuckold, do you think I could have restrained myself? Alas, there wasn't time!'

'But you did get to know her well enough to be surprised she'd fallen for, what did you call him, "a rude, crude, Australian"?'

Mark nodded slowly. 'Yes, I thought he would be totally alien to her.'

'Did you ask her what she found in him?'

'At the time I met her, I had no idea they were married. She called herself Shelley del Lucca. She admitted she had a husband but neither of us was interested in talking about him. I had a distinct impression life was not totally a bed of roses on that side but it was only when Bruce roared out that it was his ''little woman'' on the film that I knew who her husband was.'

'Must have been something of a shock?'

'Say that again!'

'I bet you contrived to suggest to Bruce you got really very close to his wife in Italy?' Darina's tone was naughty and conspiratorial.

Mark's expression was curiously shamefaced. 'If only I could have that would really have punctured his self-esteem. That girl was so attractive but just the biggest tease. Even if it had been possible, though, I would have been ever so slightly frightened of his reaction.'

A vision of the big, powerful, totally uninhibited Australian filled Darina's mind. For a moment it was as though he was present at the table with them and Darina could understand how Mark might have thought twice before suggesting he'd been involved in any way with his wife.

'She must be a very rich woman now,' she commented.

Mark arranged his knife and fork neatly on the empty plate. 'Yes,' he said. 'I suppose so.'

TEN

SHELLEY DEL LUCCA (she preferred to be known by her maiden name) stood in front of the winery at Yarramarra and looked at the rows of grapes growing under the Australian sun, their glowing lime-green leaves stretching as far as she could see, into the shimmering distance, dissolving into the far line of red hills that could hardly be discerned. It was still early but the cool freshness held the promise of later heat that made it all the more precious.

Shelley left the complex of stone buildings, mellow with age, that made up the winery. Even the new visitors' building she had helped design the previous year where wine tastings were held and groups of tourists introduced to the complex process that was wine making before being walked round the vineyard itself, even that was constructed of old stone. There was a shop, too, where not only the wines were sold but also accessories, products such as wine vinegar and preserves, books on wine and memorabilia. Amongst many items was Shelley's own suggestion, a soap moulded in the shape of a bunch of grapes and scented with the tantalizing and delicately sweet fragrance of chardonnay flowers.

Shelley walked up to the first row of vines. The thin, flexible branches of this year's growth rampaged along the training wires but the new shoots were neatly tied in and controlled. Already the grapes were formed, the small fruits had started to swell, to develop their sugars and flavour. Later in the day the automatic watering system Bruce had installed the previous year would come into play, enabling their tough, dry roots to absorb what the fruit needed to continue its development. The watering system had been a major outlay that

Bruce had justified by the increased yield he believed it would produce.

Bruce... For a moment Shelley could believe his enormous figure would stride out from behind the winery to check his beloved grapes. His fingers would heft a bunch of the immature fruit, assessing its progress, his whole being concentrated on the weight, the condition of the grapes, for that moment blocking out the rest of life, the world. The first time Shelley saw him do that, it was as though the large hand was being placed in contact with some primaeval, life-giving force.

Yarramarra was like that, it had an internal dynamism that seemed to carry them all along. Only Bruce had been able to wrest control from the vines and impose his will. What was going to happen now that he was no longer at the helm? Could Shelley continue to guide Yarramarra along the path of success? Should she try and oversee the technology and attempt to keep the inspiration and marketing techniques going that had made it into the profitable business it was today? On her own? Because there was no Kate now to help.

For a moment the vines coalesced into a lime-green blur then Shelley blinked rapidly and the landscape re-emerged. She was not going to lose control now, not when so much remained to be done. Not now that she was mistress of Yarramarra and could control her own destiny. Not now Bruce had truly disappeared from her life.

In the distance rose a small cloud of dust that travelled towards the winery. Shelley watched it with a detached interest. Who could be driving out to Yarramarra so early in the day?

The local taxi drew up in front of the winery and out stepped a tall woman of about sixty with a shock of white hair waving round a bony face that might once have been pretty. Now age had pared flesh away and with it the softness of youth. But age couldn't reduce the size of the hazel eyes that looked tired and, as Shelley advanced to meet the visitor, wary. The shadows underneath the eyes highlighted the angularity of the cheekbones.

'Can I help?' The taxi had driven off leaving a small case at the feet of the new arrival. It wasn't the first time someone had turned up at Yarramarra expecting to be able to take a room at the vineyard. Sometimes they could be accommodated but Shelley wasn't going to have visitors at the moment. Whoever this woman was, she was going to have to recall the taxi. However, first Shelley must find out if wine business was involved.

'You must be Shelley, right?' The visitor's voice was confident without being aggressive. 'I'm sorry to turn up just like this, I was going to ring you later to arrange a convenient time but I heard at the hotel last night that you were off to London today so I just dashed up here, I didn't want to miss you and it isn't a matter for the telephone.'

'Do I know you?' Shelley was beginning to wonder if in fact they had met.

'I'm Eileen Miller.'

The name meant nothing and as the visitor realized that some of her confidence faded.

'Kate never told you?'

'Told me what?'

Eileen Miller now looked distinctly uncomfortable. She glanced around the wide, dusty compound. 'Is there somewhere we could go to have a chat?'

Shelley wanted to say there was no time, she had to leave; she had a premonition about this visitor. Despite her pleasant appearance, this woman was trouble, she could sense it. But she didn't have to leave until the afternoon and all she had to do now was take her leave of the vines.

'We could go into the visitors' centre,' she said grudgingly in her low, slow voice, and led the way into its dark, airy interior, the bar swabbed clean, the chairs all neatly set on the tiled floor, the little tables ready for the day's influx of tourists.

Eileen Miller stood at the entrance and looked about her. 'This is something else,' she said with a certain amount of awe. 'I knew the Australian wine industry had grown up but I would never have imagined Yarramarra could have produced anything like this!' She walked about, running a hand over the polished mahogany, studying the wine displays.

Shelley stood by one of the small tables, purposely not offering any refreshment, waiting. 'You've visited Yarramarra before?'

The woman looked at her, seemed to drag herself back from another time and came over to the table. She sat down, looking quite at home, and gazed up at Shelley. She seemed unable to decide what to say next.

The girl sat down with her. Then, against all her better judgement, she heard herself say, 'Would you like a cup of coffee?'

'Oh, that would be wonderful. I haven't had any breakfast, I just knew I had to get here as soon as possible.'

Shelley went behind the bar, put the kettle on to boil, fixed a paper into the coffee filter then spooned coffee beans into the grinder. That was another of her innovations. 'You can't serve superb wines and offer crap coffee,' she'd told Bruce when the centre was being built. 'Instant just won't do and nor will those dreadful machines that over-extract. Beans only take an instant to grind and give so much fresher a result.' That had been in the early days when Bruce listened to at least some of the things she said.

'Have you come far?'

'Sydney.'

Shelley paused in her ladling of the ground coffee into the filter. Sydney was almost the other side of the continent. Air travel meant it was only hours away but the trip was expensive.

'You visiting friends?' Eileen Miller had mentioned a hotel but that might just be for a stopover.

'I came to see you.'

'Me?'

The woman looked rueful. 'Yes, I know, I should have rung you before starting out. But I was afraid, oh, I don't know what I was afraid of. It isn't as though I don't have a right to be here.'

Shelley brought over the jug of coffee on a tray with two cups, light cream and sugar. 'Don't you think you should tell me what all this is about?' she suggested as she put the tray on the table and poured out coffee for them both.

Eileen Miller sipped the hot, strong, aromatic liquid gratefully then put the cup back in its saucer.

'I'm Bruce's mother,' she said quietly.

Whatever Shelley had been expecting, it wasn't this. She looked at her visitor more closely. Yes, perhaps there was a resemblance to her dead husband around the eyes and mouth, that is if the soft hazel eyes could narrow and grow hard and the wide mouth could thin and tuck away its corners.

'But I thought...' she paused, not sure now what she thought.

'That I was dead?' Eileen Miller suggested with a touch of humour.

'Bruce never actually said.'

'Did he ever mention me at all?' The question was weary but held a spark of interest.

'Well,' Shelley hesitated, trying to remember now exactly what Bruce *had* said. 'I asked him once about his mother. He'd told me a lot about his father, what a colourful character he'd been, how much he'd done to build up Yarramarra, the arguments he'd had with him on his return from Europe.' Shelley remembered the exasperated affection in Bruce's voice. 'He said the old man had paid out a small fortune for Bruce to learn the business and then wasn't prepared to profit from it.'

'That would be Rory, thought he was making sure Bruce realized his father knew it all anyway. But he won through eventually?'

'After a long battle, yes. But Bruce never mentioned his mother and when I asked him he said she'd left his father when he was very young and I got the impression she'd died.'

'I think that's what his father told him,' Eileen Miller said. 'It wouldn't have suited Rory Bennett for anyone to think they could walk away from him and survive.' Her voice was ironic rather than bitter.

'Didn't you ever get in touch with Bruce?' To Shelley it sounded incredible that a mother could have a child the way Eileen Miller had and never contact him. It was no wonder Bruce had felt deserted.

'Oh, yes! I tried every way I knew. But Rory blocked all my attempts. And by the time Bruce was old enough to hear the truth, it was too late. Truth has a funny way of turning into something else.' There was a silence as Shelley looked at what had been her mother-in-law. 'Kate knew, of course,' Eileen Miller added. 'She tried to tell Bruce about his mother but Rory's influence was too strong.' She looked down at her hands holding the heavy green china cup with the gold edging. 'I knew when I left there was no hope of keeping my son but just because you know the score, that doesn't stop you hoping, does it?'

'Life must have been pretty intolerable for you here, then?' Shelley asked slowly.

The woman looked at her. 'Intolerable is one word I suppose you could use,' she said.

There was silence for a moment. Eileen Miller picked up her cup and sipped some coffee. She looked round the visitors' centre again. 'Time goes by so quickly, doesn't it? It seems only yesterday I was here, a new bride. Even with Kate to send me snaps of Bruce growing up and tell me how he was doing, it was hard to realize he'd grown into a man. Then he was in Europe and the news grew less. Kate fell out of the habit of keeping me up to date. So when I heard that he was dead, I can tell you it came as a shock. I still thought of him as my young son, not someone approaching forty.' She blinked rapidly.

Shelley wondered exactly what Rory Bennett had done to her. Part of it she thought she could imagine. 'You know Kate's dead, too? She went to London and…and died in an accident.' Shelley couldn't bring herself to say how.

Eileen Miller nodded.

'That's why I'm going. Someone has to identify the body.'

'Oh, my dear!' Eileen leaned forward and pressed her hand on top of Shelley's. 'Surely there's someone else who can do that?'

'I'm not sure that there is. Oh, I suppose Tom Jenkins, the general manager here, could go. But shouldn't that sort of thing be done by someone from the family? I'm the only one left. Anyway,' she added in a different tone, 'I want to go. I want to get away from Yarramarra and London could be good for me. I could maybe work there.' Unbidden a little voice started to sing within her. London represented hope: hope of love, of fulfilment.

'You're a cookery writer, aren't you? I think that's what Kate told me.'

Shelley nodded. 'It's time I spread my wings a bit. I'd been planning to join Bruce in London in the spring, anyway. I thought it might help my career.' No need to tell her Bruce had had other ideas.

'Bruce married a career woman?' asked Eileen in a tone of wonder.

'Sure! Bruce liked women who were independent.' Only so far, though, Shelley added to herself.

'He did?' The tone was sceptical, then Eileen said quickly, 'Well, I'm glad to hear it.'

'How did you hear about Kate's death? I'm leaving it for Tom Jenkins to go through her address book and let everyone know. It doesn't seem right to do it before we know for certain she's dead.'

'You mean there could be a mistake?' Eileen sounded startled.

Shelley shook her head regretfully. 'There doesn't seem much possibility of one. But until the body's actually been identified it seems wrong to start broadcasting the fact. So, how did you know?'

'The wine world is really quite small.'

'You mean you're still part of it?'

'My second husband is a wine merchant, we have a small chain of shops in Sydney. I've never made any secret that I was once married to Rory Bennett of Yarramarra, or that Bruce was my son.' For a moment her gaze fell to the table. 'I think maybe I hoped news of me would filter back here. Anyway, Kate Bennett's death is all round the wine trade already. I came as soon as I could.'

'But why?'

Eileen Miller looked away, fiddled with her coffee spoon. At last she said, 'Kate really never mentioned me to you?'

Shelley shook her head.

'That makes all this a little difficult. Oh, it's all such a tragedy. First Bruce now Kate, I find it all so hard to believe. Just why did she go to London?' Two deep creases furrowed their way down Eileen Miller's forehead.

'She said something about wanting to find out more about what Bruce had been up to. You know she adored him? When he died I think the shock unhinged her. She was either sitting staring at the wall or making all sorts of wild accusations.' Shelley stopped suddenly. She didn't want to think about some of the things Kate had said. 'We tried to talk her out of going but she wouldn't listen. Said it was something she had to do.'

'And exactly what happened in London? All I heard was that there had been an accident.'

Shelley swallowed painfully, this was always the difficult bit. 'According to the police, she fell out of her hotel window.'

'Committed suicide, you mean?' Eileen asked bluntly.

Shelley swallowed again. 'They said there wasn't any note but the police asked if I knew anything about her state of mind and I explained about Bruce and how het up she seemed to be. I mean, dashing off to London just like that.'

'Poor old Kate, it's difficult to think of her in that sort of state, she was always so straightforward, so direct.' Eileen Miller paused, looked hard at Shelley and said, 'About six months ago I had a letter from Kate telling me that Bruce had given her a share in Yarramarra. Did you know that?'

Shelley had no difficulty in answering this question. 'Bruce told me he felt his father hadn't been fair in not leaving Kate an interest in the winery, she'd worked at Yarramarra just as hard as he and for longer. He decided she deserved it and signed over twenty-five per cent just before we were married.' No doubt he had also thought of it as a way of ensuring Kate's home was always Yarramarra, in case the two of them hadn't got on. But she'd liked Kate, even if her sister-in-law had always been a little distant with her.

Eileen Miller sighed deeply, as if the knowledge was something of a burden. 'I wouldn't have expected it of Bruce, even though I knew he was very fond of Kate. It must have meant a great deal to her. She loved Bruce very much.'

'I know.' Shelley's mouth was dry, she had a terrible feeling she knew where this was leading.

'Kate was very fond of me, too. We were almost of an age, she was Rory's daughter by a previous marriage, and we grew practically as close as sisters.'

Shelley said nothing.

'And if it hadn't been for Kate, I'm not sure I could ever have managed to escape Rory Bennett.'

The two women looked at each other and Shelley felt her heart give an awkward swoop. For a moment she was looking at a sister under the skin. Except this woman had walked away from Yarramarra.

Then Eileen Miller said, 'I don't know whether you can

understand this, I'm not sure I understand it myself, but Kate told me she was willing her share of Yarramarra to me.'

Shelley had already guessed this was probably what the woman was leading up to. It hadn't occurred to her to wonder about Kate's will before now; she had assumed she knew what its contents would be. It wasn't the devastating shock it would have been had Eileen Miller blurted it out at the beginning of their interview but shock it none the less was.

'I thought…' Her throat was dry, making it difficult to speak. Shelley swallowed and began again. 'Kate said she would will her share back to Bruce.'

Eileen looked tired now. 'I think she had some crack-brained idea it would finally bring Bruce and me together. That if I owned part of Yarramarra, he couldn't ignore me and we would manage to form some sort of relationship.' She gave a painful smile. 'Only someone as simple and uncomplicated as Kate could have thought of that one.' She sat as though relieved she had broken her news. 'I didn't think too much of it at the time, I thought when you and Bruce had children, Kate would change her mind, decide to deed her share back to the family. But I decided that if she didn't raise the issue with me when her first nephew or niece appeared, I would. I thought there was plenty of time.' Her voice was sad. 'We always think there will be plenty of time. Instead, here we are, she's dead, Bruce is dead and it looks as though I'm your minority partner. That's why I wanted to see you as soon as possible. To tell you I'm not going to interfere and cause problems. Not that I could make much trouble with only twenty-five per cent.'

So she didn't know the full story! Shelley sat quite quiet for a moment then said, 'You're more than that, Eileen Miller. Bruce left half the rest of Yarramarra to Kate. If she has willed her holding to you, you own—' For a moment she had to think, work out the arithmetic of this ghastly fact. 'You own sixty-two and a half per cent of one of Australia's richest vineyards.' And I'm no longer mistress of Yarramarra, she added to herself.

ELEVEN

JEAN-PIERRE PRUDHOMME was rehearsing the second of his wine spots as a regular presenter for *Table* and the studio was watching intently.

Looking relaxed and cosily chic in his designer cardigan, Jean-Pierre was talking about the improvement in Provençal wines over recent years, working up to a recommendation of several available on the English market, with one in particular to be drunk with the dish Darina had just finished demonstrating. The theme of this week's programme was value for money looked at from both ends of the cost scale. Darina had shown how money could be spent producing a delicious meal with minimum effort and how effort could produce an equally attractive meal for a fraction of the cost. Inexpensive tongue had provided one dish, poached, skinned, sliced and reheated in a sauce of white wine and mushrooms. Then highly expensive turbot had been baked in the oven and served with a caviare sauce. The studio guest was to be a producer of Aberdeen Angus beef explaining how its extra cost was value for money and recommending some cheap cuts for economy. Jean-Pierre himself had begun his spot by explaining the full-bodied joys of the great burgundies and picking out a couple of good examples that hadn't priced themselves beyond their value.

As Jean-Pierre picked up one of the lesser bottles from the table at his side and showed the label to the camera, Lynn's exasperated voice rang out, 'Bloody hell, Mark, leave that alone!'

Jean-Pierre stopped his rehearsal in full flight, Alison, the floor manager, angrily called for quiet and Darina, leaning on her demonstration counter, switched her attention from the

Frenchman to the long work table at the end of the studio where Lynn was preparing the plate of small eats with which the session round the table would open the programme.

Mark was once again causing trouble by pilfering bits of food. To begin with Darina had been amused at his seemingly endless need to consume something, anything. Time and again he demonstrated his wholehearted love of food had little to do with sensitivity of palate. Everything was consumed with the same gusto whether it was half-stale left-overs or the fruits of a top chef's inspired creativity. But her amusement had long since vanished as his constant pecking away interfered with Lynn's preparation. Over the last few weeks the home economist had become more and more vocal over his invasions of her territory.

This time his fingers were in the dish of tongue. 'Have a heart, Lynn,' he whispered. 'I'm starving! This is only the half-finished dish and, anyway, you must have another one tucked away somewhere.'

Darina watched the girl give Mark a withering glance and push a loaf of bread his way while rescuing the gratin of tongue. As the presenter tore off a hunk, she returned to her task of spreading carefully made scrambled egg on tiny rounds of brown bread and butter, topping each with either a small piece of gherkin or a fragment of anchovy. Already in the fridge reposed mangetout stuffed with a mixture of Stilton and cream cheese plus brown bread triangles topped with the best quality smoked salmon. The small electric hob on the work table was heating water for boiling quail's eggs, to be served with celery salt. A mixture of the expensive, cheap, simple and time consuming, the canapés would provide an entrée into the programme's theme.

Darina could see Lynn cursing under her breath as she arranged her little rounds of bread on a long plate while snatching a glance at her watch. Neil wanted to capture the introductory shots for the programme before lunch and it looked as though Lynn was in trouble with time.

Darina went over, picked up another knife and started to help. Lynn shot her a look of gratitude.

Nothing remained now of the terrible bruise she had sported during the two days of shooting the Christmas programmes. By the time the production team had met in the New Year, its spectacular purple and green had faded completely. But she still looked as strained as she had before Bruce's death.

As the recording of Jean-Pierre's talk came to a finish, Mark's hand reached for one of the little bits of bread and scrambled egg and Darina gave it a light slap. 'Wait for the recording,' she hissed at him. He gave her a grin that said it was only a try-on and wandered off.

'Bugger that man,' muttered Lynn. They worked in silence for a little then she said, 'Thanks, Darina, I think that's everything ready now.'

It was only just in time. Neil had almost finished setting up for the table talk.

Alison called Darina to join Mark, Jean-Pierre and the Aberdeen Angus man at the table.

The Frenchman greeted her with a smile, his face creasing into a map of attractive wrinkles, his dark eyes sparkling. He rose as she approached. 'I 'aven't 'ad a chance to wish you *bonjour* yet.' Viewers had already reacted favourably to the charm of that accent. What with that, his lived-in face and air of careless authority, Darina was sure Jean-Pierre was going to prove a worthy replacement for Bruce.

Mark sat back in his chair; he watched while the studio lights were tweaked, checking the result in the monitor and complaining he looked twice his age. Alison told him to wait until they'd finished before criticising and suggested an early night before recording day wouldn't come amiss.

'If only some people knew their business, we'd have finished here by now.'

'Mark,' said Alison wearily, 'everyone here knows their job, including you. If you will kindly shut up, you will be able to get on with it.'

'I like very much the atmosphere in this studio,' said Jean-Pierre, his face crinkling with good humour. 'Everyone is so professional. The standards of television in England are very 'igh, more so, I think, than in France. Certainly the programmes are better, apart from the Meteo, that is, there we 'ave presenters who are such fun; 'ere you are professional but not so much fun.'

The French tact put glue back on the production so that they were soon commencing a quick run through of the opening sequence but Darina was left wondering what devil had got into Mark. He was soon at it again, holding up the dish of canapés, then complaining the camera wasn't set up for the shot. Since Darina could see the monitor in her sight lines showing a perfect picture of Mark and the plate, she couldn't imagine what he thought he was up to.

Alison, grim faced, told him in pleasant tones that belied her expression that the camera was indeed in place and could they please go back to the beginning of the run through so that the correct angle of the plate could be achieved.

They began again.

Jean-Pierre started to look less relaxed and Darina to worry that she was going to lose her spontaneity for the recording, she hated too much rehearsing. And she could sense the restiveness of the studio's technical team under Mark's constant needling, she was conscious they felt under attack, their professionalism questioned.

Finally Neil and the gallery were happy to start recording. Then there was a long pause while Alison, one hand held in the air, listened to voices in her headphones only she could hear. Her hand dropped. 'Sorry, everyone, it's just coming up to one and we have to break for lunch. We'll record this first thing this afternoon.'

'Bloody hell,' said Neil, coming forward. 'That's going to put at least thirty minutes on the afternoon session. What's happening, Jan?' he asked into the air. 'Why can't we take lunch later? Another five minutes and we'd have this in the bag.'

Jan's tall figure marched down the steep steps from the gallery. She was as smart as always in navy blue trousers and a matching sweater attractively appliquéd in turquoise and was carrying an attaché case. She strode up to Neil. 'We can't break for lunch later,' she enunciated as crisply as she could through clenched teeth, 'because the technical manager won't ask the crew if they're willing to postpone, he feels they have had to suffer enough over the last half-hour or so. Frankly, I don't blame him! If we run into overtime, it won't be *my* fault.' She shot a virulent look at Mark and stalked out of the studio.

Neil gazed after his director, then advanced towards Mark.

Darina hastily left the studio, pausing as she saw Jan in the corridor, standing rigid with rage, hurling her attaché case down with the force of a power drill. 'Bloody motherfucker!' she screamed as the case bounced and skidded along the polished composition flooring until it finished at Darina's feet.

Silently Darina picked up and returned the case to the furious woman.

Jan took it, examined the leather carefully, placed it under her arm and said in a conversational tone, 'I'm sorry about that. You see, stopping now means extra time spent getting back into the swing of things after lunch, checking the technical side again and reminding all of you exactly where we were, when we were just ready to get the whole thing in the can.' She paused, looking at Darina thoughtfully. 'Can you throw any light on what's rattled Mark's cage? He seems to grow more bolshie with every programme.'

Darina shook her head. 'No idea, I'm sorry. Come and have some lunch and forget it.'

'Difficult when you don't know the next little trick he's going to pull. Ah, Alison,' Jan tucked her free arm into the floor manager's as she came out of the studio. 'Do you think this afternoon you could relay to Mark my exact words rather than your usual tactful translation?'

'Bloody prima donna he is, wants us all to know who's top dog,' Alison said cheerfully as they went across the corridor into the hospitality room for lunch.

HAD ALISON put her finger on the cause of Mark's behaviour? Darina wondered about it as she drove back to Somerset after recording had finished. Did he just enjoy throwing his weight around? Like disrupting the programme for the sense of power it gave? Was he really not running the risk of being thrown off by Neil? The executive producer had looked angry enough for murder let alone a firing.

Darina remembered the way Mark had complained about Bruce's attitude.

He seemed to believe the Australian had been jealous of him and trying to undermine his position on *Table*.

But Bruce was gone now and Mark should be happy. Instead he seemed to be trying to sabotage everyone's efforts to produce a successful programme.

Had he been trying to mislead Darina over Bruce? Trying perhaps to cover up for earlier attempts of his own to rock the boat?

Back in Somerset that evening, Darina looked out the video tapes she had recorded of *Table*. William was, once again, working late and had said he wouldn't need any food when he got in.

There had been six *Table* programmes with Bruce, including the last one when he had collapsed. Darina placed the first cassette in the video player and switched it on. She sat alternating between hating her own performance and finding Bruce's vivid personality here in the room with her almost more than she could bear. All that energy, all that throw-away charm, all that gusto for life, gone.

The programme ended and Darina realized she had noticed nothing of the exchanges between Bruce and Mark. She rewound the tape and started it again, then changed her mind, stopped the cassette and removed it from the player.

The tapes needed concentrated viewing. Better to look at them in the morning when she was fresh. Also she didn't want William to return and find her absorbed in them, she was determined to be welcoming, to ask intelligent questions about what he was up to and to demonstrate just how much she cared about him and his work.

It was after eleven when he returned. Darina had tidied up the cottage, given the kitchen a good clean and had just taken a tray of his favourite biscuits out of the oven. It was, she hoped, the perfect scenario for a weary man to find.

'Hi,' he said, giving her cheek a peck, assailing her with beery fumes. 'I'm starving, you haven't got something solid I could eat, have you? Not that these aren't delicious,' he wolfed down a couple of the still hot biscuits, 'but a growing man needs proper feeding.' He leant against the dresser and looked at her hopefully. His top shirt button was undone, tie loosened and skew-whiff and his eyes seemed to have trouble focusing.

'I'm sorry, darling, you said you were getting something to eat with the boys so I didn't bring anything back.' Darina was equally tired, her day had started very early and been particularly stressful. She tried to sound sympathetic. 'What are you involved in, I hope it isn't anything too nasty?'

'No, we're almost on top of things for once. But there's been another complaint about the con man. An otherwise seemingly intelligent woman allowed him to take a valuable figurine up to London to try and sell for her. When she eventually realized she wasn't going to see either the china or the man again, she complained to us, rather shamefacedly but said he ought to be caught before he ripped off others. I despair of saving the public from itself sometimes.' He helped himself to some more biscuits.

'So what have you been up to?'

'The idea was for us to catch up on the paper work aided

by an Indian take-away but we finished earlier than we'd thought and went to the local. The others drifted home, leaving Don and me to put the world to rights.' Don was a detective sergeant William worked closely with, Darina had never realized the attractions of his company were greater than her own. 'I had to call a taxi when they chucked us out, couldn't run the risk of being picked up, d'you think you can run me to the pub in the morning so I can collect the car?' Suddenly his face brightened and, taking his morning lift for granted, he said, 'Tell you what, I think there's a tin of corned beef in the larder and there's some cold potato somewhere.' William opened the fridge and started rummaging around the contents Darina had sorted out only an hour or so earlier.

'I'm afraid I threw the potatoes away, another few minutes and hairs would have grown on them.' She didn't even try to sound regretful.

He stared at her with open curiosity. 'What's got into you? Usually you wait until a dog wouldn't look at something before you bin it.'

'New Year resolution.' Darina forced herself to maintain her temper. 'I will keep both the fridge and the kitchen in perfect condition.'

'Well, see you keep a good set of left-overs around as well, can you? I really fancied some fried pots.'

'Then fried pots is what you shall have.' Darina reached for a pan and the olive oil and set some gently heating while she peeled a couple of potatoes.

'Get us something to drink, will you, this won't be long,' she said as she tossed cubes of potato into the pan and added a couple of rapidly chopped shallots.

William flopped into a kitchen chair. 'Had more than enough at the pub, thanks. Tell you what, I could do with some coffee.'

Darina ground her teeth, put the kettle on and got out the bottle of white wine she had put in the fridge earlier, imagining them having a quiet chat while sharing a glass or two together. She opened it with an angry pull of her wrist on the corkscrew, poured herself a glass and made herself relax as she tasted the cool, flavourful Australian chardonnay. It was a bottle of Yarramarra wine and while she drank she saw again, vivid before her, Bruce's face, laughing as it had been on the tape.

Darina made the coffee, poured out a cup for her beloved and placed it before him. He drank, munched more biscuits and read the daily paper he'd picked up from the hall table as he came in. She looked at the crisp brown curls of his hair, the attractive way his ears were set against his head and the aquiline nose. She noted the worry lines that the years were deepening beside his generous mouth and held her tongue.

Slices of corned beef joined the potatoes and shallots in the pan. Darina added a couple of eggs and a few minutes later placed the plate of food in front of William.

'That looks wonderful, darling,' he said absentmindedly, turning a page of the paper before starting his supper.

A few minutes later he put down his knife and fork. 'Do you know, I think those biscuits have done the job. I'll have this for breakfast tomorrow. Shall we go up now? I'm shattered.'

Left in the kitchen, Darina carefully placed the plate of congealed food in the fridge, cleared away the coffee, realized she had no need to get out the biscuit tin as all the biscuits had been eaten, then sat at the table slowly finishing another glass of wine and mulling over thoughts of murder.

TWELVE

WILLIAM APOLOGIZED as she drove him to the pub where he had left his car the previous evening. 'If it's any consolation, I've got a splitting head and I know it serves me right. If I'd come back after a quick pint we could have had a nice evening, you wouldn't be mad as hell with me and I'd be feeling like a human being. Tell you what, I should be able to leave at a decent hour this evening, why don't I take you out for a meal?' He smiled at her in guilty supplication.

Darina kissed him goodbye and said she'd look forward to that. She returned home feeling slightly more cheerful, went and found the *Table* tapes, inserted the first one in the video player and settled down to concentrate on Bruce's performance and his interaction with Mark.

By lunchtime her eyes were tired and her mind alive with questions.

Answers were difficult.

Looked at from the point of view of an ordinary viewer, the programmes offered a bantering relationship between the two men that was amusing. The viewer could identify a pleasurable air of tension but remain secure in the knowledge that it was all good fun. Except, was it? Seen one after the other, the programmes offered a more disturbing interpretation, the brash, iconoclastic Australian jokes at the expense of the urbane English man started to look relentless. Darina thought she could see what Mark had meant by having to work hard at defusing the little charges Bruce kept setting up. But was Mark actually right? Had Bruce been trying to undermine his confidence and authority and was it only Mark's refusal to be rattled, his ability to turn it all into an ongoing joke, that meant the show retained its watchability?

Or had it been just Bruce's heavy handed down-under humour with Mark over-reacting, perhaps because he felt insecure after what had happened to his two co-presenters?

After all, what reason was there for Bruce to want to get at Mark? It was in Bruce's interest, surely, for them to work well together. The Englishman was the long-term presenter, Bruce was a newcomer, had his name to make.

Darina thought back to their relationship off camera, had the same tension existed there as well?

When she had met the *Table* team, Darina had been nervous and anxious to suss out how everyone interrelated. She had watched each member of the team with close attention at that first meeting. With almost total clarity she could remember the good humour that existed between Mark and Bruce. Mark had appeared genuinely amused by the Australian and Bruce had seemed anxious to establish good relations with him. It had contrasted well with Mark's behaviour towards David Bartholomew. All the barbed comments in that meeting had been between the two of them.

Darina picked up the tape of the first show. The atmosphere between Mark and Bruce had already been set by the time that had been recorded. Italy had been its theme.

The moment she remembered that, Darina could identify exactly when the relationship between Mark and Bruce had changed. It had been after Neil had shown the film taken at Theresa Mancusa's Italian cookery school, when Bruce had identified his wife amongst the foreign journalists there. Shelley del Lucca, that had been her name. Thinking back, Darina saw again Mark's shocked reaction, David Bartholomew's amusement.

There had been a little scene with Mark drawing out enthusiastic comments from Shelley del Lucca on both the cookery course and Italian food in general. They had been sitting on the terrace at the palazzo where the courses were being held, at a table over drinks, very relaxed. It might have been a trick of the filming, but the interview had definitely suggested the two of them were getting on extremely well.

As if in a replay, Darina could see again the sharp look Bruce had shot Mark after the showing of the film, quite at variance with his roar of delight at seeing his wife on her first appearance.

Was it simply a case of the jealous husband?

Bruce had left his wife behind in Australia, had hinted to Darina that their relationship left something to be desired, and had certainly behaved as though he was free to have affairs.

Mark had suggested Bruce had been having an affair with Anthea, Neil's wife. Having looked again at the brief appearance of Shelley Bennett in the Italian programme, Darina felt she'd been right in identifying the two women as similar in type, though Anthea must be some ten years or more older. Not older than Bruce, though.

Was he the sort of man who held there was one extra-marital law for men and another for his wife?

Darina realized she still knew very little about Bruce Bennett. Also that she was hungry, last night she'd only eaten a bit of cold tongue, more or less on the run during her frantic cleaning-up activities. She found some bread and cheese, went back to the living-room and sat eating, looking at the set of tapes sitting on the table.

Could Bruce possibly have been murdered? What was it Neil had said about the autopsy report—that cause of death was unknown but there was no evidence it was anything but natural, something like that. Just what did that mean? Darina knew she had to get hold of the full report before she could be satisfied. It must say something else, give some explanation. And what was it that Kate Bennett had been going to tell her?

Bruce's sister had come all the way from Australia to meet Darina and tell her why she thought Bruce had been murdered.

And now she was dead herself.

Kate Bennett had announced her arrival via a letter which could have been read by anyone connected with Cantlow Productions. Neil had apologized for opening it but hadn't been able to remember when it had arrived. Over the period of the holiday break, he had had most of the team in at one time or another for discussions on how the programme should proceed. If Bruce had been murdered, it had to have been in a diabolically clever way and by someone connected with *Table*. If it had been murder and the murderer had discovered Kate Bennett was coming over, could he have guessed why then taken steps to protect himself—or herself?

A shiver ran through Darina and she rubbed her arms through her thick jersey. If that was what had happened, there was someone extremely ruthless and determined connected with *Table*.

Darina had now been involved with television long enough to know that everyone in that world was determined and most were ruthless. They were two requisites for success. The murderer, if murderer there was, just had to be that bit more determined and ruthless than the rest.

But she had to keep coming back to the question of how murder could have been committed. The only thing Bruce had consumed before his collapse had been the fruit drink and they'd all, Darina, Mark and that week's guest, drunk from glasses filled from the same jug, there couldn't have been anything toxic in it. Anyway, the autopsy had ruled out poison. Could something else have happened, something nobody had noticed because their attention was on the main action?

Darina suddenly remembered that recording had been going on when Bruce collapsed. What had happened to the tape? Did it still exist? If there was anything to be seen, surely it would be on there.

There was one person who would almost certainly know what had happened to it. Darina went and found a copy of one of the *Table* production lists, with the telephone numbers of most of the production team. She looked up Jan Parker's number, rang the director and asked if she'd like to come round to supper one night the following week. 'There are one or two things about the show I'd love to talk over with you,' she explained, 'and it would be nice to get to know you a bit better.'

Jan sounded delighted and a date was decided.

Darina put down the phone and belatedly remembered that she wasn't supposed to be looking into Bruce's death. Feeling distinctly guilty she went and found a duster and attacked the sitting-room.

JAN TURNED UP at the Chelsea house promptly at 7.30 p.m. on the evening they had agreed.

'What a lovely place,' the director said, shrugging off her baggy leather jacket. 'I have a small flat in Wandsworth and sometimes I long for more space. Now that prices are lower, I'm thinking of trying to get somewhere larger. I couldn't aspire to anything like this, though.' Her gaze took in the two rooms, connected by wide doors that always remained open, furnished with antiques and *objets d'arts*.

'I'm very lucky, the house was left to me by a cousin, together with an income that's just about enough to cover the expenses. I certainly couldn't afford it otherwise.'

'But you really live in Somerset, isn't that right?' With a glass of white wine in her hand, Jan wandered around the room, examining Victorian card cases and small wooden netsuke, then peering at a collection of fans, mounted in deep, glazed frames and arranged artistically on one of the walls.

'My fiancé is in the Avon and Somerset Police force, he has a cottage not far from Frome. It's been our home for the last year or so.'

'Fiancé? Is this him?' Jan picked up a photograph of William that stood on one of the side tables. 'Very tasty! Distinguished looking too, not what one expects from a policeman.'

Darina said nothing.

'Have you any marriage plans?'

'We've set a date in March, just after we stop recording *Table for Four*.'

'Ah!' said Jan.

'Actually, that was luck. When we set the date, I had no idea I was going to be involved with television. And it's not all that lucky, I never seem to have time to attend to all the details my mother thinks we should be deciding on. I keep telling her there's lots of time but it's racing past and I must get down to sorting things out soon.'

'It sounds a bit of a schizophrenic life for you.'

'And how!'

'I think I'd find it very difficult not to be able to concentrate entirely on the programme.'

It was a relief to Darina to be able to talk about her problems and frustrations to a listener who was not only sympathetic but could understand the background and almost before she realized it she was spilling out her difficulties with William as they ate the meal she had prepared.

'It's almost as though he's jealous of my career!' she wailed at one point. 'He never used to be like that.'

'Probably he was never greatly inconvenienced by it before,' Jan said drily.

'I'm sorry for boring you like this, it's all just got to me. Thanks for listening.'

Jan gave her a warm smile. 'No problem. Part of the trouble, as I see it, is that you are over-tired. It looks as though you are writing books, charging up and down from Somerset, keeping two homes running *and* doing your piece on the programme, no wonder you haven't got time to decide on a wedding dress!'

'But it's not as though I'm involved in the whole programme,' Darina protested. 'All I have to do is a bit of cooking and some chat. It's not even as though I have to prepare the food.'

Jan cocked an eye at her. 'You don't spend time rehearsing your food spot? Don't have to work out exactly what you are going to do and how you're going to do it? Don't have to sort out exactly what Lynn will have to prepare and order? You don't give any thought to what you can say during the chatty bits that will sound well and maybe score a point or two off the other presenters? In the nicest possible way, of course?'

Darina laughed. 'All right, there is a bit more to it.'

'And there are the production meetings, the filming sequences, not to mention the wear and tear of nerves. Don't tell me you don't suffer from those?'

'Do I ever! There are times I wish I was anywhere but in a television studio. There are times, in fact, when I seriously consider telling Neil it's no good and he'll have to find someone else.'

'Don't even *think* that. You're coming over really well.'

'But if it's going to ruin my relationship with William?'

'Sod that! What's your relationship with him going to be like in a few years' time if you've given up a great chance like this merely to pamper his sense of self-esteem?' Jan looked keenly at her. She smiled suddenly. 'There are better ways to ensure he feels good. For instance, it seems to me part of your trouble is non-delegation. Get someone in to look after the cottage. It's ridiculous either of you having to turn to and clean after the sort of work you're both doing. Equip yourself with someone who can sort out the cottage and produce the odd meal for William as well. If he's comfortable while you're away, I guarantee his attitude will improve immediately.'

'Jan, you're a genius! Why couldn't I think of that?'

'Why couldn't William?'

'We're both too close to the problem and too tied up with trying to keep on top of our jobs. Have you ever been married?'

'Briefly, a long time ago. It fell to pieces when I discovered all he really wanted was a bedmate and someone to housekeep.'

'There's much more than that between William and me.'

'You're lucky!' Jan said briefly.

'You've never found anyone else?'

Jan shook her head. 'Not to marry. Frankly, I think until men change their attitude, accept us on a completely equal basis, marriage is just not on.'

'Times are changing! After thirty years of women rethinking their roles I'm sure men are now undergoing the same process. I know I've been complaining about William but he really does accept that I have a career of my own to follow, that I'm not going to give it all up and become the little woman.'

'As I said, you're lucky!'

'And then there's Neil. Isn't Anthea a publishing editor? That must involve a lot of her time.'

Jan gave a small snort. 'Anthea has the same sort of problem as you. Neil will invite the whole production team to his home on a Sunday without a second thought and expect her to provide us all with lunch. No consultation as to whether Anthea had set the day aside for something else, everything has to bow before the mighty television producer.'

'What about Mark and Milly? I gather they were an item, who was top dog there?'

'Oh, Milly,' said Jan instantly. 'But they were always having rows. Sometimes they didn't speak at all in the studio apart from when they were actually involved in the programme. Like so many men, Mark's basically insecure; I think if you'd asked him who, between the two of them, he thought Neil would fire, he'd have said it would be him.'

'Did you think Neil made the right choice there?' Darina asked curiously.

Jan spread her hand out on the polished mahogany of the table, and studied the long, strong-looking fingers unencumbered by rings. After a moment she said, 'I think Neil had made up his mind to bring Bruce on board, Milly didn't really stand a chance.'

'The other day you said you thought *Table* was doomed without Bruce. Have you changed your mind now that you've seen Jean-Pierre in action?'

'I think it's too early to tell but he comes over well, there's been a good response to him and it's possible we can squeak our way through.'

Darina realized she hadn't really got round to the ostensible purpose she had asked Jan over to dinner for, let alone the real one, which she was now not at all sure she wanted to carry through. 'Mark was saying the other day he thought I should be more relaxed, do you think he has a point?'

There followed a discussion on Darina's contribution to *Table,* with valuable advice from Jan on how she should present herself to the camera. 'Mark's right about television being an intimate medium,' the director said finally. 'The viewer is watching in his own home, it's as if you are an invited guest. The last thing you want is to appear to be addressing an audience of more than one. But don't worry,' she added kindly, 'you improve with every programme. After all, Mark's an old hand now.'

'Bruce seemed to take to it very easily.' Darina couldn't resist bringing the conversation back to the Australian.

'Bruce was a natural. No inhibitions, no stage fright, nothing. He spoke to the camera as he would speak to you or me. The man may have been a shit but he was Heaven's gift to a television director.'

'A shit? I thought he was great fun and rather charming.'

'Oh, come off it, Darina! Don't say you're another of the well-brought up, well-educated, refined ladies Bruce always felt challenged to get into bed!'

'Is that how he operated?'

'Well, look at Anthea, it's common knowledge he came on in a big way as soon as he met her and Neil.'

'Where did they meet?'

'It was when Neil visited Australia last year. We were doing a programme on Australian food and wine in the last series and he went over there to record some footage and do a little research. One of the first places he visited was Yarramarra.'

'Did he take a film crew?' Darina wondered if anyone else connected with *Table* had been on that visit.

Jan shook her head. 'He decided it was cheaper to hire a team out there. Anthea went with him and they were treating it half as a holiday. Apparently they had a marvellous time. Bruce took both of them around, showed everything off and entertained them. Shelley wasn't there at the time, apparently Bruce told them she was in New Zealand on some PR trip, like the Italian one.'

It was no good, Darina couldn't resist this perfect opening. 'You were on that as well, weren't you? Tell me, Mark's been suggesting he and Shelley got on really well together, did it seem that way to you?'

'Really?' Jan looked startled. 'Do you mean he meant they were having an affair?'

'I don't think exactly that,' Darina said hastily.

'Oh, well, Mark's always trying to suggest he's God's gift to women.' Jan sounded dismissive.

'Did she talk about her husband at all?'

'Shelley? Not really. She wore a ring but that doesn't seem to mean much to many of the women on these trips, or the men either! But she didn't seem to me to be looking for...' Jan paused, searching for the right phrase.

'A quick fling?' Darina offered.

'Well, that sort of thing, yes. She was rather quiet, in fact. I thought she might be unhappy but I didn't have much time to find out, I knew Neil was considering giving me the series to direct and I was anxious to make sure we got as much good material as we could.'

Darina was willing to bet Jan had seen more of what had gone on in Italy than she was telling. Those sharp eyes, trained to observe, wouldn't have missed a thing. She wondered exactly what it was that Jan wasn't telling.

'So it was as much of a shock to you as to Mark when you found out Bruce was her husband?'

Jan smiled. 'It was rather funny, wasn't it? Bruce was really taken aback.'

'It certainly wrecked the good feeling between him and Mark.'

Darina watched for Jan's reaction to that one.

'Ah, so you noticed that, did you?'

'Only the other night, really, when I looked through all the tapes again. I'm afraid I'd been too wrapped up in what I was doing before that.'

'Up in the gallery we see everything.'

'Of course, Bruce had no right to be resentful of anything Shelley might have been getting up to, he didn't appear to be the most faithful of husbands.'

'I'd say not! Quite apart from Anthea, as soon as he met the *Table* team he was after Lynn.'

'Then I was right! She was involved with him!' Darina looked at the director curiously. 'How did you know? Very little seemed to go on between them in the studio or at meetings.' There had only been that one short confrontation she had noticed, just before Bruce died, and that certainly couldn't have been seen from Jan's gallery.

'Oh, Lynn and I are quite close. She spends the week in a bedsit not far from where I live. Sometimes she borrows my kitchen if she's got some cooking to do and her landlady can't make hers available.' Jan shot a quick glance at Darina. 'Did you know Lynn has a small son?'

'No, I'm afraid I haven't had time to find out much about her.'

'She had an affair with the manager of a hotel she was working in. Married, of course. The moment he heard a child was on the way, he ran a mile, typically male! I suppose, though, that the poor sod couldn't do much anyway, the hotel went into receivership at the same time and everyone was out of a job.'

'How awful!'

'I think it was pretty grim. But Lynn's mam in Wales came to the rescue. She offered to look after the baby during the week provided Lynn came home every weekend. From what Lynn says, she sounds pretty much of a gorgon, won't babysit for her if anybody asks her out, but it's the only way Lynn can manage to keep the child and she's dotty about him.'

'How old is he now?'

'Henry? About six months, I think. She is still breast-feeding him, anyway. Freezes the milk during the week and takes it with her in a coolbag to Wales. During recording there's always a shelf of the studio freezer stacked with the stuff. After she knew she was expecting him, Lynn left restaurant cooking and went freelance, doing the usual sort of thing, cooking directors' lunches, private dinner parties, testing recipes for cookery writers, you know.' Darina did, it was how she had started herself. 'Then someone suggested her to Neil when the previous home economist left and she's proved a treasure. She does a bit of moonlighting as well, fills people's deep freezes, that kind of thing. I think she finds it pretty difficult to make ends meet, what with paying her mother and keeping a car going so she can drive to and from Wales every weekend.'

'No wonder she's looking so tense and tired! I'm amazed she found time for Bruce. She doesn't seem to fit your pattern of the type he went for either.'

'I think Bruce went for anything in a skirt that was available. He just found women like Anthea a particular challenge.'

Darina looked at Jan thoughtfully. The director laughed. 'No, don't even think it! Bruce would never be my type and he sensed it immediately. He had all the instincts of some jungle animal.' She gave a sigh. 'Poor Lynn, I don't think she got much joy out of their little affair. She hasn't told me much about it, just that she wasn't seeing him any more. I worry about that girl, she's one of life's natural victims. She was mugged just after she started working for the programme.'

'No!'

'If someone hadn't come along at the critical moment, she'd have been raped as well. You can't be too careful these days, especially in London. When Lynn told me, I gave her the name of a really good martial-arts course, it's only common sense to be able to defend yourself.' Jan looked at Darina's tall figure. 'How are you at karate?'

'Useless.'

'Of course, with your build you've got more of a chance than someone small like Lynn but it wouldn't hurt to learn some useful tricks. I can put you in touch with a good course if you're interested.'

Darina said that it sounded like a good idea, particularly now she was spending so much more time in Chelsea. Then, over coffee, she found herself gradually working the conversation round to the fatal recording when Bruce had had his attack. 'It must have been such a shock to see it happening,' she said. 'At least on the studio floor we could try to help, up in the gallery you must have felt so helpless.'

'God, yes! I can see him now, gasping in pain, pulling at his clothes. It looked just like a classic heart attack and I can't say I was surprised he was dead by the time the ambulance got him to hospital.'

'Don't you think it's strange that apparently the autopsy didn't find any damage to his heart?'

'I sometimes think the medical profession is as ignorant about the body as most of us are. Life is such a fragile thing at the best of times, isn't it?'

'What happened to the tape that was being recorded at the time?' Darina asked. As Jan stared at her, she added hastily, 'It's not really morbid curiosity, I just thought it might show when the attack started. Perhaps if the medics had seen that, they'd have known a bit more.'

Jan's eyes narrowed. 'Didn't you say on that chat show

you'd solved several murders? You don't really think Bruce was killed, do you?' There was shocked surprise in her voice.

'Good heavens, no!' Darina hoped she sounded sincere. She added for good measure, 'Surely there can't be any question it was anything but natural? I mean, the autopsy didn't find anything sinister.'

'And the undetectable poison belongs to crime fiction!' Jan laughed then apologized. 'I'm sorry, it isn't a joking matter. Anyway, it's most unlikely the tape still exists. After editing, everything that hasn't been used is wiped. If you don't keep the stuff down, it'd end up taking over.'

THIRTEEN

'EVER SEEN A BLACK SNOWMAN?' David Bartholomew brushed the melting flakes from his hair and gave Pam a sparkling glance. He stood in the front office of Cantlow Productions, small epaulettes of the snow that was falling in fairylike profusion outside decorating the shoulders of his track suit.

'Heavens, don't say you jogged here?'

'Took the tube to Victoria then ran the rest of the way through the parks with the snow falling all around me. It's lying now, everything will soon be buried in the stuff. There's something about weather like this that's magic.' He shrugged a rucksack off his back. 'I only hope the suit's not hopelessly creased.'

David went off to the small office bathroom, showered and dressed himself in his business clothes. Good cloth and master tailoring was definitely an investment, he smoothed down a jacket that hardly looked as though it had been off the hanger. A quick adjustment of the silk tie and he was ready. He hung up track suit and running shoes to dry then went back to the main office.

'I know I'm early, I wanted a word with Neil before everyone else gets here, is he available?'

'Give it a go, why don't you?' Pam returned to her typing.

David gave a last brush to his wet head, picked up his briefcase and went through to the executive producer's office.

The snow seemed to have had much the same exhilarating effect on Neil. He stood by the window watching the large flakes dance down, obliterating the building opposite, his hands in his trouser pockets, humming the catchy opening tune of *Table*. 'Come in, come in,' he invited expansively as David opened the door and enquired if he was free.

'You look as though something's gone right for once,' David said, coming in and sitting down on one of the chairs put ready for the meeting. 'Or is it the child in you excited by the weather? Shall we all go out and have a snowball fight?'

'Great idea!' Neil came and sat behind his desk. 'Well, David, what is it? Not a financial crisis, I hope?'

'More personal, Neil.' David hitched one leg over the other and adjusted the set of his trousers. 'The thing is, Neil, I wondered if we could talk about my being given some creative responsibility.'

Some of Neil's good humour disappeared. 'David, you're not ready, you need more experience.'

'Neil, you've been promising me creative experience for two years now and I'm still stuck with the bloody figures!'

Neil winced. 'Don't shout, I'm not deaf. I know how difficult patience is for you but it won't be long now, I promise. You just have to wait for the right moment.'

'I'll drop down dead before the right moment comes along! I warn you, Neil, if I don't get this, I'm off. Off with my budgeting ability, my ideas and, who knows, perhaps other things as well.'

Neil's gaze narrowed. 'Are you threatening me? I don't like that. Don't think you're indispensable.'

David's anger rose bubbling to the surface. Just in time he prevented himself from throwing his job in Neil's face. That was no part of his plans. What was it his father said, 'Always go forward from a position of strength; never give up one job before you've organized the next. A chap in work is worth three times an unemployed.' Well, the old man should know. He'd worked his way up the executive ladder to the boardroom of a powerful industrial conglomerate. Not bad for a darkie! Deep within David were hidden the slights and insults thrown his way ever since he could remember. England not a racist society? Forget it! Never mind his father's position, never mind the fact his mother was a leading lawyer, never mind the comfortable house, his public school education, all the trappings of an upper middle-class background; if your skin was black you soon learned life had to be tackled head on. And then that there were ways of dealing with prejudice that could earn more satisfying dividends than bashing someone's face in. Eton had taught him that, amongst other things.

'Neil,' he said placatingly, swallowing the bitter gall that threatened to spew out. 'Neil, you know I love working with you. Cantlow Productions has taught me everything. It's just that you did promise I would get on the production side.'

'And you will, you have my word on it,' Neil said soothingly, settling comfortably into his chair again. 'As I said, it's just a case of waiting for the right moment to come along. It won't be long now, I'm sure.'

Oh yeah? It wasn't as if Neil couldn't do with the help, either. No wonder he didn't have the time to come up with another winning programme idea. David glanced down at the slim document case on his knee. Well, Neil was going to have to sing for his production manager. It would have been advantageous to have had a little extra experience before he started up on his own but, hell, he could hack it without and the time had come.

The door to Neil's office opened and the production team started arriving. Soon everyone was assembled in the office and Pam was bringing in coffee.

The meeting had been under way for an hour and a half when Neil's phone was buzzed.

David noted Neil's annoyance as he picked up the phone and he wondered what was sufficiently important for the production secretary to ignore the time-honoured rule that nothing interrupted the meeting.

'A visitor? Didn't you tell them I wasn't available? What? Who? Good heavens, quite right!' He put down the receiver and bounced to his feet, thrusting his way through the tangle of chairs and people to greet the visitor Pam showed in.

David caught his breath as he saw it was Shelley del Lucca. Her thin face was pinched with the cold, her dark hair was curling from the damp and a heavy black overcoat swamped her slim figure. Under the intensity of the Italian sun she had been vivid and glowing, totally at ease in her bright summer clothes. Here the English winter appeared to have eaten into her spirits and washed out the attractive touch of bravura.

But, of course, she was now a widow, in mourning for her husband, not a journalist enjoying a foreign press trip.

Neil was welcoming her to Cantlow Productions, expressing the regret that they all felt at the sad death of her husband. 'It's so good of you to visit us,' he said. 'And how lucky we are having one of our production meetings, now you can meet everyone. Let me take your coat.'

Shelley allowed him to remove the black overcoat. Underneath she was wearing a grey wool dress brightened with scarlet touches. Colour was beginning to come back into her pale face.

Neil introduced each of the production team. Shelley nodded, smiled at each person, warmth beginning to seep through the frozen exterior.

Jan offered her hand. 'We had that lovely time together in Italy, filming for *Table* last September.'

'I remember,' Shelley smiled at her. 'It was my first time abroad and you were all so kind to me.'

'Jan was just like a mother hen,' said David coming forward. 'Protecting you from the big bad wolves.'

Shelley flushed.

'You couldn't call me a wolf.' Mark edged up, displacing Jan.

Shelley seemed happy to see him. 'Mark, how lovely that you're here as well.'

Mark grasped her hand in both of his. 'We must get together, what are your plans?'

Shelley looked towards Neil. 'I hoped to be able to have a few words,' she said. Her voice was as David remembered, low and unhurried, the slow delivery giving a sense of importance to everything she said.

'Of course.' Neil was warmly expansive. 'We've nearly finished. Why don't you sit over there while we run through the last few details, you might find it interesting.'

Neil quickly wrapped up the last details of that week's programme and dismissed the production team.

'Now, my dear,' he was saying as they all left his office, 'sit over here and tell me all about Yarramarra.'

Yarramarra…David smiled to himself as he thought of acres and acres of productive vines.

There was the usual dash to make telephone calls or leave the office. David heard Mark ask Pam to make sure she got the details of where Shelley was staying. Then the presenter claimed an urgent appointment with some food chap and left the office. David smiled to himself, to the hunter went the spoils.

He opened the door to the small office that was his and sat himself down at the desk. By shifting the chair slightly, he could see Neil's door. He opened a filing cabinet, brought out some papers and sat down.

It wasn't long before Shelley emerged from Neil's office.

'You must come out to the house,' Neil was saying. 'How about tomorrow evening? Anthea would be thrilled to meet you.'

He sounded so sincere David wondered for a brief moment if Neil really hadn't known about Anthea and Bruce.

Shelley's eager acceptance of the invitation certainly suggested she was in ignorance of her husband's affair.

Neil asked Pam to give Shelley his address and arrange for a taxi to collect her from her hotel.

David walked out of his office. 'Are you free for lunch?'

Just for an instant her gaze flicked towards Neil then she smiled warmly at him. 'I'd like that.'

Neil held out his hand. 'I'm sorry I can't offer to take you to lunch myself but we'll be looking forward to seeing you tomorrow. I'm sorry about that other matter, too, but I'm sure you understand the position.'

Something flickered in Shelley's eyes then she smiled and shook hands. Neil disappeared back into his office.

David found her coat and helped her into it, his hands lingering for the briefest of moments on her shoulders. 'I know a nice little place just round the corner from here.'

Shelley pocketed the piece of paper Pam gave her with Neil's address and telephone number and they left the office.

'Is it always this cold and miserable in England?' Shelley asked after they'd slushed their way the short distance to the quiet restaurant David had decided would be ideal.

'Most of the time,' he said, straightfaced, as they settled themselves at a comfortable table towards the rear of the small room and the waiter handed them the menus.

'God, how did Bruce stand it?'

'Actually, this is pretty exceptional. What will you have to drink?'

'It'd better be whisky, I need something warming.' She rubbed her thin hands together.

'It's wonderful to see you here. I didn't think you'd be making it quite so soon.'

Shelley wrinkled her nose. 'I wasn't going to but, I don't know if you heard, Kate, my sister-in-law, died over here the other day.'

'I'm so sorry.' David tried to project the right amount of concern.

'I had to identify her body.' The low voice was so quiet he had to strain to hear.

'No! You poor thing!' He reached across and put his hand over hers. 'Was anyone with you?'

His sympathy was rewarded by a small smile, the soft lips, coloured to match the red flashes on her dress, briefly curving like a slice of some small, exotic fruit. 'There wasn't anyone I could ask to go with me.'

'I would have gone, you should have rung me.'

'Sweet of you, David.' Eyelids loaded with dark lashes

swept down, blanking out the grey eyes, a grey so soft it was like the fur of a Persian kitten.

'Was it very dreadful?' he asked, his warm hand still holding hers.

The lashes swept up again, the eyes now shiny with tears. 'I only saw her face. They said her body was…' She hesitated, gave a small gulp. 'Had been crushed in the fall. And one side of her head. But her face was unmarked.' Another small gulp. 'She looked so shocked, as though she couldn't believe what was happening.'

David took out a handkerchief and handed it over.

'Thanks.' Shelley carefully wiped away her tears. 'At least, that's how it seemed when I first looked at her.' She paused then added, 'But then I thought it might be a look of determination. The police think she jumped, you see.'

'While the balance of her mind was disturbed?'

'She was so very odd before she flew to England. Bruce's death seemed to have sent her completely off-beam. She didn't leave a note but I can understand that she could have been so confused and depressed she just decided to end it all.'

'Poor you, one thing after another,' David said, his voice full of sympathy.

'You don't know the half of it!' The drinks arrived and Shelley took a reviving swallow of her whisky and soda, then another.

David sipped at the Negroni he'd ordered because he thought it might recall Italy to her. He remembered the bitter sweet taste of her lips that day they'd gone driving together, the expensive fragrance of her lipstick mingling with the saltiness of the tiny beads of sweat that had bedewed the skin around her mouth on that hot day. That was all the time they had had together but for him it had seemed rich with promise.

'My shoulder is at your disposal, highly absorbent for crying on.'

Another small smile.

'Let's order,' suggested David, picking up the menu.

'You choose,' she said listlessly. 'You know the food here, something light.'

He ordered two *saltimbocca alla romano,* for the same reason as the Negroni, preceded by soup, the kitchen here was rather good on soups, plus an excellent Italian light red wine.

'All right, now that's out of the way, tell me everything.'

Shelley seemed to have her thoughts in order now. 'You know Bruce had invested in Cantlow Productions,' she started.

David drew his breath in with a hiss.

It was as though a light had been switched on. So that was where the cash injection had come from! Several months ago Neil had been desperate for money and David had helped him prepare a number of financial proposals to be given to various sources the producer thought might be prepared to invest in his company. At the time, David hadn't felt at all confident the proposals would prove sufficiently enticing. The UK revenue barely covered direct production expenses, viability depended on overseas and other sales and at that time they weren't attracting enough of those. He had prepared himself to see the company fold. But the money had arrived. It had come from 'a City source', Neil had said.

Now he knew it was nothing to do with the City, it explained so much. Why Bruce had suddenly turned up out of the blue, why Neil had tolerated all that crap from the Australian, why he had turned such a blind eye to what was going on with Anthea, why Bruce was allowed so much of a say in the programmes.

'No, I didn't know,' David said. 'Neil and Bruce kept it quiet.' He could understand Neil not wanting it general knowledge, confidence in the company and all that. But why not tell him? Because Neil didn't trust him, that's why. David fumed silently.

Shelley glanced up at him through her lashes. David smiled at her. 'I'm sorry, you were saying Bruce had invested in Cantlow Productions?'

'He was desperate to make it big, to be *the* wine personality not just in Australia but all over the world, the first person anybody thought of when an authority on wine was needed. He reckoned television was an essential part of the process.'

'I thought he said he was a regular on Australian television?'

'Oh, he'd appeared on one or two shows but that wasn't good enough for him. He said no one watched Australian programmes but Australians. If he could be part of an English programme, it would probably be shown all round the world.'

'We are now selling *Table* to a number of foreign countries,' acknowledged David.

'I think he got the idea after Neil visited Yarramarra last year. I didn't meet him, I was on some promotional trip in New Zealand. When I got back Bruce was full of this hotshot Pommy producer and his ambition to make it in the UK TV world. I thought it was just one of his lines, Bruce was always spinning some sort of tale, I'd learned not to believe half of them.'

'I reckoned he was some sort of con artist myself,' David offered in support.

'But all the time we were in Italy, Bruce was negotiating long range with Neil. He didn't tell me a thing, just said he was off to fame if not much fortune in the old home country.' She shot him another look from under her lashes. 'I wanted to come too but, well, as you know, things between us weren't too good and he said he wasn't having me cluttering up his life in London. I was amazed when I learned he'd got himself a spot on *Table,* such a coincidence!' David thought the wide-eyed and candid look she gave him was just a little overdone but he wasn't going to criticise. Then she added, 'Bruce's lawyer took me through his will.' Once again her eyes were veiled by the long lashes and David wondered what it was she didn't want to tell him. 'And that was when I heard about the investment.'

Shelley raised her chin and lifted away the dark hair from

the back of her neck, fluffing it out with her fingers now that it was dry again. The strong dark curls shone against the sheen of her lightly tanned skin. She looked such a soft little creature.

'So I told Neil I was very interested in keeping the investment with him, that I wanted a chance in a UK show, told him about the TV I've done back home.' She paused as the soup arrived. 'I didn't actually say if he didn't offer me something I'd withdraw the money…'

'But you managed to suggest that would be the case?' How long had it taken Neil to recognize the steel under the softness?

Shelley nodded, her eyes sparkling with something that wasn't amusement.

'And what did Neil say?' He could have felt in somewhat of a quandary, David thought. Desperate for the cash but knowing that if he ditched Darina and took on Shelley the further change of format might be fatal to *Table*. David felt he could be desperate himself. This was the most unexpected of developments.

Then he saw that the sparkle was the sparkle of anger. 'He told me Bruce's investment had been protected by insurance and that his estate would shortly be receiving a cheque repaying the capital he'd put in.'

'Did he, by God!' David was relieved but resentful. Neil had the luck of the devil, he now had the capital that was so vitally important without the aggro of an interfering partner. 'Well,' he said, 'at least you will get the money.'

'But not my start in British television! Neil said he'd try and help but he didn't sound as though there was much he could do.'

No, Neil wouldn't be interested in setting up a cookery demonstrator in a rival show.

'Shelley,' David said softly, 'didn't I say to trust me? Wait until you hear what I've got planned.'

FOURTEEN

'WENT WELL, your cooking spot today.'

The technician who'd come up beside Darina as she stood in front of the monitor watching the run through of Jean-Pierre's wine spot was the one with a squint and a penchant for loudly patterned sweaters. Darina knew most of their names by now but couldn't remember what this one was called. Normally he avoided socializing, concentrating on being available should one of his lights need tweaking into a different position, or looking in the general direction of Lynn, though his squint made it impossible to know whether she was the attraction or not.

'Might have a go at stuffing a chicken skin myself, you made it look much easier than boning out a bird.'

'It is! You do a lot of cooking?'

He shrugged his shoulders, giving a little jerk to the hump on the intarsia camel decorating that day's sweater. 'Not really, but every so often I have a go, cheaper than eating out, isn't it? Look—' He shot a glance around, seemed satisfied no one else was within hearing distance and said, 'I heard you were interested in a copy of that tape, the one where the Aussie snuffed it?'

Darina's stomach did a quick flip. She had casually mentioned the tape during a quiet moment to the technical manager soon after make-up and costumes had finished with her early that morning. She hadn't said she wanted a copy, merely wondered out loud if one existed. The technical manager had given her an odd look and said nothing. Darina had smoothly moved the conversation on to another topic and nothing more had been mentioned about it.

Now it appeared her enquiry had borne fruit. 'You've got one?' Darina asked in an uninterested way.

'Could have.' His look was furtive. 'Cost you, though.'

Darina felt a deep distaste, the tape was obviously being sold for purposes she would rather not identify. 'I want to check something,' she said, hoping he wasn't thinking the worst.

'I understand.' The look he gave her was far from comforting.

A few minutes later it was all organized. At the end of the recording session, Darina handed over most of the contents of her wallet, recharged the previous day for the weekend shopping, and received in return an unmarked video cassette. The transaction was effected quickly and silently and Darina placed the tape in her bag confident that no one else had seen what had happened.

It was something of a shock, therefore, when, as she turned away from the electrician, David Bartholomew materialized from round the dresser that backed her part of the set. 'There you are!' he said. 'I've been trying to catch up with you all day. You haven't let me have your expenses for visiting that chicken farm last week yet.'

It had been Darina's contact, an organic chicken farm in Somerset. She had met one of *Table*'s researchers there the previous Monday when they had talked to the proprietor with a view to seeing if an appearance on this week's programme was a possibility.

'I'm sorry,' Darina said to David, 'I didn't think there was anything to claim. We didn't take her out to lunch or anything.'

'What about your car expenses? Didn't you drive there? And Jenny says you paid for the lunch you both had after the visit.'

'Oh, that! I didn't think that qualified; it was only a pub and we would have had to eat anyway. But I should have given you a note of the mileage. I'm sorry. Will next Monday do?'

'Fine,' said David and went off to chase up somebody else.

Darina looked after him thoughtfully. Had he seen her taking charge of the tape?

Would it have mattered if he had? People were always handling tapes of one sort or another. It surely couldn't have been identified as one of Bruce's death, it would never occur to him anyone could be passing it around anyway.

Unless, of course, David had been responsible for killing Bruce, in which case he might well be ultra-suspicious.

Could David Bartholomew have had a motive for killing the Australian?

Vividly Darina remembered the scene in the hospitality room on her first recording day when Bruce called David 'a little Abo'. She recalled the anger that had been clearly seen on David's face and the way Theresa Mancusa had defused the situation.

Could a slight like that be sufficient motive for murder?

There could be another one.

Darina had finished recording her cookery demonstration that morning to find Shelley del Lucca standing by Lynn's preparation table with David Bartholomew. Neil had invited Shelley to come along, David had said. He thought she might be interested to see in action the programme Bruce had made such a hit with.

Shelley had stayed until about four o'clock, watching what went on, seemingly fascinated. During lunch David had behaved as though she was his exclusive property, helping her to food, introducing her to various members of the team, never leaving her side. He seemed to have forgotten he was not the only one to have met her in Italy. At one stage Shelley had asked where the cameraman was who had been there. 'He's film not a studio cameraman.' Jan Parker had joined the group round Shelley. 'Have you seen the film we took? There are some good shots of you on it.'

'Really?' Shelley had looked excited.

'I've been trying to get hold of you, I thought you might like to see them, but you're very elusive.' Jan had sounded more than a touch peeved and guilt had crossed Shelley's face, warming the creamy skin.

'There's been so much to organize, what with identifying Kate's body, making all the arrangements and everything,' she had said apologetically.

Jan's tone had immediately become warmer. 'Of course, you poor thing, it must be awful for you. But remember I'm here and I can always help, you've only to ask.'

David had moved closer to Shelley. 'I'm making sure she's being looked after,' he had said protectively.

Jan had looked at him thoughtfully. 'I'm sure you are,' had been her only comment but it was as though she understood a great deal more than had actually been said. Then she had taken out a small diary and looked at Shelley. 'Well, shall we make a date?' They had just about managed to arrange something before David whisked Shelley away again.

Mark had been furious at the way David had monopolized her.

'Shelley, my darling,' he'd said, coming up behind her and David as they chatted to Alison, the floor manager. 'You are for ever connected in my mind with all the delights of Italy. Come over here and let me renew our friendship.' Neatly cutting Shelley out of the little group, he'd taken her into a corner, together with a bottle of wine he'd lifted from the buffet table. David had been left looking abandoned but it wasn't long before he'd found someone else to bring up and introduce to Shelley.

The pursuit had quite amused Darina.

'Just like young bulls round a heifer on heat,' said Jan, standing beside her at the buffet table and cutting into a good-looking Brie. There had been an acid note in her voice.

'She's very attractive,' Darina had commented, watching

David take Shelley off to another part of the room, both of them deep in conversation.

'Quite a little stud, isn't he?' Mark had come up with a slight swagger. 'Have you noticed how David never likes being next to someone really tall when there's a pretty girl around? Coffee, anyone?'

IN SOMERSET there was a message from Darina's mother on the answering machine. She had found someone who might possibly be able to help in the cottage and, unless Darina rang back to say it was inconvenient, Mrs Hope would be coming round at ten o'clock the following morning. And would Darina please ring her mother about her wedding dress as soon as possible.

Hope, what a marvellously apposite name! Darina immediately picked up the phone. 'I can't wait to meet her, Mother, thank you so much for finding her.'

'It's nothing, darling, I just put the word about.' Lady Stocks' voice was brisk. 'Thank heavens you're being sensible at last, you should have done something about help months ago. I told Gerry you were mad to think you could manage everything and he agreed with me.'

General Sir Gerald Stocks was her mother's second husband. Widowhood to the Hon. Anne Lisle had meant an active social life but little to involve her emotionally beyond her daughter. No one had been more pleased than that daughter when her engagement to the elderly widower had been announced. Both William and Darina liked Gerry Stocks enormously and he knew exactly how to handle her mother.

'Now, I've also found someone in Glastonbury who designs and makes the most marvellous wedding dresses. I know you said you'd find something in London but you don't seem to have done anything and time is getting on. I've had a word with her and she says she could just about get one done in time if you decided on the style immediately. I thought we could meet there tomorrow afternoon, unless you would rather go alone,' she added.

'No, let's do it together,' Darina said, stifling the urge to put the whole thing off yet again. 'I can tell you how Mrs Hope turns out then as well.'

Darina rang off and looked at her watch. It was half-past eight. William wasn't home yet but he'd said he wouldn't be late. The tape was burning a hole through her handbag, it couldn't be very long, a matter of minutes, no more.

Still in her overcoat, Darina slipped the tape into the video machine and switched it on, bracing herself to watch Bruce's final agony.

The tape ran for a little longer than she had expected and so involved had she been in what it showed that it wasn't until it came to an end and she tried to wipe away the tears streaming down her face that she was aware William was standing behind her.

'I'm sorry, I didn't hear you come in,' she said apprehensively.

'Is that what I think it is?' he asked, slipping on to the sofa beside her. As she nodded, unable to do more, he placed an arm around her shoulders and drew her against him. 'It can't have been an easy thing to watch, sweetheart.'

She relaxed against him, it was going to be all right. 'I told myself to pretend it was a television play, that he'd pick himself up off camera and everything would be all right. But, of course, it wasn't like that at all. He was so alive, so vital and then he collapsed, so suddenly.' Darina buried her face in William's chest and struggled to control herself.

He held her and made soothing noises.

'I'm sorry.' She pulled herself away and pushed back her hair. 'You're earlier than I expected, I was going to be all welcoming with supper ready when you got back. I didn't realize what seeing the tape would do, I thought it would only take a few minutes.'

'Hush, I understand.'

Yes, he would understand. William had had to view crime scenes far more horrific than anything the tape had shown and control himself in far more stomach-turning situations. But with his cases there was no personal involvement and Darina was aware that William understood this as well. It was such a relief that he seemed to have conquered his jealousy of Bruce, she was overflowing with love for him.

She stood up, smiling. 'Thank you, darling. I'll get supper ready, it won't be a moment, it's prawns marinaded in Thai spices with a pasta salad.'

'To someone who's existed on beefburgers and oven chips for the last few days that sounds ambrosial and even if I'd been living high on the hog it'd still sound pretty good.'

Darina turned to go to the kitchen. William stayed where he was and picked up the video control. 'Mind if I just run this through again? A tape like this is unique.'

'When you're dead, they'll find calluses on your heart,' Darina said lightly and left the room before the tape could be played through again.

She went through to the kitchen and switched on the grill before taking off her coat or retrieving the marinading prawns from her coolbox.

By the time she was ready to place the skewered shellfish under the heat, William had come through, taken a bottle of wine from the fridge and started opening it. While he pulled the cork and poured out two glasses, he said, 'Are you sure the autopsy didn't find signs of a heart attack? The sort of poison that would produce those symptoms would have to have been administered in that jug of whatever it was.'

'Apricot, mango, passion fruit and sparkling mineral water,' Darina automatically responded. 'I know, that's what I told you when you mentioned poison the other day. I angled to get hold of the tape because I thought it might show something else. But there was nothing.' She turned the prawns under the grill. 'Both Mark and I sampled that drink, not to mention that specialist grocer. There couldn't have been any-

thing in Bruce's glass before the juice was added, either. You
have no idea the care that goes into presentation with these
programmes. Everything has to be just so. Just before the
recording started Neil called for clean glasses and I watched
as each was polished before being set on the table. *And* they
were all polished with the same cloth.'

William handed her one of the glasses of wine and started
laying the table. 'Pudding?' he asked hopefully, pausing at
the cutlery drawer.

'You're in luck, I managed to snitch one of the orange and
cognac *crème caramel* Lynn prepared for the programme by
swearing on my honour to take back the dish on Monday.'
She produced it, covered with cling-film, from her basket.
'Made with organic eggs.'

'And didn't you say the autopsy hadn't found anything
toxic in the stomach?' William asked, laying the table.

'Yes, according to Neil, and he couldn't have been lying,
the police would have been all over the place if they had
found anything.'

'Just as I said, the death was natural.' William sounded
annoyingly smug.

'Only if a hale and hearty man of not quite forty suddenly
keeling over and dying for no explainable reason can be called
natural.' Darina's tone was terse.

William sat at the table he had prepared, his wine glass in
his hand. 'I did find one thing slightly odd. That chap gave
no sign of feeling unwell until he drank the fruit cup. Normally if people are going to keel over there is at least some
warning. They feel faint, or have vague pains. Yet he was
joking and appearing to feel absolutely nothing wrong. Still,
I expect a macho Aussie like him would have covered up any
sign of weakness, he must have been something of an actor
to come over as well as he did.'

Darina slid the grilled prawns off the skewers on to a serv-
ing dish and poured over the juices. 'Don't you believe it, the
more macho a man, the quicker he collapses when illness

strikes! And you should have seen Bruce a few programmes earlier when all he had was a bad cold, there was no attempt at covering up the fact he didn't feel well, everyone knew about it.'

Darina remembered the occasion well. Bruce had been rude to one of the cameramen, snapped at Mark and herself and fluffed his recording three times. Afterwards he had apologized and explained he was afraid he was coming down with 'flu. But by the time of the next Monday's production meeting, he was back to his normal self and the episode had been forgotten.

'I'd swear Bruce felt perfectly fine until just after we all tasted the fruit juice. There he was, asking us if it wasn't the most delicious thing we'd ever tasted, and I was just about to agree, when this look of panic comes over his face. You can see it on the recording.'

'From what I could see, he then clutched at his heart and seemed to go into some sort of seizure. After that everybody crowds around and you can't see anything more.'

'We all wanted to help. Neil shouted for someone to call an ambulance and Mark and I went to try and see if we could do anything. It was dreadful, he was panting for breath and we just sort of lowered him to the floor. A first-aid class I went to once explained that when people are having a heart attack you need to try and make them as comfortable as possible and relieve the pressure on the chest. So we made him sit up and lean forward.'

'And did that help?'

'It didn't seem to. It was as though he was trying to fight us, his hands kept going to his throat, his breathing was terrible. He tried to speak but it was impossible to make any sense of what he said.'

'Some of that comes across on the tape. You can just hear something that sounds like "Yamaha".'

'I'm sure that was Yarramarra, Bruce's vineyard in Australia. The rest was just rubbish.' Darina put the prawns and the dish of pasta salad on the table. 'If it wasn't for what Kate Bennett said on the phone to me, I really wouldn't have thought there could be anything odd about Bruce's death, apart from the fact that nothing was actually found to account for it.'

'There's no evidence to suggest she didn't jump, either.' William started eagerly helping himself to the food.

'None that we know of.'

'I've been in touch with the chap in charge of the investigation. Don't look so astonished, aren't I always the supportive partner? Helpful wherever I can be, even to shoving my nose into other police forces' cases?'

Darina was, frankly, amazed. 'What did they say?'

'My opposite number on Chief Inspector Gatting's team, Inspector Barnes, says nobody asked for her at reception, nobody saw anyone go into her room but she did receive two calls.'

'Two?'

'Apparently.'

'One was me, I can't think who the other one could have been. Unless, of course, it was my first call, before she arrived.'

'That could well have been it.'

'On the other hand,' Darina said excitedly, 'it might have been someone else. Could you ask Inspector Barnes to check?'

William sighed. 'I don't see where you're going to get if I do. Oh, and Barnes said the hotel receptionist who checked her in remembers a small woman who seemed very distrait. She complained of not knowing what the time was and feeling dreadful. She asked if the hotel had any aspirin.'

'She'd just arrived from the other side of the world.'

'Well, Barnes said they'd just had the body formally identified and they expected the inquest to return a verdict of accidental death or suicide while the balance of the mind was disturbed.'

'Shelley, Bruce's widow, is over here, she turned up at the production meeting on Monday. I suppose she identified the body.'

'Perhaps the other call Kate Bennett received was Shelley ringing from Australia.'

'I suppose it could have been. Switchboards can't tell if it's an incoming international call these days, can they? Poor Shelley looked pretty shaken on Monday. But,' added Darina consideringly, 'she had cheered up remarkably between then and today, when she came to the studio.'

'Amazing what a good night's sleep can do,' commented William drily. 'I'm sure if there was anything to back up your story that Kate Bennett knew something to prove Bruce had been murdered, the Shelley woman would have told the police. God, those prawns were good, no more, I suppose?' He surveyed the empty dish in disappointment.

'That lot was supposed to do four people,' Darina said severely, clearing the table.

'Of course,' she added, placing the *crème caramel* before her fiancé, 'if Shelley del Lucca had been involved in the murder, she wouldn't tell the police anything, would she?'

Half the delicate custard was now on William's plate. 'A black widow, like the spider? You are, I trust, having me on or have you anything to back up your allegation?'

'Hardly an allegation, just a small cast not expected to catch so much as a minnow, but I've been thinking, you couldn't get hold of a copy of the autopsy report on Bruce, could you? There must be something in it apart from a statement that cause of death was unknown even if they couldn't find evidence of anything unnatural.'

William sighed. 'I don't understand how your black widow could have had anything to do with his death in any case, she was safely on the other side of the world when both victims died.'

'But you will try?'

'Well, I'm quite intrigued myself,' he confessed. 'All right,

I'll see what I can do. I've established quite a rapport with Barnes, it turns out we played rugger together one time. I'd prefer it, though, if you left the detecting to me and concentrated on the cooking. Your body's pretty good to have around but what I really miss is your food.' William polished off the last of his pudding.

'That's Lynn's cooking.'

'As long as it tastes as good as this, I don't mind whose it is.'

Darina opened her mouth to explain the possible advent of Mrs Hope, then shut it again. The woman could turn out to be a disaster. Lulled by the reassuring feeling that her and William's relationship was once again sailing smooth waters, she let her eye travel over the ancient sink and dark brown cupboards with which the kitchen was furnished.

'We really ought to do this place up, you know, darling.'

'Why, what's wrong with it?' he asked stiffly.

'Well, if you don't mind my saying so, it looks as though it belongs in the Middle Ages. Kitchens these days are sleek engine rooms kitted out by designers who care as much for the finish as the ergonomics.'

'You mean if it wouldn't make the pages of *House and Garden,* you wouldn't be seen dead in it?' His tone was grim.

'And while we're at it, we could do something about the living-room as well, the chairs and sofa need recovering and the curtains have never gone with the carpet.'

'Gone where? Down to the local?' He didn't make it sound a joke but Darina didn't notice.

'Don't be silly, darling. I can't do anything with those stains on the bath enamel either and that room's so wretchedly designed that if we redid it, with proper advice, we could probably add a shower. You know you're always complaining it takes you so long to have a bath.' Darina stopped, suddenly uneasy.

William surveyed her coldly. 'I realize to you television types the look of everything is all. Perhaps you'd like to tell me if there is anything about *my* house you do like,' he said at last.

FIFTEEN

DARINA ARRIVED at Cantlow Productions on Monday morning to find most of the production team standing around the outer office not even trying to look as though they weren't listening to the row that was going on in Neil's office.

'For God's sake, Mark,' the executive producer's voice thundered through the door. 'What the *hell* do you think you've been playing at?'

The presenter's words were inaudible.

'It's unacceptable, completely unacceptable. If I'd had the least idea...'

'Come on, Neil, it's no big deal,' Mark could be heard to say.

'No big deal!' Neil's door could have been open, his words were so clear. 'You're fired, Mark. And I'll see you never work again in television.'

The production team looked at each other then at Pam.

The secretary held up her hands in mock surrender. 'I haven't a clue! Mark arrived just after I did, saying Neil had asked him to come round early. Then Neil said I wasn't to let anyone in until he buzzed through.'

A moment later Mark stalked through the assembled company, his face set, his eyes blazing and his mouth a thin line. He said nothing to anyone, merely shrugged his way impatiently into his crombie and disappeared.

David Bartholomew grabbed his own coat and hurried after him.

Neil appeared at his door. He looked at the startled company filling the outer office as though he couldn't understand what they were doing there. His face was rigid with fury.

'All right to come in, now, Neil?' asked Jan.

She could have been the Avon lady, he looked at her with such incomprehension. Then he said abruptly, 'Meeting's off. We'll hold it tomorrow. No calls, Pam, no calls whatsoever.' He turned and went back into his office, closing his door with a dismissive click.

The company stood stunned for several minutes. Then Alison said, 'Any bets on whether we still have a series?'

Nobody answered.

Lynn collapsed into a chair and began to cry, great tears welling up and running down her drawn face. She tried to wipe them away with the back of her hand.

There was an awkward silence. Then Pam pulled some tissues out of a box of Kleenex and handed them to the girl. Jan went and knelt by her. 'Come on, Lynn, it can't be that bad. Neil will patch things up with Mark or find a replacement. We'll keep the show going, you see.'

'Let's go and have a coffee somewhere and relax,' Darina suggested.

Lynn used the tissues to mop up. 'I'm sorry, I don't know what came over me,' she said but still looked as though her world was collapsing.

Fifteen minutes later Darina was ordering coffee for them both in a small café not far from the office. Jan had said she couldn't join them, there were a number of urgent calls she just had to make. Darina wondered whether any of them was connected with finding another job if *Table* folded.

Darina brought over the coffee. 'I've ordered a proper breakfast for you as well, Lynn. You look as though you need it. Have you been saving money by cutting down on your food?'

There was no need for the girl to answer. She drank coffee and sniffed away some of her distress. Darina sat quietly and waited.

A plate of fried egg, bacon, sausage, mushrooms and chips arrived. 'Just the sort of meal we're all being warned against but it'll do you nothing but good,' Darina announced and watched as Lynn, slowly at first and then with increasing speed, worked her way through the food.

While the other girl ate, Darina sipped her coffee and wondered about the best approach.

'I don't think we need really worry too much yet about the programme folding,' she said when the plate was nearly clear and buttered toast had arrived. 'At least not immediately. You heard what Jan said, Neil will probably patch things up with Mark.'

'I hope he doesn't! I can't stand having that man around.'

'You mean, the way he keeps on interfering with your food?'

'He's not a nice man. Comes over well, I give you that, but he can turn really nasty. Before you joined us I told him off in a big way after he'd pinched some expensive chocolate and there wasn't enough left for a retake. When Neil complained, I said straight out whose fault it was, well, I wasn't going to find myself in the cart for him, was I? So later I find all my milk's out of the freezer. My breast milk for the baby,' she added as Darina looked blank. 'I bring it in on recording days so it's all ready to take home to Wales. The poor bugger had to be fed on formula for the next week.'

Darina filed away the little story for future thought. 'Well, anyway, I'm sure what's under threat now is not this series but a possible future one. Have you any plans for what to do when the *Table* recordings stop?'

Lynn placed her knife and fork together with a sigh. Already she looked a little better but she didn't seem any more cheerful. 'I'm not sure. I think someone's going to ask me to do some recipe testing for a book and there's the possibility of a job in Wales, working at a local restaurant for the summer.'

'That would mean you could see more of your son, wouldn't it?' Darina suggested. 'Sounds as though it could be a good idea.'

'But the hours are terrible! At least this way I get three

good days with him. Working in that restaurant could produce a couple of hours in the afternoon if I'm lucky with me totally exhausted on the one day I'd get off. And the money's not so good.'

'I don't suppose it would be easy to have much of a social life, either.'

'I don't get that anyway.' Lynn added marmalade to a piece of toast and ate it listlessly. 'Me mam doesn't approve, she says she's not having me collecting bastards like a schoolboy conkers. Got a nasty tongue on her, my mam has, but she's great with little Henry.' Lynn's tone softened.

Darina eyed her closely. The way Lynn could banter with the production team and the technicians suggested she was a girl who enjoyed social contact. 'It must be difficult having a demanding job then looking after a small baby at weekends, never going out.'

'Oh, I wouldn't say I *never* go out!' Lynn grinned suddenly. 'I manage the odd night out in London. Not often, mind, but sometimes.' She looked almost cheerful and gave Darina a big wink.

'You went out with Bruce a few times, didn't you?'

Tears started once again to pour out of Lynn's eyes, she dropped the toast and dived for her bag.

Darina sat and watched her apply the wodge of tissue. 'I'm sorry,' she said when the fountain looked like becoming more of a trickle, 'I really didn't mean to upset you again but don't you think you need to talk? I hate to see you like this.'

She waited. Lynn put the wet tissue on her dirty plate and uselessly stirred the sugarless coffee. Darina felt if only she knew the right thing to say, Lynn might start to confide in her. 'Have you got a close friend you can talk to?'

Another large tear welled up and fell down Lynn's cheek. 'I tried to talk to Tricia about Bruce, she's the friend I rent my room from, but because she never met him, she couldn't understand what I was on about.'

More tears fell.

'Talk to me about him, after all, I knew what he was like.'

Lynn looked at her, smudged mascara, eyes red, face pinched and thin. 'I don't expect you did. Not unless you went to bed with him.' She paused and looked across the table, her eyes suddenly alert. 'Did you?'

'No!' Darina caught herself. 'I'm engaged but I thought he was very attractive, my fiancé was quite jealous.'

'At first I thought he was wonderful. When he asked me out I couldn't believe my luck. I knew what he was after, of course, but that suited me. I hadn't had anyone since Henry's father, he was a big man too, I like big men, and I was randy as all hell.'

Talking seemed to be doing Lynn good. Her tears had dried and she was more composed, stirring sugar into her tea and downing several pieces of toast and marmalade.

'He seemed great fun,' prompted Darina, hoping Lynn wasn't going to dissolve again when she reached, as she inevitably was, the point of explaining that Bruce had dumped her after he'd grown bored.

A moment later she regretted her glib analysis of the situation.

'He was an *animal*,' Lynn snarled suddenly. 'He shouldn't have been allowed near any decent girl.'

Darina gazed at her. 'What, exactly, do you mean?' she asked, her eyes narrowing, wondering how unsophisticated this girl from a Welsh valley was.

Lynn looked back at her with eyes that belonged to a woman older than history.

'You wouldn't understand, nobody could understand!'

'Try me,' Darina suggested. 'You have to talk about it to someone, you can't keep it all bottled up inside you and you can't tell me anything I haven't heard about already from my fiancé. He's a policeman, a detective, and some of the things he has to deal with are unbelievable. Some of the stories he's come home with make animals seem civilized.' Darina hoped William would forgive her the exaggeration.

Lynn started playing with the remaining piece of toast on her plate, tearing the dry bread apart with nervous fingers, scattering crumbs around the plate.

Darina waited.

At last the girl looked up at her again, her face drained of emotion. 'It was fine at first, he was a really good fuck.' She used the word lightly, as a technical term. 'I like to be active in bed.'

There was an attempt at a giggle. 'Burns the calories off, doesn't it? Not that I've got anything to worry about in that department. First time I've had anything to show upstairs was when Henry was born.' She glanced down at the swelling little breasts decorating her thin body. Her hands played again with the bits of toast, adding more crumbs to the table. 'Anyway, at the start it was just a thundering good time and we both enjoyed ourselves.' She paused again.

'When did you stop enjoying yourself?' asked Darina gently.

'When he started bashing me around.'

'You mean, that bruise you had?' Darina remembered the livid purple mark on the side of the girl's face that she claimed had been the result of walking into a door.

Lynn nodded. 'That wasn't the worst, the worst were hidden by my clothes. It wasn't too bad at first, you expect the odd love bite and a bruise or two when things get too, too, well, athletic. But then he started going beyond that.'

'How long did this go on for?' Darina gazed at the girl unbelievingly, Lynn made it sound as though she had had no choice in the matter.

'Until he hit me in the face. That was the buckle on his belt, you know, that big leather job he liked to wear?'

Dimly Darina remembered a studded cowboy effort with an ornate metal buckle. She tried to control her shudder. 'How could you have let him? I mean, Jan said you attended some lessons in self-defence. I know he was big but surely there are ways?' Her voice trailed away as she registered the cold self-disgust in Lynn's eyes.

'I can't explain. He did something to me. It's not like someone beating you in cold blood. He makes you excited, leads you on…' Her gaze dropped. 'I told you you wouldn't understand, you can't if you've never experienced anything like that. Your body is separate from your mind, you stop thinking, it's just all feeling, it's like drugs, your body wants it. And then, afterwards, you feel dreadful. Hate yourself. Swear you'll never see him again, that you don't care how much your body aches to be touched. Until you hear his voice, see the way he looks at you…God, no one can understand, no one.' Lynn looked despairingly at Darina, her eyes hot and dry. 'But that last night, when the buckle caught me like that, that was too much. I told him he'd gone too far and I wasn't seeing him again.'

'But he wanted you to?' It wasn't really a question.

Lynn sighed, a deep sigh full of self-disgust. 'He reckoned he knew me, he thought it was just a matter of time and I couldn't resist another night with him. He said I did things to him nobody else could. Well, I bet he said that to all the girls!'

A sudden vision of quiet, elegant, dark Anthea came into Darina's mind. What had her relationship with Bruce been?

'But you told him no.'

Lynn nodded vigorously. 'He didn't like it, he rang me several times. Even tried to persuade me one time at the studio. Normally he kept away.'

'Didn't want the rest of the team knowing he was involved, I suppose.'

'That, and the fact I told him Pete would slaughter him if he knew how he was treating me.'

'Pete?' Darina failed to work out who this new man was.

'Sparks, you know, that electrician. He's taken me out once or twice.' She fell silent for a moment, thinking, then added, 'I can't say I really like him, but he's got this idea I need protecting and that's always nice, isn't it?' She looked hopefully at Darina. 'I saw him beat a man up outside a pub one night who'd been what he called fresh with me.' She gave a small shiver of excitement. 'He's not all that big but he knows how to handle himself.'

Even so, Darina wouldn't have thought the electrician would have stood much of a chance against Bruce and said so.

'No,' agreed Lynn, a trifle sadly.

'Now,' said Darina in what she hoped was not too much of a nanny voice, 'why don't you tell me the rest of the story. You don't have to worry about Bruce any more but, if anything, you've looked worse since he died than you did before.'

More tears arrived. The tissue wodge was now too wet to be of any help; Darina fished out some dry ones from her bag and handed them over. She waited until Lynn had herself in hand again then asked, 'You haven't got into a similar situation with Pete, have you?'

Lynn's reaction was instant. 'No!' Her voice shook with intensity. 'I never, ever want to be involved in anything like that again.' She fell silent, stirring away again at her tea then finally said, 'I'm pregnant, that's the trouble.'

'Bruce?' asked Darina.

Lynn nodded wordlessly.

'Oh, Lynn, no wonder you're worried. Didn't you take any precautions?'

'I thought as a nursing mother I didn't have to.'

Darina couldn't believe she could have been so naïve.

'And my mam is going to kill me!'

TRYING without much success to sort out Lynn's problem made Darina late for her lunch date.

What had promised to be a relaxed, enjoyable session with an amusing wine merchant was now overshadowed by the revelations of Bruce's sexual proclivities.

All the time Richard Godney was rattling away, Darina's

mind was occupied with the implications of her new knowledge.

'Would you call these the chattering classes, Darina, my dear? They certainly chatter louder than the starlings in my Sussex wood,' her host was saying and Darina wrenched her attention back to survey the Ritz restaurant clientele.

'Chattering classes are a journalistic invention to save creative effort,' she retorted crisply.

'What a relief, I do so dislike being made to feel ignorant. You always give me such a good impression of myself. And how delightfully you come over on *Table for Four,* the programme is a vast improvement over the previous format, it's even survived the loss of Bruce Bennett.'

'He was good, wasn't he?'

'Good? My dear, he was brilliant; he made the most ignorant of viewers feel that with only a little attention he, too, could be an expert. He removed pretentiousness from the wine world; showed you could talk about claret in words a sensible man could accept.'

'Amazing to hear someone like you, Richard, talk that way. Don't you make your money from spinning webs of words around bottles, just as spiders spin them in the cellars?'

'Now, now! I believe to bemuse a client is as bad as to confuse. Let him understand how to judge for himself, learn to trust his palate. No, Bruce Bennett was refreshing. His death is a tragedy, particularly, I should think, to Yarramarra.'

'Is it really a big business?'

'Big? My dear, does champagne bubble? In ten years Bruce Bennett took Yarramarra to the top of the Australian wine league and made himself a fortune in the process.'

'So he wasn't just a big mouth. And now we have another vintner on *Table*; have you seen Jean-Pierre in action?'

Richard nodded.

'That French accent must be worth a million in viewing figures.'

'And I hope it manages to increase his sales figures as well.'

'Does he need them increased? I thought the Prudhomme vineyard was highly respected.'

'Respected, yes; doing well, I'm afraid not.'

'Really, Richard?'

Richard Godney laid down his napkin and beckoned the wine waiter to recharge their glasses. 'He's had very bad luck over the last few years. That terrible frost killing off most of one year's growth; hail destroying another year's grapes just before the *vendange* and then losing his master vintner for the second time in ten years.'

'Second time?'

'Yes, the first I think was carelessness, we'll not go into that, our good friend Jean-Pierre is more than a little careless with his most precious possessions, then blames everyone but himself after it's too late, his vintner isn't the only thing he has lost through inattention. But this time it wasn't Jean-Pierre's fault, the poor fellow died from cancer. It meant more disruption and Jean-Pierre having to turn his attention from marketing to production; within two years he found the Prudhomme wines were no longer commanding the prices he was used to. I understand he's now found a worthy replacement and I'm sure the exposure he's getting on *Table for Four* will provide a welcome boost to the Château Prudhomme vintages.'

Over coffee Richard Godney at last came to what Darina, later, decided must have been the whole purpose of the luncheon invitation; a description of some new Chilean wines that had been added to the Godney list.

'Richard, they sound fascinating. Why don't you send the details in to Neil? I'm sure he'd be interested in considering them should there be another series but I'm almost certain everything for the remaining programmes in the current one has been decided on.'

He bent his head slightly, a little acknowledgement of her

message. 'I will certainly follow up as you suggest but a little personal word from you would help pick the suggestion out from the pack, hmm?'

No such thing as a free lunch, thought Darina, and gave her assurance she would, indeed, mention it to Neil.

Richard smiled at her. 'Now, we've spurned dessert but I think we deserve the *petits fours,* don't you? Ah, heaven!' He popped a truffle covered in white chocolate into his mouth. 'What message do you think the Almighty has sent us by making the grape and the chocolate bean all but incompatible?'

As Darina took her leave with thanks, her host pressed her hand between both of his. 'The pleasure has been entirely mine. Have I mentioned we have a yacht in the Mediterranean? Unkind souls have been known to murmur the words ''gin palace'' but really it's more a brandy boozer, excessively comfortable and hardly leaves Cannes harbour unless the weather is divinely fair set. Might we perhaps tempt you and your charming William down some time? If television commitments allow?'

SIXTEEN

THE POSTPONED production meeting took place on Tuesday morning.

Neil looked as though he had been up most of the night, might, indeed, have slept in the office, but he was triumphant.

'I've got Mike Darcy to join us as presenter in place of Mark,' he announced to astonished gasps.

'Bloody hell,' said someone. 'He must be costing a fortune!'

'That's incredible,' said someone else. 'I knew his show was in trouble but not that much!'

Neil held up his hands. 'Hush, children. I've been talking to Mike for some time, sounding him out to see if he'd agree to join us for a new series.'

The production team hung on his every word. This was the first time the definite possibility of another series of *Table* had been mentioned.

'Up until now he hasn't known what was to happen with his own show, which has just finished its current run. We've all heard the rumours, seen the way the figures have slipped despite his personal popularity, and the decision has just been taken, no new series. I rang yesterday at exactly the right moment. You know how fond he is of his food and he feels a return to his journalistic career is the right way to go.' Neil grinned at his team. 'I don't think I'm exaggerating when I say he leapt at the opportunity to front the remaining shows in the series, especially as he will be able to pursue other opportunities as well. Needless to say, with him on the programme, our viewing figures should increase dramatically.'

There was silence for a brief moment then it seemed as though everyone was talking at once.

Again Neil held up his hands. 'Children, children! We are behind with our schedule! Mike sends his apologies for this morning, he couldn't clear his diary to join us but he's coming in this afternoon; he and I will go through this week's show—Jan, I'd like you to join us at about three thirty, we should be ready for you by then—and he'll join us at the studio on Thursday. Now, can we get on?'

'Neil, what happened with Mark?' It was one of the researchers who actually asked the question everyone wanted answering.

Before he could respond, Pam entered the office carrying a daily newspaper. 'Anthea's just rung. She says have you seen this?' Pam folded the paper to an inside page and put it before Neil.

He read rapidly, his face darkening. 'Right!' he said to his secretary. 'We go on the offensive. I told Mike I wanted to release the news today and he's given his go-ahead. Call a press conference for twelve thirty this morning, here.' As Pam hurried out, Neil looked up from the newspaper. 'You want to know why I fired Mark? I'll tell you. I found out he was taking bribes from food manufacturers and others who wanted to come on the programme.' He paused and there was dead silence.

'I can't believe it!' Jan sounded stunned.

Neil's euphoria vanished, he sat back in his chair and surveyed the meeting. 'Neither did I. But it's true. That organic chicken farmer who was to appear in last week's programme, the one who got caught with hormone-treated food, he rang on Friday and asked me for his money back.

'To start with I couldn't understand what he was talking about. After he explained, I began ringing around and making enquiries. There's no doubt about it.'

Astonished comments broke out from the assembled team but Neil lifted up the newspaper Pam had brought in and raised his voice to quell the hubbub. 'I think you'll be interested in this item from today's diary column.' He started to read. '"The trouble-beset food programme *Table for Four*, popularly known as *Table*, suffered another blow yesterday when Mark Taylor, sole remaining presenter from the original series, announced he was leaving the programme to join producer David Bartholomew. The pair are to make a rival series investigating all that's new and controversial in the food world. The new programme is expected to hit our screens in the autumn. David Bartholomew is another refugee from the luckless *Table*, currently providing a merry-go-round for presenters. Before setting up his own company, David was production manager for the series. Financial backing is rumoured to be coming from Shelley del Lucca, widow of Bruce Bennett, the wine presenter who recently died during a recording of *Table*. Miss del Lucca is an Australian food writer with a big reputation down-under. It is expected that she will provide a cookery input to the new programme.'"

Neil put down the newspaper to consternation.

Until that moment, Darina hadn't realized that David was not amongst the production team crammed into Neil's office.

What a coup for him!

'He can't have picked up a slot just like that,' said Jan. 'It takes months of negotiating, you don't just walk in and put down your name. He must be bluffing.'

'What about the *Table* slot?' suggested one of the researchers bluntly. 'Suppose the channel's decided to take us off and give him a chance?'

'Without even a pilot to show them? Come off it!' protested Alison.

'We don't know he hasn't got a pilot,' retorted the researcher. 'Who knows what they've been up to. If Mark can take backhanders like that, he's quite capable of sneaking off with David to make a sample programme. No wonder he's been so difficult lately.'

'But if Shelley is producing the backing,' contributed someone else, 'the company can only just have been set up. I mean she only arrived from Australia the other day!'

'Fast work on David's part,' came another voice. 'But didn't they get together in Italy last summer? On that cookery school story?'

Neil looked at his studio director. 'You were there, Jan, did they seem close to you?'

She thought for a moment, her face white and set. 'Honestly, Neil, I wouldn't have said so. In fact if you'd asked me that a few days ago I'd have said both David and Mark would have liked to have got a good deal closer to Shelley than she allowed.' She paused for a moment then added, 'The way David behaved with her at the studio lunch last week suggested differently though.'

'You arranged to show her the Italian film last night, didn't you?' asked Darina. 'Did she say anything about her plans then?'

Jan's face was controlled but a muscle twitching in her jaw betrayed just how deeply this development was troubling her.

'She rang yesterday afternoon asking if we could postpone it. Something had come up, she said.' She glanced towards the newspaper on Neil's desk. 'I think we all understand what that was.'

'Well, now we've got Mike Darcy,' the floor manager said buoyantly, 'I don't see them getting very far.'

'Right, Alison! This is an amateur attempt that is doomed to disappointment.' Neil attempted to recapture his earlier mood of enthusiasm but it was obvious the development had deeply shaken him as well.

'If only,' Jan said, 'you could have announced Mike Darcy was joining the programme before Mark and David went public. Now it looks as though we're just battling to keep things together, inviting a has-been to join a sinking ship.'

'Right on, Jan!' murmured somebody.

Neil slammed his hand hard down on the table. 'Look, people, we are not a sinking ship and Mike Darcy is no has-been. A few moments ago you were all delighted when you heard he was joining us. I will not have a defeatist attitude. David hasn't a hope of getting together any sort of a show, even with Mark and Shelley. He has no creative experience, no technical team.' He looked again at the studio director. 'I'd appreciate you letting me know if you get an approach from them, Jan.'

She nodded. 'Be quite an experience to be that much in demand,' she said lightly, looking thoughtfully at her notepad.

'Can we, please, now get on?' asked Neil.

As the meeting proceeded, one thought was uppermost in Darina's mind. David and Shelley; the combination provided a tangible link between Australia and the studio of *Table for Four*. Could Shelley have been involved in whatever it was that Kate Bennett had wanted to tell her about?

SEVENTEEN

DARINA WAS BACK in her Chelsea house that afternoon when she received a phone call from a secretary in the features department of the *Recorder*. A woman had rung from Australia, very anxious to get in touch with her. Of course, the secretary said, she'd told her it was newspaper policy never to give out contributor's telephone numbers, usually Darina rang callers back, but, said the secretary, the woman had been so insistent she had agreed to ring and ask if Darina would allow it on this occasion, after all, she wouldn't want to incur international charges, would she?

Australia could only mean one thing to Darina but it was hard to imagine why anybody connected with Bruce Bennett should be calling her from there. It was more likely to be some cook wanting to discuss a problem with one of her weekly recipes; the paper got sent all over the world and readers could be astonishingly persistent.

'She says her name's Eileen Miller,' the secretary continued. 'But that it won't mean anything to you. She wants to talk to you about the death of someone called Kate Bennett.' The secretary giggled. 'It all sounds desperately mysterious, do you think we should ring MI5?'

'Give this Eileen Miller my number, I'll be delighted to speak to her.'

'You will?' The secretary sounded astonished. 'OK then. She said she'd ring back later this afternoon, it'll be the early hours of the morning there so she must be keen.'

Darina put the telephone down with excitement bubbling through her. She had absolutely no idea who Eileen Miller could be but if it was anything to do with Kate Bennett that meant it had to be concerned with Bruce's death as well. Not that she had any intention of doing any investigating into this case that refused to turn itself into a case as far as the police were concerned but it would be very interesting to hear what this woman had to say. She started preparing for a session of recipe testing hardly able to concentrate on anything but the possible implications of the promised call.

When the telephone rang less than thirty minutes later, Darina picked it up full of expectation. It was William.

'Hey, I'm sorry if I'm interrupting anything,' he said after Darina had been less than welcoming. 'I thought you'd be interested to know what the autopsy report said.'

Darina stopped wondering how she could get him off the telephone as quickly as possible. 'You haven't managed to look at it, have you?'

'Didn't I promise I'd try?'

'Well? Don't tease, darling!'

'I'm not sure it's going to help much. As far as I can gather there's only one little bit that could be of interest. There's all the stuff we already knew about, that there weren't any specific findings, that the cause of death was unknown but that there was no evidence that it was due to anything unnatural.'

'And?'

'Well, don't hold your breath but amongst all the negativity there was one positive bit, the report mentions evidence of angio-neurotic oedema of the glottis.'

'What on earth does that mean?'

'I'm not too sure at the moment but I think it's something to do with a swollen throat.'

The disappointment was crushing.

'I'm chasing our local police surgeon to see if he can throw some light on it but I thought you'd like to be kept in the picture.'

Darina thanked William profusely and rang off. She sat looking at the telephone wondering if Bruce had been coming down with something nasty and whether that could have contributed to what ever had caused his death. But with no medical knowledge, it was a hopeless exercise.

The Australian call came through an hour later.

Eileen Miller's voice sounded pleasant but strained. 'I can't imagine what you're thinking and I hardly know how to start,' she said. 'Are you in the middle of something? If so, I'll call back because I think I'm about to make the Australian telephone company very happy.'

Darina reached a long arm and took a saucepan off the stove. She then hooked a foot round a chair leg, drew it towards her and got hold of her cookery notebook and pencil. 'I'm sitting comfortably with nothing to concentrate on but you,' she said.

'I think Kate got in touch with you?'

'She did but I'm afraid she died before we could get together.'

'I know. I've just received a letter from her. Most of it was written on the plane going over to England but it was finished in her hotel room after she arrived. She must have posted it just before she died.'

'Did she mention anything in it about suicide?'

'Not a word. It was very positive, very Kate.'

Darina took a deep breath. 'Did she tell you why she came to England, why she wanted to speak to me?'

'That's why I'm ringing. Look, the letter should have reached me several days ago, it had to be forwarded from my home in Sydney.'

'Where are you now, then?'

'At Yarramarra.'

'Yarramarra?'

'I think I'd better start at the other end otherwise you'll never understand what I've got to tell you.'

Darina contained her impatience with difficulty. Why couldn't the woman tell her what Kate Bennett had said? They could fill in the background afterwards. But she didn't dare interrupt, the other woman was paying for the call, after all.

'Kate Bennett was my stepdaughter.'

'Stepdaughter? Then you're...?'

'Bruce's mother. His father and I divorced when he was quite small. Kate wasn't a whole lot younger than I and we've been good friends ever since I first arrived at Yarramarra.'

Darina wondered what had caused the divorce.

'Anyway, I didn't see anything of Bruce after I left his father but Kate used to keep me in the picture, send me snapshots and stuff, you know?'

'Right, I understand.' What it amounted to was that Eileen Miller only knew her son by proxy. The Miller bit no doubt belonged to a second husband. No wonder Bruce had been so fond of his sister, it sounded as though she had been something of a substitute mother.

'But what are you doing at Yarramarra now?'

'Just before he went to England Bruce gave Kate a share in the vineyard and in his will he left her half of the rest of his holding. Kate's will left it all to me. At the time she made it, of course, she thought she only owned twenty-five per cent but because Bruce died before she did, it means I'm now the major shareholder. And, let me tell you, no one could be more surprised than I!'

Except perhaps Shelley del Lucca, who it now turned out wasn't the Queen of Yarramarra after all? Darina's thoughts were racing round the possible implications of that. 'Well, that's the background. Now for why I'm ringing you.' At last, thought Darina, taking a firmer grip on her pencil. 'Until I received Kate's letter, I had no idea that Bruce's death was anything but natural. Apparently she'd tried to ring me before she left Australia but I was in Brisbane visiting my daughter and she couldn't get hold of me. That's why she wrote.'

'And?' asked Darina, consumed by the violence of her curiosity.

'Kate said as soon as she heard how Bruce had died she was sure there was something wrong. Because of what she knew about him, you see.'

'And what did she know?'

'Bruce couldn't eat nuts.'

It didn't make much sense to Darina, she asked Eileen Miller to explain.

'Bruce was allergic to nuts; according to Kate if he ate any sort he had a terrible reaction. He always carried a syringe of antihistamine, if he didn't immediately inject himself, he wouldn't be able to breathe and would die of asphyxiation.'

Swollen throat, thought Darina. Could that be what had happened to Bruce? What they thought was a heart attack was him trying desperately to breathe as his throat closed right up?

'She wrote that she was hoping to talk to you,' Eileen Miller continued. 'She said she was sure you could find out just who wanted him dead. You see, if it had happened in Australia, she would have suspected Shelley, Bruce's wife. But she was here when he died, she hadn't had anything to do with anyone he was involved with in England.'

But Eileen Miller didn't know the full story. Darina couldn't rule Bruce's widow out of the running, especially now she knew how Bruce had been killed.

'Was there any particular reason for her suspecting Shelley Bennett might have wanted Bruce dead?'

There was silence from the other end of the phone for a little, then Eileen Miller said, 'I gathered from Kate a little while ago that the marriage wasn't turning out well. She didn't say much but, reading between the lines, I think she believed Shelley was only staying with Bruce because of the money. They were rowing all the time, she said.'

People could row without wanting to break up their relationship.

'Did Kate think Bruce was treating Shelley the way her father had treated you?'

There was silence on the other end of the line before Eileen Miller said warily, 'You seem to know something about the Bennett men.'

Then Rory Bennett had been a sadist as well.

'Yet you left Bruce behind?'

The other woman followed the jump in the reasoning without effort but her voice was strained. The phrases came easily, though, as if she had said them to herself many times. 'Rory adored Bruce, I didn't think he was at risk, not the way I was, and it seemed wrong he shouldn't grow up on Yarramarra. Kate promised to watch over him. I was desperate, I couldn't do anything else,' she added in a different tone, one that rang with truth.

So Bruce grew up watching his father bully his way through life, achieving what he wanted through ruthless exploitation. Had Rory Bennett covered his ruthlessness with the same sort of charm his son had deployed? Or had Bruce learned that from someone else, Kate perhaps? Or had it been another thing he'd brought back with him from Europe? No point now, though, in exploring his upbringing.

'If Kate ruled out Shelley, had she any ideas over who else could have wanted Bruce dead?' Darina might have her suspicions but she wanted the full picture.

Some of the strain vanished from Eileen Miller's voice. 'She said Bruce had invested quite a large sum of money in the company that was producing the food programme he was appearing with. Well, where money is involved there can always be trouble.'

Invested money in Cantlow Productions, had he? That could explain why he had been able to throw his weight around so much.

'I'm sorry,' the Australian woman was continuing. 'I know I should have come over and spoken to you in person but I couldn't face it.'

'It's very expensive to fly here and a long journey,' soothed Darina, wishing she could be speaking to this woman face to face.

'It's not that! I'm used to travel but Kate Bennett died over there. I'm certain she never fell out of that window by herself

and I don't want to run the risk of ending up the same way
if the murderer found out why I was coming over. I'm such
a coward. That's why I ran away from Rory, Bruce's father.'

'Look, this call must be costing you a fortune. I don't want
to keep you but I must ask you, how many other people be-
sides Kate knew what you've told me?'

'Difficult to say. Kate said there wasn't any secret about it
when he was growing up, it was only after he came back from
abroad that he kept it quiet, claimed it didn't do his image
any good. There are people at Yarramarra who've been here
over thirty years.'

'And Shelley?'

'Kate thought she would have been told. On the other
hand,' Eileen added thoughtfully, 'if Bruce really was like his
father, he may have tried to hide what he would have seen as
a weakness.'

Except he would have been running a huge risk and, judging from what Darina had seen of his behaviour, Bruce wasn't
taking that sort of chance.

Eileen Miller appeared to have reached the end of her information. Darina thought rapidly but there was nothing else
she could think of to ask for the moment. 'Are you staying
on at Yarramarra?'

'For a little. I thought as the major shareholder I should
find out how things are going here. I know something about
the wine trade, I've taken various courses and my second
husband has a small chain of retail shops in and around Sydney.'

'Give me the telephone number in case there's something
else I need to get back to you on.'

'You think you can crack this thing?'

'I'm not a detective, Mrs Miller, whatever Kate Bennett
may have thought. But this definitely needs pursuing by someone. I'll speak to you soon.'

DARINA put the phone down thinking hard. Such a simple
thing. How silly of Bruce to have kept it so quiet. He had

handed his murderer a lethal weapon that could be used without fear of discovery.

Because of his stupid pride, Bruce had been killed in a way
that was simple, stunningly clever and now undetectable.
Could Kate Bennett have started an investigation that would
have uncovered the truth?

Darina thought about her murder for a little, she was sure
it had been murder; then she wondered if the killer hadn't
panicked. Even if Kate had told everything, what could have
been proved?

What, indeed, could be proved now?

For Darina was almost certain she knew who had killed
Bruce Bennett and why. Several details had slotted into place
during her conversation with Eileen Miller and made a le-
thally plausible picture. The question was, what could she do
about it?

Darina rang William, waiting anxiously as he was tracked
down at the station. His experience and sound common sense
were needed here but she wasn't sure how he was going to
react. After she'd upset him the previous week, it had taken
time before she could persuade him all she'd meant was that
the cottage needed a lick of paint. What she had to say to him
now was not going to improve his temper. She'd have to try
and convince him she didn't want to take things any further
herself.

Eventually he came to the phone and she told him everything. Afterwards there was a long silence then he said, 'So
you think lover boy, this David Bartholomew, carried out the
murder then waited for the grieving widow to join him with
her millions?'

'There's no proof, I know that, but it all hangs together.
She could have told him about Bruce when they met in Italy.'

'But surely she didn't know he was joining the *Table* programme then?'

The advantage of discussing things with William was he

never forgot a detail, you didn't have to repeat things, he had everything clear in his mind even when you didn't think he'd been listening.

'It might just have been something said in passing that David remembered after Bruce joined them.'

'He must have established a pretty close relationship with the widow, then.'

'Perhaps they wrote to each other, or exchanged phone calls. It could have been after Bruce joined *Table* that Shelley saw how they could get rid of him and suggested the method to David. The way he was looking after her in the studio the other day suggested they knew each other well. And the proof of the pudding, surely, is that Shelley is providing the financial backing for his new company and he's using her for his programme series. There's another thing, Bruce was terribly rude to David, called him an ''Abo''. You should have seen David's face!' Darina remembered a chat she'd had with him one day during the lunch break, interested to know more about the intelligent, prickly but attractive production manager. 'He was at Eton and Oxford, his father's a prominent industrialist and his mother's a barrister. You'd have thought he'd be above being insulted in that way, it was such a stupid thing for Bruce to have said, but I think he's very touchy.'

'So murdering Bruce would have paid him back for insulting him as well as turning Shelley into a rich widow? And you think not only did he dispatch him but his sister as well?'

'He was in the Cantlow office every day, he could easily have seen that letter from Kate and understood what it meant. And he was in the hospitality room while I talked to her on the phone.' Guiltily Darina remembered her astounded repetition of the word 'murder'. What else had she said to Kate?

'Then popped round to the hotel and pushed her out of the window?'

'Darling, be serious!'

'My sweet, I'm deliberately trying *not* to be serious. The possibilities if you are right are not funny. Two people are dead. Once someone's killed once, he's got nothing to lose by killing again, and everything to gain if it prevents exposure.'

A chill went through Darina. William not taking her seriously was exasperating but William in earnest could be frightening.

'I'm not nearly as convinced as you all the facts add up to your total but I do think some things need checking out. Incidentally, I was talking to the police surgeon when you rang. He said that angio-neurotic oedema of the glottis would have been an indication of an allergic reaction. So that fits in with what Eileen Miller told you. I take it you'll be contacting Gatting?'

That was Darina's intention but she felt she had to say, 'Is Chief Inspector Gatting really going to believe this changes a great deal? We've no proof of anything. But I don't see how either David Bartholomew or Shelley del Lucca are going to know I'm even interested in the case let alone try to stop me interfering.'

'I wish you'd come back down here. I don't like the idea of you all alone in that big house.'

'I'll be all right! A moment ago you were suggesting the whole idea was complete nonsense.'

'Wishful thinking, darling. Now call Gatting. You do understand this isn't something you can handle?'

'Yes, darling, don't go on about it!' Darina wished William could trust her ability to do the right thing.

DARINA CALLED the chief inspector as soon as William had rung off. She received an immediate invitation to come round to the station.

There, Gatting listened while she related all Bruce's mother had told her.

'And you think this is proof Bruce Bennett was murdered and that his sister was thrown out of her hotel window?'

Darina flushed. She hadn't expected him to be very open

to the information but how could he be so deeply sceptical? Even William had appeared to understand the possible implications.

'I think it deserves looking into,' she said simply.

The policeman sighed. 'Look, Miss Lisle, if you can produce some real evidence, of course I'll be interested in reopening the Kate Bennett case and in investigating her brother's. But at the moment all we have is a death officially classed as natural and another that the coroner decided was suicide.'

'But surely Kate Bennett's death needs further investigation? You told me yourself she didn't leave a suicide note and the facts show she sent a perfectly sensible letter to her stepmother explaining why she thought her brother had been murdered just hours before she died.'

'We only have Mrs Miller's opinion as to the sense of the letter,' said the chief inspector, but the tone of his voice was thoughtful. He picked up his pen and started drawing a neat series of interlinked boxes on his notepad. 'Shelley Bennett seemed very upset at her sister-in-law's death, she broke down when she identified the body.'

Darina nearly asked if he usually accepted that as a sign of innocence.

'No harm in asking Australia to send someone out to talk to Mrs Miller and get a copy of the letter,' Gatting said at last.

'And you'll question David Bartholomew about where he was on the night Kate Bennett died?'

'One thing at a time, Miss Lisle.' Gatting rose. 'Thank you for coming in.' Unexpectedly, he smiled at her, his severe face with its watchful eyes revealing a softer side. 'I appreciate your interest, I wish we had more co-operation from the public. But it's easy to let instinct run ahead of evidence.'

It might have been William speaking.

Darina left the police station feeling both triumphant and frustrated. Enquiries might very well be made in Australia but she had no confidence they would lead anywhere further. A motion-going-through exercise, that's what it would be.

She really didn't intend getting involved in this case but, as she returned to her cooking, she couldn't help wondering just how it could be proved that David Bartholomew and Shelley del Lucca had conspired to murder Bruce Bennett.

EIGHTEEN

DAVID BARTHOLOMEW let himself out of his flat and shivered in the early morning dark. His track suit gave as much warmth as tissue paper.

He fought, as always, with the desire to return to his warm bed and have another hour of sleep, he had been up late the previous evening, going over yet again all the plans for the new company. Discipline won. Now more than ever it was necessary to maintain his physical fitness.

His compact body moved smoothly into action and he started to jog his way to Wimbledon Common. There was almost no one around at this hour. A few souls, of course, when was London devoid of people?

Despite the cold and the protest from his body, David was soon relaxed and happy. He enjoyed feeling his muscles, already warmed up from a short exercise session in his bedroom, respond to challenge. His stride lengthened. He was on his way. In every sense.

He thanked Heaven he had been in the office when Neil fired Mark, it was perfect timing. Now Mark was free of his contractual obligations to Cantlow Productions and had become involved with Bartholomew Programmes before he had had time to wonder if there wasn't something else that would suit him better.

The way they'd launched the company meant any story Neil put about now on Mark accepting backhanders wouldn't receive the attention given a gnat. And David had made Mark swear he wouldn't pull a trick on him like that. What an idiot! The money involved surely couldn't have been worth the risk. For a disquieting moment David wondered just how badly Mark needed cash.

As he encountered the hill up to the Common, David felt his legs and breath start to labour. He told himself he would soon be through the first barrier, that point when the urge to give up, to stop punishing himself, miraculously melted away and he would feel renewed vigour flowing through his limbs. He forced his legs to move faster.

Pushing aside the physical discomfort, for a brief moment David wondered about any obligations he might have to Neil Cantlow. He dismissed them. Neil had had his pound of flesh, and blood, and sweat, toil and tears as well. David had given him everything he had and what had he had in return? Sweet FA, that was what.

David negotiated the road he had to cross to reach the Common, the traffic never stopped completely, and then, at last, enjoyed the sensation of running on grass-covered earth. The ground was frost-hard but it didn't feel as hard as the concrete pavements. He struck out on his usual path. Away from the street lighting the Common was mysterious, the bare trees and bushes just discernible through the gloom. David always took the same route, it enabled him to concentrate on working out things in his head if he didn't have to wonder which way he should go.

Of course he'd been paid well by Cantlow Productions, but who wasn't in television? And in return David had worked his butt off. The nights he'd sat up worrying over those figures. Well, now it would be his own figures he'd worry over.

Figures! He stumbled slightly over a small branch, victim of a recent storm, recovered himself and ran on. Money could be a problem. He had Shelley's backing, of course, but that wasn't proving as generous as he'd expected. He was going to have to explain again about the necessity for adequate funds. She had all the wealth of Yarramarra behind her, and David had researched as well as he could exactly what that was. This was not the time to be mean.

Of course, he suddenly realized, probate was bound to take time and, until that had been passed, there would obviously be limits as to how far she could commit herself. Why hadn't she explained that? Come to that, why hadn't he thought of it himself before this? David smiled and thought it was all working out perfectly. Who would have thought, last autumn when they met in Italy, that things would develop like this? They made a perfect team, he and Shelley.

Behind him he could hear another figure running. For a moment his body tensed. His mother worried about his early morning exercise. You heard of dreadful things happening these days, she said, why take such risks in such a lonely area? Why not go out later, when people were about? For an intelligent woman who could run rings round most other barristers in court, David thought she could be uncommonly stupid. The last really nasty local incident had happened midmorning in broad daylight. If your time was up, fate came along, there was not a lot you could do about it. Anyway, nothing had ever occurred to worry him during his early morning runs. Now, however, in the chilly darkness, the sound of those footsteps and the heavy breathing behind him struck fear. Later in the year it was quite usual to meet other joggers but not now, not when it was so cold and dark.

David quickened his pace. The figure behind increased his also. Fighting down panic, David tried to glance over his shoulder.

For a moment all he could see was a white headband, a pale track suit and running shoes. Then he realized who it was.

Relief flooded through him and he slowed his steps. 'Hi! What on earth are you doing here?' he said, turning to welcome the other runner.

Only at the last moment did he see the heavily weighted sock being lifted. Only then did the fear flow back. Fear and astonishment. Why? What had he done?

Then the expertly wielded weapon caught him behind the ear and all went black, blacker than night, blacker than his skin, blacker than anything he'd ever known.

NINETEEN

LIKE SO MUCH ELSE connected with *Table* the book that should have accompanied the television series was in a mess and way behind its publication schedule. The chef Darina had replaced had failed to produce his recipes, then most of the wine notes had to be scrapped when Bruce took over from Milly. The book could not possibly now come out until after the series was over but Neil was convinced it would still have a worthwhile market. Darina had had to work desperately hard to complete her contribution and it was an enormous relief to be able to deliver her copy to the publishers. There were enough complications in her life, getting rid of the book meant one less.

Darina handed over her manuscript to the editor, a young woman in her late twenties with a briskly professional manner that inspired confidence.

'I'm so pleased to have been able to go into certain points more deeply,' Darina said. 'There's never enough air time to explain technical details properly, Neil's always gingering me up to get the recipe over in the shortest possible time. That's fine if your audience understands cookery technique but there are thousands of people out there who seem totally ignorant. Pam in the office is always receiving enquiries from viewers who want to know more.'

'Oh, quite! But our trouble is space. As well as your recipes there are the background food pieces and the wine essays.' The editor started reading through one or two pages. 'But I don't see too many problems with this, you've managed to be concise as well as informative.' She put the manuscript to one side and rose. 'I shall look forward to going through it before sending it out for editing and I shall certainly be trying some of the recipes.'

Then she was leading Darina down the publishing company's graceful staircase.

Coming up the stairs was Anthea Cantlow.

'Good heavens,' said Darina. 'I'd completely forgotten you worked here!' How stupid, she chastised herself, of course Anthea's company would be publishing Neil's book.

Neil's wife greeted her cordially and asked how the work was going. 'I'm on the fiction side myself, I have nothing to do with the *Table* project.'

'Anthea's a director, she commissions most of our modern fiction,' said the other editor proudly.

'It must be so interesting and not like work at all, being able to read all day without feeling guilty!' Darina never found enough time for all the books that interested her.

Anthea smiled. 'That's exactly how I feel!' She looked at her watch. 'Are you free for lunch? There's a nice little place not far from here.'

'I was just going to suggest the same thing,' Darina exclaimed.

Anthea took her to a French restaurant, not large but with a pleasant atmosphere and an interesting menu.

They consumed fish soup followed by red mullet accompanied by the most delicate of orange butter sauces and talked about books, the problems involved in writing them, the difficulties in marketing them, the delights of reading them.

As the bottle of Sauvignon they had ordered went down, Anthea opened up. Darina had met her before but always with the Cantlow production team milling around, when Anthea seemed to be friendly but withdrawn, as though she inhabited a different world from that of television and, indeed, found it difficult to focus on anything outside the narrow parameters of fiction. Now she was pulsing with energy, talking freely and amusingly, her slight air of reserve banished.

'Is Neil settling down again after the upset with Mark?' asked Darina as they finished their fish.

'Wasn't that extraordinary? I couldn't believe it when Neil told me. Mark, taking bribes!' Anthea exclaimed, her eyes bright. 'I can't think why he should need more money. Except, everything in that flat of his is beautiful, I believe he had most of the furniture specially designed, perhaps he overstretched himself. All the same!' She gave her head a little, bewildered shake.

'The production team was shattered. And, yet, I suppose it's a narrow line between accepting a present, like the produce so many manufacturers hand out, and a bribe.' For a brief moment Darina remembered Richard Godney's happy invitation to his yacht in Cannes. If she and William accepted, would there be air tickets made available as well, she wondered? And if she took them, where would that place her?

Anthea looked politely sceptical anyone could muddy morality like that and Darina went on, 'Neil has the most amazing ability to produce new presenters. Fancy being able to enlist Mike Darcy like that! Were you surprised?'

'Not the way I was when Bruce suddenly appeared on the scene,' said Anthea.

'You didn't expect him to come over after you met at Yarramarra?

'I? Why should I expect anything?'

Darina, who hadn't meant to suggest anything that personal, took another look at Anthea. 'I only meant something might have been said to Neil during your visit.'

'Oh, I see. No, nothing was said.'

'What was Yarramarra like?' asked Darina curiously.

'It's beautiful,' Anthea said dreamily. 'Acres and acres of vines surrounded by hills. There's an air of magic to Australia, it's so different from anywhere else. The one thing I regretted about our trip was that we didn't have time to go into the interior. When you fly across the continent, you can see most of the civilization is concentrated round the edges and there's this huge, empty space in the middle, just like an ethnographic doughnut. There's thousands and thousands of miles of what looks like reddish earth with almost nothing there apart from the odd track. I must go back, I'd love to explore the bush.' Her eyes had a far-away look.

'Backpacking, you mean? That sounds very uncomfortable.'

'Neil and I used to do a lot of fell walking when we were first married,' said Anthea unexpectedly.

'William and I had a short holiday in the Lake District a little time ago and I loved scrambling over those hills. But the weather could change so quickly, half the time we ended getting drenched!'

'That's all part of the fun!'

Darina encouraged her to talk more about the joys of long-range hiking and gradually realized that Anthea's air of fragility was no more than that. Beneath the soft clothes and delicate features was a steely determination.

'You must have to be very fit,' she said thoughtfully.

'I've always kept myself in trim, these days you never know when you're going to need your strength.'

It echoed what Jan had been saying about self-defence. And William had been on about much the same thing. 'You must know how to defend yourself,' he'd insisted only the other day. 'I've seen the results of too many nasty incidents lately. I know you're tall and strong but if you don't know how to use that strength, you could be helpless. Attack is not always a matter of brute strength ruthlessly applied, small chaps can be just as deadly if they know what to do. And even when women are at a physical disadvantage, if they've learned to defend themselves, they're in with a chance.'

Anthea was continuing, 'I've been wanting our non-fiction side to commission a book on the martial arts. It could be beautiful as well as practical. Bruce said…' She paused for the briefest of moments then continued, 'I find it difficult to realize he's not still with us. Didn't you find him a vital person?' It was as though she had to talk about him, had to bring in his name whenever possible.

'Incredibly so!' Darina responded. 'He had a way of producing just the right remark that relaxed you and put a sparkle into whatever was going on.' She looked at Anthea thoughtfully. 'I've heard lately, though, that he had his darker side.'

Anthea flushed. 'I suppose that came from Shelley?' Darina said nothing. 'You know their marriage was a sham?'

'Really?' Darina had no trouble in sounding interested.

'My own opinion is that she married him for the money. Bruce said…' There was another brief pause as Anthea shot Darina a little look. 'Bruce told me once that he just got carried away when they met. It was a moment of madness that he later regretted.'

Darina wondered if this bore out what Kate Bennett had believed. Or was it a case of Bruce off-loading responsibility for his own brutal behavior? She looked reflectively at Anthea, no suggestion from this woman she had been abused by the Australian. Was she a masochist or hadn't things gone that far between them?

'You seem to have known Bruce quite well.'

'I suppose you could say that.' Anthea twirled her nearly empty wine glass slowly. Darina poured in the last of the bottle, she had consumed less than half the wine herself but her companion's glass had been constantly empty. 'I think most women found Bruce physically attractive but with me it was his mind that was fascinating.' Anthea's brown eyes were cool and looked at Darina with a certain amount of challenge. She drank more wine then, in a different tone, asked, 'I suppose you and your fiancé talk? Really talk, I mean? Neil and I used to. We'd discuss art, politics, books, television. He tried out ideas on me, I did the same on him. We were involved in each other's lives.' She fell silent.

'And now?'

'Now?' Anthea gave a short laugh. 'Now we live in the

same house, argue about the children and meet for meals, sometimes.'

'Neil seems to be very involved in his company and the programme?' Darina suggested.

'His programme!' Anthea suddenly exploded, an unexpectedly coarse streak breaking through the quiet, well-bred manner. 'Bloody fucking television! It takes over! All he ever thinks about is that programme. Even when we do manage to get away for a weekend or a holiday, his mind is back in the office, wondering how he's going to deal with this problem or that, working out how the next programme is going to go, thinking up ideas for the future. And the company is constantly threatened by bankruptcy. I tell you, if the whole thing folded, I, for one, would be delighted. You on for coffee?' she asked abruptly.

Coffee was ordered while Darina stored away another bit of information about Neil's financial position and mused on the unexpected side to her personality Anthea had revealed. Had it been that latent coarseness that had attracted Bruce?

'So Bruce must have been a welcome change?'

'Like going out into the sun from a cold room.' Anthea's smile was warm with memories.

Darina allowed her to bask in that sunlight for a few minutes before she asked, 'If Bruce hadn't died, do you think your relationship could have led somewhere?'

Anthea leaned back to allow a coffee-cup to be placed in front of her and it was as though she retreated emotionally as well as physically. 'No,' she said distantly.

'Your decision or his?'

Anthea picked up her coffee spoon, reluctance with the turn the conversation had taken plain on her face, but eventually she said, 'It's difficult to keep any relationship completely cerebral.' Did that mean they had gone to bed or not?

'Is that what you wanted, really?'

'I thought I did.'

'Until?'

But Darina had pressed her too far.

'I really don't think we know each other well enough for this conversation.' The cool, remote woman was back, the defences had been raised.

'I'm sorry, I've been intrusive and I apologize, I get too interested in other people, that's my trouble.'

Anthea inclined her head in a gracious acceptance of the apology and they finished the lunch talking about nothing in particular.

BACK AT HER HOUSE, Darina got out her recipes for that week's programme and started concentrating on exactly how she was going to handle the demonstration. She had already supplied Jan with a step-by-step run-through of each stage, what she had to do now was work out the best way to describe what she was doing. 'It's a combination of sound and pictures,' Neil had explained at the start of her involvement with *Table*. 'We must never forget the sound. What you say must add something to what is being shown on the screen, open up the viewer's mind, not tell him something he can see for himself.' He had made it sound simple!

No sooner had she started work than the telephone rang.

It was Mark. 'You haven't heard from David today, have you?'

'David Bartholomew? Not since he dashed out after you at Monday's meeting. Haven't you both left the programme?'

Mark ignored her asperity. 'He never showed for a meeting Shelley and I were supposed to be having with him at my place this morning. He hasn't rung and I can't understand it. There's no reply from his flat, not even the answering-machine is on. So I've been contacting everyone I can think of, you were a last hope.' He rang off.

Darina went back to her task.

Two hours later she had the demonstration worked out; she decided she would take a short break then run through the whole thing again to make sure she had everything firmly fixed in her mind.

She made some coffee and switched on the little television set she kept in the kitchen.

It was news time. On the screen was a picture of what looked like a common. Police tape closed off an area of grass and trees and part of it was shielded from gaze by screens. A frozen-looking reporter was saying, 'The body was found this morning by Mr Ron Pickles, who was exercising his dog. The police have stated the victim is a man in his late twenties who was probably attacked while out jogging. They have appealed for anyone who was on Wimbledon Common early this morning to ring this number.' While the reporter signed off, a stunned Darina scrabbled for paper and pencil and scribbled down the police telephone number. It must be someone else, she kept thinking, David can't be dead! But he did live near Wimbledon Common and he was well known for his early morning jogging routine.

She switched off the TV and looked for Mark's number.

TWENTY

THE STUDIO next day was agog with the news. David Bartholomew had not been popular with everyone, budget controllers seldom are, but no one could fail to be shocked at what had happened.

Mark had rung Darina back late the previous evening, sounding unnerved. The police had contacted David's father and he had identified the body as his son's. The morning newspapers carried the story, referring to David as the 'up-and-coming television producer'. Mark was quoted as being 'devastated' and Shelley was referred to as 'too upset to comment'. The police, according to the papers, were 'also investigating a mugging that had taken place on Wimbledon Common the previous day but were cautious about making a connection'.

When the *Table* team broke for lunch, conversation concentrated on little else. 'He was mad to go out jogging all alone like that,' said Lynn. Of them all, she appeared the most shaken by the news. 'He knew about what happened to me when I was nearly raped.'

For a little while the talk was of the perils of modern life but it wasn't long before it returned to David and the way he had departed the programme as well as life.

'I wonder what Mark is going to do now,' said Jan, attacking a piece of Cheddar.

'You are right, 'is new career is finished before it 'as started!' Jean-Pierre didn't sound too upset. He and Mike Darcy had established an instant rapport and the opening chat round the eponymous table that had been recorded just before lunch had gone with a new verve and sparkle.

'Strange that we should have another death connected with

the show,' said Darina. Her mind had been turned upside-down with the news and now she was wondering whether she had to revise all her ideas about Bruce and Kate Bennett's murders.

'You mean you think it wasn't a mugging?' exclaimed someone excitedly.

'I just mean it's strange to have two deaths in a small company like ours one after the other. Especially since Bruce Bennett's sister died as well.'

'Oho, it's the detective at work,' Mike Darcy announced. 'I said your fiancé had to watch out.'

Darina caught Jean-Pierre looking at her quizzically, as though the idea was new to him. Of course, he wouldn't have seen the show Bruce and she did with Mike.

'But Bruce wasn't murdered!' exclaimed Alison. 'He had a heart attack.' By now most of the production team had been attracted to the discussion.

'Quite,' said Darina repressively. 'Mike's just talking nonsense.' They didn't want to leave it there but she refused to be drawn further.

After lunch Neil decided to leave the wrap-up session back at the table until after Mike had recorded his interview with that week's guest, a professor expounding on a new nutritional theory. 'It goes more successfully when we can pick up on something that's been aired in the interview,' he explained.

As Darina waited for the last stage of the recording, she watched Neil taking charge of the show with a new confidence. There was no doubt that Mike was easier to work with than Mark had been. There were no little snide remarks, no air of uncertainty, no suggestion he might suddenly turn everything upside down with an unexpected development in the interview.

She found her mind going back to David Bartholomew. Had he been killed by a psycho roaming Wimbledon Common? Had a quirk of fate meant some jungle justice had taken over from the due processes of the law?

After Mark had confirmed it had been David's body, Darina had tried to get hold of William but he'd been out on a case; a seventy-year-old woman had been mugged and raped in her council flat. Darina had replaced the telephone thinking the whole world had gone mad. Mugging joggers was bad enough but who could want to rape a septuagenarian woman?

The rain had been lashing against the glass of her front door with an intensity that suddenly sounded threatening. All at once her Chelsea house had seemed very large and the street outside very dark.

Darina had wanted to get into her car and drive down to Somerset and be with William. But not only had there been the programme to record the following day, Thursday, William was to join her in London on the Friday evening, they had planned a weekend of visiting exhibitions, eating out and generally enjoying the capital. Somehow she had to pull herself together and cope with being on her own. She had never been nervous before.

By the time it came to record, Darina had more or less recovered but as she now watched Mike run the professor through the main points to be covered in their interview, her mind was being nagged by doubts about her theories surrounding the Bennett deaths. Had she been too quick to jump at the implications offered by the way David and Shelley had teamed up? Perhaps she should give more consideration to other possibilities. She had a nasty instinct that David's death couldn't be coincidence, the jungle wasn't that close.

Darina wished she knew what the police had discovered and then realized recording had started and Mike was already half-way through his interview. She made a determined effort to concentrate on what was going on, she might need to pick up on something for the round-table session at the end.

'But a number of nutritional theories have arrived only to be shot down in the last ten or so years. Is someone going to come along shortly with evidence that shows you've got it all wrong?' Mike's lazy charm removed any sting from his words.

The professor hunched forward earnestly. 'We're all still learning. Science is a constant process of reinterpreting facts in the light of new knowledge. We can only act on what we know now. For many years most of us paid less attention to what we put in our bodies than most car owners do to the petrol they put in their cars. What could be more foolish? Our health is directly affected by our diet and we need to pay it the most careful attention. We all need to be far better informed. For too long we have been too trusting. Food is not universally good for us. Even fresh and unrefined it can, literally, bring us death rather than life.'

'You make that sound very dramatic!'

'Diet is dramatic, it's what we live on! Look, for years we've paid more attention to feeding our animals than ourselves. How long did it take us to understand we could benefit from bran as well as our horses?'

Alison was making winding-up circles with her hand at Mike.

'Professor, thank you for a most illuminating discussion. Can I suggest we go back to the table and see what Darina has been cooking up? Somehow I doubt it's feednuts!'

After the cameras stopped, Neil seemed to be having something of a conference with Jan in the gallery. Then he turned to the guest. 'Professor, I'm a bit worried about that reference to the dangers of food, I think we've either got to expand upon it or cut it out. What exactly were you getting at?'

The scientist was only too happy to explain. 'Well, there are a number of things I had in mind. For instance, there are people with very low tolerance levels to such things as wheat, or dairy products. It can make their lives exceedingly uncomfortable, sometimes ruin them.'

'Not exactly dramatic!' said Neil.

'Their recovery when the culprits are removed from their

diet can be. Then there are foods that, if not properly understood, can turn into killers. Red kidney beans are toxic until boiled, the Japanese blow fish in the hands of a careless chef can be lethal. Or...' But the executive producer was holding up his hand and listening to his headphones. He nodded his head to something Jan said in the gallery.

'Sorry, Professor, but we think this is too large a subject to touch on here. Can we go back to your plea for us being more informed about our bodies and nutrition? Perhaps if you bring in that nice bit about our paying more attention to animal diets than our own, I think we'll have got it. Mike, just ask your question again, can we have the exact wording?'

The tape was run through, Mike happily repeated his question and recording was once again under way.

Darina realized that she had been holding her breath while the professor was speaking. Had anybody else in the studio realized what it was he could have been leading up to?

She looked around. Alison's attention was given to the action being recorded, the cameramen were intent on their shots. Neil, frowning with concentration, was watching Mike and the professor. Everyone else had their attention riveted to the monitor screens, studying the effect of what was being recorded. Except Lynn. She was standing behind her preparation table looking at nothing in particular, her tasks all completed, seemingly uninterested in what was going on, her face pale and strained.

After the recording had finished, a technician came up to remove Darina's microphone and battery, always a complicated business that required burrowing beneath layers of clothing. After it had been successfully concluded, she looked around for the professor.

'He's gone,' Mike said. 'He had a plane to catch, I think he's off to the States. Was it important?'

'Not really, I just wanted to follow up on something he said, that was all.'

'Yeah, he was interesting, wasn't he? Pity we didn't have

the time to develop that bit about not all food being good for us.'

'Well done, Mike,' said Neil coming up and putting a hand on his arm. 'I think that was a very successful show.'

'Your car's here, Darina,' said Pam, bringing up a burly young man.

'Not dashing away to Somerset tonight?' asked Jan, arriving down from her gallery.

Darina explained about the weekend.

'If you're not doing anything tomorrow evening, would you like to come round? I'm not that much of a cook but it would be fun to return your hospitality.'

'Thanks, Jan, but we're due to be dining with some of William's relatives.' Relatives who would understand if a hard-pressed detective was late arriving in London.

'Love's young dream back on course, then? Sorry I can't offer tonight but I'm otherwise engaged. Take a rain check?'

'I'd love to.' Darina smiled at the director and went to get her things.

THE LUXURY of being driven back to Chelsea allowed Darina's mind full licence to speculate on financial troubles in the TV world, joggers who made no secret of their early morning activities and fatal foods.

By the time the driver drew up outside her house, Darina was feeling distinctly uneasy. There was one definite result from David's death. *Table* had lost a possible rival. A rival that had looked, on the face of it, to have dangerously promising potential. William's words about killers having nothing to lose by committing second and later murders rang in Darina's head. Then she realized her driver was holding open the door for her. She thanked him and went inside.

She was too tired for serious work and not hungry enough to cook anything, so spent the evening in her cosy study catching up on some correspondence. Around ten o'clock she undressed and put on a warm, comfortable dressing-gown and slippers. She was now starving and she went downstairs.

She switched on the light in the kitchen and realized she hadn't drawn down the blind over the window earlier. The dark rectangle looked naked and vulnerable. She went and leaned across the sink, reaching for the wooden acorn on the end of the blind cord. Then she froze. The window looked out on to a small paved garden and there, by the little statue, just outside the area of light that spilled from the window, Darina could swear she saw a figure. A dark figure that almost melted into the back wall sparsely furnished with bare rose-bushes. The indistinct outline gave no clue to sex or size.

Darina hoped she drew down the blind as if she had noticed nothing. She found her hand was trembling. She moved quickly upstairs. Without switching on lights, she crossed the floor of a bedroom that overlooked the garden and stood at the side of the window, trying to peer down into the darkness without being seen. Was that a figure or not?

She made a quick decision, went to her study at the front of the house and rang the police.

Ten minutes later a male and a female constable knocked on her door. The WPC waited with Darina and made them both a cup of coffee while her partner went through the kitchen and out into the garden. Two minutes later he was back.

'Nobody there,' he announced. 'I couldn't see any trace of an intruder but in the dark it's impossible to be certain. We'll put in a report and ask for someone to call again in the morning. Meanwhile, we'll check the premises at intervals during the night. Now, let's go round and make sure everything's secure.'

Darina was grateful he hadn't made her feel an idiot. After she relocked the front door behind the police, she wondered what she should do next. Ring William? But he was involved with the mugged and raped victim. She hadn't even mentioned David Bartholomew's death to him during the brief conversation they'd had earlier that evening and it seemed he hadn't picked it up from the newspapers. Probably too busy to read them.

She decided not to ring again, there was nothing he could do, it would only worry him and, anyway, she could have been mistaken.

But Darina was certain she hadn't. There had been somebody in the garden, she was sure of it. Firmly repressed was the mental picture of David Bartholomew thudding along Wimbledon Common in the murky morning light, unaware of fate following on his footsteps.

TWENTY-ONE

FRIDAY MORNING provided Darina with a succession of visitors.

First to arrive was another pair of constables.

'I'm afraid you were correct about the intruder,' the older of the two said after they had inspected the garden. 'There are marks on the back flower-bed where someone has got over the wall and jumped down. They've done a good job of making sure no identifiable footprints have been left but, after the rain we've had recently, there's no doubting someone's been there.'

Darina thought of the little terrace's high brick wall that backed on to a small passage lined with garages and workshops. How had anybody managed to scale that? 'They must have brought along a ladder,' she commented.

'Ah, well, as to that, there's a scar on the top of the wall, looks as though someone used a grappling hook of some sort.' He looked closely at Darina. 'Your visitor seems to have been well prepared.'

She thought of the dark shape she had seen in the garden, sinister in its anonymity, then resolutely wiped the image from her mind. She couldn't believe anyone would consider her a sufficient threat to need removal. But this weekend she would bring William up to date and get him to help her sort out the tangle of information she had somehow managed to collect. Chief Inspector Gatting wasn't going to welcome yet another theory from her without some hard evidence or at least an impressive amount of circumstantial data. Darina had to convince him, though, that David Bartholomew's death had been no mugging. She had been wrong to cast him as murderer but amongst the *Table* personnel, continuing to act as normal, was a killer who had no hesitation in killing again.

'We'll get a couple of SOCO boys round to see if there's anything they can pick up, it could be a chap we're chasing for several burglaries in the area, but evidence doesn't look hopeful.' The constable looked at her searchingly. Was he wondering if she was the nervous type? 'The question is, will your intruder be back? Do you have anything worth stealing, may I ask?'

Darina took him through the house, pointing out the odd nice painting, the collections of *objets d'art*, the antique furniture, with a growing conviction that her intruder had had burglary on his mind.

'Enough to be tempting but, if you'll forgive me saying so, miss, not nearly as much as most of your neighbours have.'

Darina had been invited in to a couple of houses in her street. She remembered exclaiming over a Monet painting on the wall of one and noticing a cabinet of antique silver in another. Either the picture or the silver could have bought her house, contents and all. No self-respecting professional burglar would be bothering to break into hers.

'There's nothing you haven't shown me? No safe, no valuable jewellery?'

Darina shook her head.

'Then it was probably an amateur looking for an easy job. Unlikely he'll return but shall we go round and check your security?'

Once again Darina took the police round her house, displaying the metal grilles that covered the windows and the steel bolts that secured front and back doors.

'And these are all in place at night-time and when you're out?'

Darina assured him they were.

'Then you're not an easy job and last night's effort will probably have demonstrated that. Provided you activate all your security, you should be all right.' He sounded eminently reassuring.

No sooner had the two policemen departed than a team of cleaners arrived. Having hired Mrs Hope for the cottage, Darina had rung an agency in London and arranged for a spring clean in Chelsea, to be followed by a weekly contract. What was the point of earning money if you were too tired to enjoy it? She didn't know yet how the arrangement in Somerset was working out but the determined assault on her London house filled her with joy.

Closing her ears as best she could to the noise of the vacuum cleaner, Darina retired to her study and began to work on her weekly cookery column for the *Recorder*. It had to be in by the next day and so far all she had was an idea and some recipes.

After a couple of hours' concentrated effort Darina had finished all but the final polishing of her column and found her mind returning to David Bartholomew's death.

Just how seriously could his proposed company have threatened *Table?* The programming complexities of the television world were beyond her but Darina realized the pertinent question was whether the Bartholomew company could be perceived as a threat rather than whether it actually was.

The telephone rang.

It was William, full of apologies. The case of the elderly woman looked like breaking. 'She's given us excellent descriptions of her two attackers, one of them matches a young man we've had an eye on for some time. We should be able to pick both of them up today but it looks as though I shan't be able to get away for the weekend. I was really looking forward to it, I'm so sorry.'

'Don't worry, darling, I'll come back to Somerset. I've just got my article to finish then I'll pack up here and be with you by this evening.'

'It's such a long way down, why don't you stay in town? Not that I don't want to see you but that's just it, I probably won't anyway. You know how these things go, I'll be tied here the whole weekend.'

Yes, Darina did know how these things went. William would be totally involved with interviewing the suspects and putting together the case against them. Even if he managed to get home for a few hours, his mind would still be back at the station. When he was on a case like this, he had no time and no energy to spare for anything else, even her. Particularly he wouldn't have the time or energy to discuss all the possible angles involved in Bruce Bennett's death. Indeed, he seemed to have forgotten about it already.

His one acknowledgement of any interest in her life was the dutiful question, 'Did the recording go well yesterday?'

'I think so.' For a brief moment, highlighted in Darina's mind was the little scene at the end of recording, when she announced to the entire production team that she wasn't going back to Somerset that evening but would be at her Chelsea house. Some of them knew the address, those that didn't could find it quite easily from the phone book.

'Oh, and your mother rang first thing this morning. She hadn't realized you wouldn't be back this weekend, she wants a session with you as soon as possible on wedding arrangements.'

Darina dragged her mind back to her personal life, her heart sinking. She knew what a meeting with her mother would entail, hours of listening to tedious arrangements. They had sorted out the wedding dress and outfits for her attendants but there were a thousand and one other details to be decided.

'How about eloping with me next weekend?'

His warm chuckle came down the telephone wires. 'Remember, she'll be my mother-in-law, how could I do that to her?'

'Not to mention depriving *your* mother of her day either!'

'Who is also anxious to have a heart-to-heart when you have a minute.'

'You know, I think you're right about staying in London.

If you really aren't going to be around, I'll take your advice, I'll get much more done up here.' On Darina's desk were her notes for the outline of a book a publisher wanted her to write. The outline was supposed to be delivered the following week. A free weekend in London was a Heaven-sent opportunity to work uninterrupted on it. More importantly, she had come to realize there were realities that had to be faced about marriage and William and now was the time for some dispassionate thought, it wasn't something she could put off any longer.

'That's fine, then. If things break the way they seem to be doing at the moment, I should be free next weekend. Then we'll really hit the town.'

'I'll use that thought to keep me going.'

It wasn't until she had replaced the phone that Darina began to feel uneasy, a feeling that had nothing to do with her disappointment over not seeing William that weekend. Nor was it that she wouldn't be able to discuss David Bartholomew's death. Obviously William hadn't watched the news and she hadn't had the heart to worry him over what was happening around her when he was deep in the middle of a case. And somehow her problems didn't seem very important put beside innocent seventy-year-olds being brutally attacked.

No, what was unsettling was the realization she would be on her own in this house for the entire weekend.

The doorbell rang. The Scenes of Crime Officers had arrived and soon her little terrace was full of men and equipment.

Darina made everyone cups of coffee and went back to her article.

She had finished the polishing process and had just started printing it out when the doorbell rang again.

This time it was Shelley.

Darina blinked at the sight of the Australian girl standing on the doorstep, her tanned skin a glowing reminder of all the sun they were missing on this cold January morning.

'I should have rung,' said Shelley. 'But I was afraid you

mightn't agree to see me, so I took the chance of finding you in.' Her low, slow voice charged her words with consequence.

Darina took her inside, out of the harsh chill. She hung her coat in the cupboard under the stairs then opened the door into the big downstairs room. The two young men from the agency were in possession, brushes, dusters and vacuum cleaners all over the room. 'Sorry,' said Darina, 'we'll have to go upstairs to the study, it's the only place we'll be safe.'

She led a bewildered-looking Shelley up the stairs. 'You're lucky I'm here, I usually go down to Somerset immediately after recording.' She cleared a bunch of papers from the little sofa so Shelley could sit down and realized the girl was more than bewildered. A nerve was twitching at the corner of one eye and her face was strained. She sat cautiously where Darina indicated, looking far from happy, and started to pick nervously at a loose thread on her thick, hand-knitted sweater.

'I rang your Somerset home yesterday.' Shelley's low voice shook slightly. 'Someone there told me you were staying in London for the weekend so I thought I'd come over this morning.'

'Someone' must have been Mrs Hope. Darina was relieved that at least something was in place in her world.

The printer had finished rattling off her article, all it needed now was faxing off to the paper. That could be left until later.

'Can I offer you some coffee or how about a drink?' Shelley accepted chilled white wine. Darina went down to the kitchen, found the cleaners had just started in there, and came back up the stairs carrying wine and some home-made cheese straws.

In the study Shelley was looking about her surroundings in an abstracted way.

'Now,' Darina said, handing over a glass of wine, 'to what do I owe this visit?'

The other girl huddled into a corner of the sofa, shrinking inside her sweater. 'I'm scared!'

'Scared?'

'It's David, his being murdered, I mean.'

Darina looked at her thoughtfully. 'You don't think he was the victim of some psycho on the loose, then?'

The girl shivered. 'Do you? After Bruce and Kate's deaths?'

At last there was someone else who saw things the same way as Darina. But it was Shelley Darina had suspected of being behind the deaths. Could she now remove her from the murder frame?

'Bruce's death was supposed to have been natural. What makes you think it could have been anything else?' Darina waited with sharp interest to see what Shelley would say.

Shelley's face was a study of doubt and confusion. At last she blinked extremely slowly and said, 'Bruce had an allergy.'

'An allergy?' Darina had to make Shelley spell out what she already knew from Eileen Miller.

'He couldn't eat nuts.'

'Let me get this straight. Are you telling me that Bruce had an allergy, if he ate a nut, any sort of nut, he could die?'

Shelley nodded, starting to look a little happier. 'He was paranoid about it. The last time he accidentally ate one, that was nearly it. It was on the menu as a wild mushroom risotto but the chef had added tiny nibs of almond. All Bruce took was one bite and he reacted immediately. Afterwards he said it had never happened that quickly before and the doctors told him the next time it would be even quicker. So then he refused to eat anything he hadn't cooked and prepared himself unless he could be absolutely certain that it didn't contain nuts, they get used so often these days and it only needed one tiny taste. I was toasting almond flakes under the grill one day for something and Bruce had to leave the kitchen, he could feel himself beginning to be affected just by the aroma, that's how sensitive he was.'

'And you think someone else knew about this and used it to kill him?'

'He tried to keep it secret, he didn't think it would do his image any good, but there were people in Australia who knew about it.'

'Did his sister tell you why she was coming to England?'

'No, she just said it was business. I thought it had something to do with the wines.'

'But you think now she might have suspected Bruce's death hadn't been natural?'

'She was so odd after he died. She'd get hysterical then become completely withdrawn.'

'But you didn't suspect anything when Bruce died? Or when you heard your sister-in-law had fallen out of her hotel window?'

Shelley shook her head but there was something in her expression. Shifty wasn't the right word for it, the look had been too fleeting, but for an instant Darina knew Shelley del Lucca was not being completely honest. Then the girl gazed directly into her eyes. 'I think I was too relieved Bruce had died.'

'Yes, I gather your marriage wasn't exactly a success.'

'Success! It was a disaster!'

'In what way?' Once again, Darina had to hear it from Shelley.

Another low, throaty sigh. 'He was such fun to begin with. Meeting and falling in love with him was like being taken on to some terribly exciting roller-coaster. We met on a television programme, I was doing a cookery spot and he'd been asked to judge some wines. It was instant combustion! He asked me to come away with him for the next weekend but I said I couldn't, I had too much work to do.'

Shelley paused, a slight smile on her red lips. Darina would have been willing to lay a more than small bet Shelley had decided accepting Bruce's first invitation was not the way to keep him interested.

'But that wasn't the end of it?'

'No way! I've never been chased like it!' Another, satisfied little smile. 'Before I knew what was happening, we were married.'

'When did it all start to go wrong?'

Shelley lost any trace of a smile and Darina noticed there were shadows under her eyes. The air of wellbeing given by the tan was spurious, now she could see the girl looked as though she hadn't slept for days.

'Almost at once. I don't think Bruce had realized quite how well I was doing. He got jealous of my work, suggested I retired and concentrated on him and Yarramarra.'

'But that didn't suit you?'

'You kidding? I haven't spent years working every moment of the day, researching trends, working out recipes, doing dems in tiny one-hole places, wooing magazines, radio and TV stations to give it all up just when I was really starting to get somewhere. I told him no way, I was going places and if he didn't like it, well, he knew what he could do.' There was nothing even faintly amusing about Shelley del Lucca's determination. Not even the charismatic Bruce Bennett could have stood a chance against her ambition. 'And Yarramarra isn't exactly the centre of the world, you know? I don't know how Kate stood it, buried away there the whole of her life, no wonder she never found a man.'

'So it was really a case of male jealousy that came between you?'

Darina watched Shelley struggle with trying to work out whether to leave it there or say something more. She decided a small prompt wouldn't come amiss. 'There's a rumour going around that Bruce was, well, more than a little physical in bed.'

Shelley glared at her. 'Physical is putting it mildly! He was an animal!' Exactly the word Lynn had used. 'There was some kind of terrible devil in him. Most of the time he was charming, fun, even considerate. Then something would spark him off and he'd turn into a brute. Talk about being raped by your own husband—and that wasn't the worst!'

'So why did you stay with him?' Darina asked bluntly.

Shelley's eyes narrowed. 'He would have liked me to run off and leave him, then it would have been my fault. But I wasn't going without a fair settlement. I wanted him to pay for the agony, mental and physical, he put me through.'

Shelley had shed her soft and pliant image, this was an extremely obdurate woman.

'So,' Darina said. 'His death was such a relief it never occurred to you to wonder if someone had wanted him out of the way?'

'Right!' Shelly concurred vigorously.

'And I suppose you now own Yarramarra?' Darina thought she might as well get everything out in the open. She watched as Shelley's grey eyes hardened.

'The brute fixed me in the end! He altered his will just before leaving Australia. He'd already given a quarter share to Kate, just before we were married, he said it was only right she had a financial stake in the place. She was so much older, I thought she was bound to go first and leave it back to him, there wasn't anyone else.'

'But Bruce died first instead?'

Shelley pouted. 'And then I found out he'd left her half of what remained.'

'Making your sister-in-law the major shareholder?'

'And she left it to Bruce's mother, a woman he'd never known and I never knew existed until the day I left to come to London!' Bitterness rang through her voice.

Poor Shelley, thought Darina, just when she must have felt everything was going her way.

'But even a share of Yarramarra must be worth a considerable amount of money?'

'But I can't sell it! The shares have to remain in the family and Eileen Miller won't buy them. She says she hasn't got the money and she won't go to the bank for a loan. She says the income should be enough for me.' Another pout, like a little girl who's been told Father Christmas can't bring everything on her list.

'I suppose David Bartholomew needed more money than you could supply?' suggested Darina.

'Television's so expensive! Bruce only left me a bit of money apart from the shares in Yarramarra, he spent money like water. But Neil said he'd insured Bruce's investment in his company and was paying me out, so I said David could have that when it came through. But David needed more. That's what we were all going to talk about on Wednesday morning, only he was dead!' Her mouth trembled and tears welled up in her eyes. 'Oh, Darina, I'm so scared.'

Darina handed her the box of tissues from her desk then answered a knock on the door.

It was one of the scientific officers. 'We've done everything we can,' he told Darina, giving an interested look to the girl wiping her eyes on the sofa. 'I'm afraid it won't amount to very much but if there's another attempt we might be able to add to the evidence.'

Darina thanked him and escorted him quickly downstairs to the front door, where his companions waited. She shut the door behind them and leant against it. Another attempt? What made him think the intruder could be back? Almost she opened the door to call after him but decided there was no point. Everything was speculation.

She clambered over a stack of cleaning materials and looked into the kitchen. The table was piled with things that lived on the top of working surfaces together with the contents of several cupboards that were having their shelves scrubbed down by one of the two astonishingly cheerful young cleaners.

Darina returned to the study, finding Shelley looking a little more composed.

She sat down and started to say, 'I don't understand...' when the telephone rang.

It was Neil.

'I want a meeting with you, Mike and Jean-Pierre tomorrow afternoon,' he said abruptly. 'We need to talk. I'm sorry about your weekend with William but it's urgent. Two thirty all right with you?'

'I couldn't come a little earlier?' asked Darina. She glanced at Shelley. 'There are one or two things I'd like to discuss with you before the others arrive and William won't be coming this weekend, he's working.'

'Fine, why not come at one and join us for a quick lunch?'

Darina thanked him, repeated the details, and rang off. 'Sorry,' she said to Shelley, 'I hope we don't have any more interruptions. Now, what I can't work out is why you've come to me with all this. If you really think Bruce was murdered, and your sister-in-law and David, you should go to the police.'

'But what can I tell them? I have no idea how it could have been done. I mean, Bruce never ate anything he wasn't sure about, never. And why didn't he inject himself with anti-histamine and, oh, all sorts of things I don't know. On that chat-show tape Bruce sent Kate it said you'd solved lots of murder cases and I thought you could find out who killed him.'

'If, indeed, anyone did. Tell me, why are you so sure? You've just pointed out how unlikely it was anybody could have got Bruce to eat a nut.'

'But what about Kate? Do you think it could have been suicide? I mean, she had been more than a little strange since Bruce died but not that strange.'

'Yet you didn't mention any of your doubts to the police when you identified the body?'

'They seemed so sure she had jumped out of the window. I mean, who was I to suggest they could be wrong?' Shelley's eyes were large and round as she looked at Darina with blank innocence.

It suited your book not to make waves, Darina decided.

More tears welled up as Shelley continued, 'But when David was killed, I started to get scared. I mean, all these people, all dead! And what if it should be me next?'

'Why should it be you?' Darina asked shortly. This innocent, lost little girl air was beginning to exasperate her.

'I don't know!' wailed Shelley, all control lost. 'But David and I were partners, if someone wanted him dead, why not me?'

Could anyone be that self-centred? Yes, Darina believed, Shelley could.

Darina started to explain that if it had been David's company that had provided the motive for his murder, it was unlikely Shelley had to be removed as well, but she had to break off in the middle to answer another call. It was the cleaning agency. 'I'm terribly sorry,' the girl at the other end of the phone said, 'but we appear to have double-booked your team. Can you put one of them on, they're supposed to be in Putney this afternoon. They haven't finished your place, have they?' she asked hopefully.

'Finished?' Darina vented her exasperation. 'They've only just started getting down to the dirt. You can't take them away now!'

The girl was apologetic but said the prior booking had to take precedence. 'The only thing I can do is ask them if they'd come in tomorrow. I know it's a Saturday but they're often keen for as many hours as possible, most of them are out of work actors desperate for money. Can you ask Charles if they're willing?'

Darina apologized to Shelley and went downstairs again.

Charles and his partner were more than happy to work the next day as long as it could be in the afternoon, they had something on in the morning.

'That's going to be difficult. I've got to go out for lunch and a meeting,' Darina said.

'Leave us the house, you don't want to be around when the dust's flying anyway. Lots of our clients give us keys and tell us to get on with the job.'

He looked reliable, the agency had a very good reputation and Darina thought it could be no bad thing to have the house occupied while she wasn't there.

Back upstairs, Darina explained to the girl from the agency what had been agreed, received their assurance that the pair were thoroughly reliable and rang off. She returned to explaining to Shelley how her fate needn't be inextricably linked to David's.

At last the girl seemed to grasp the message. 'You mean, someone might want just him dead, not me as well? Are you sure of that?'

'No,' Darina confessed. 'I'm not sure of anything. But it seems likely.'

'So why were Bruce and Kate killed? I mean I'm connected with both of them as well.'

Darina took a deep breath and prayed for patience. 'I don't know why Bruce died but I think Kate was killed to prevent her telling me about Bruce's allergy, which would have explained how he could have been murdered.'

'But I know about that, so I could be in danger, too! I told you!' Shelley was now near hysterics.

'But you've told me now.'

'But does the murderer know that?'

For once Shelley seemed to have got hold of a point.

'If you were going to be got rid of so you couldn't spill the beans on Bruce's allergy, it would have happened before now,' Darina said tersely, wondering if in fact that was the case. 'But why don't you go to the police, tell them everything and then let everyone know that's what you've done.'

'Who's everyone?'

Who indeed?

'Everyone connected with the *Table* programme,' said Darina.

'You mean, just ring them up and say I think Bruce was murdered because someone fed him a nut and I've told the police that?'

Darina nodded.

'They'll think I've gone bananas.'

Darina asked if that wasn't a better alternative to being dead and Shelley slowly nodded.

'In fact, you could suggest to the police that it might be interesting for them to listen to the reaction of everyone you spoke to.'

Shelley looked at her unblinkingly. 'You mean, it could give them a clue as to who the murderer is?'

Personally Darina thought the killer was far too in control to give away the slightest hint but anything to suggest the police were brought into the picture seemed a good idea.

'I suppose you could be right,' Shelley said reluctantly.

'Do it,' urged Darina. 'That way you know you'll be safe. Shall I ring and make an appointment for you?'

Shelley shook her head, said she didn't want to be rushed into anything but she would think about contacting the police. 'And you will try and work out who it could be?' she urged as Darina took her downstairs at last.

'Oh, Shelley, I'm not a detective, I just struck lucky in those other cases. If anything does occur to me, though, I'll let you know, where are you staying?'

Shelley gave her the name of a hotel, then added, 'Mark has asked me to go and stay with him, he thinks I'll feel safer. I told him, you see, I was scared and that I was coming to see you, in fact it was from his flat I rang your house yesterday. Maybe I'll move in with him.'

'For Heaven's sake,' Darina said. 'Not until you've been to the police.'

Shelley looked at her full of amazement. 'You surely don't think *Mark* could have killed Bruce, do you?'

Darina sighed, the girl obviously hadn't listened to much she had said up in the study. 'Until you know for certain, isn't it best to assume *anybody* connected with *Table* could have killed him?'

Shelley glanced unhappily up at Darina's superior height. 'But that would include you!'

At last she seemed to have got the point. 'Quite!' Darina said.

Shelley's face lightened for an instant. 'Now you're being ridiculous!' Then she grew wistful. 'It would have been nice staying with Mark, they're all so snooty at that hotel.' She chewed the corner of a finger and Darina remembered she was on the other side of the world from home, an alien in an unknown country that had not proved at all hospitable.

For a moment she almost weakened and suggested the girl come and stay with her. Then the memory of the figure in the garden the previous night came back to her. No one connected with *Table* was going to slip under her guard until this case was cleared up, and that included Shelley del Lucca.

TWENTY-TWO

DARINA closed the door behind Shelley. In the kitchen Charles and his partner had nearly finished and were now packing up their gear.

'Back tomorrow before twelve,' they promised.

Darina faxed her article through, then arranged herself comfortably on the small sofa in her study, pushed her long hair away from her face, poured out another glass of wine and pulled closer the tin of cheese straws.

In the matter of murder, means, opportunity and motive were the vital factors.

How Bruce had been killed didn't now present any problem. Opportunity was more troublesome because it seemed it had been available to everyone during that pre-Christmas lunch party. As well as the *Table* team, Anthea had been there and even Jean-Pierre had unexpectedly popped in.

The studio hadn't been locked and sitting on Lynn's preparation table all during the lunch break had been Bruce's jug of fruit juice. It wouldn't have taken a moment for someone to go in there and add a few drops of nut oil. From what Shelley had said, it seemed even one would have been sufficient to trigger off his fatal response but Darina reckoned his murderer would have added more than that to be on the safe side. Almond would have blended beautifully with the apricot flavour and even Bruce's keen palate was unlikely to have noticed its presence, not under the stress of recording.

What, though, of the syringe Shelley insisted Bruce always carried? Perhaps he hadn't been clutching at his heart at all as he collapsed, perhaps he had been reaching for his breast pocket. Had the syringe been removed by the murderer? If so, an investigation might have something to go on, wardrobe wasn't nearly as easy to gain access to as the studio.

Darina found the telephone number of *Table*'s wardrobe girl, Mary Burgess, and rang her.

Mary was home and happy to talk.

She said Bruce had wanted to put something that looked like a spectacle case in the inside breast pocket of the jacket chosen for him to wear on screen. After he'd been told nothing was allowed to spoil the line of the material, he had reluctantly agreed to leave the case in his other jacket.

In all the confusion after Bruce's collapse, Mary had forgotten about his other clothes. It wasn't until later she had found and given them to Neil.

Darina had a sudden memory of Mary handing over a coat hanger draped with some men's clothes to Neil as he talked over with Mark and the rest of the team the tribute to Bruce he wanted recorded. He had hung them over the back of a chair.

What, Darina wondered, had happened to them after that? Had they been returned to Australia and had the absence of a syringe alerted Kate Bennett?

And what about Kate Bennett's death?

Theoretically, at least, most of the *Table* team could have called on her that last evening of her life. The open letter at the Cantlow offices with Kate's arrival details and hotel had been all too available for anyone to glance at. A quick call could have established her room number and maybe the fact she wasn't seeing anyone until the following morning.

It would take the resources of the police to check everyone's whereabouts that evening.

How about David's death? Here, again, there was little to go on; everyone had known where he lived and about his early morning jogging.

So much for opportunity, what about motive?

Without too much effort, Darina could think of an embarrassingly large number of people who could have felt easier with Bruce Bennett dead.

There was Lynn, angry and disgusted at the way Bruce had abused her. A cook, she might well have somehow come across Bruce's allergy and realized that a drop of nut oil could turn into a lethal weapon.

But had she really feared Bruce's attentions so much murder was the only answer?

Anthea could have been outraged at Bruce's treatment of her, if things had progressed that far. Darina was by no means sure they had.

What, though, if Neil believed they had?

But wasn't Neil the one person who had most to gain from keeping Bruce alive? It was Bruce who had brought new life to the *Table* series, Darina had no illusions about the part she played in it; compared to the Australian's success, she was a minor feature.

Yet, *Table* was surviving without Bruce, wasn't it? A thought to ponder. Just as it might be as well to remember Jean-Pierre's success in taking over the Australian's mantle. Bruce had worked at his vineyard, it was more than possible Jean-Pierre knew about his allergy and he had been in Neil's office over Christmas discussing the possibility of joining *Table*. Might he have seen David as a threat to his new career? If he'd killed twice already, another death might have been unimportant. But could Bruce's appropriation of yeast and a master vintner be sufficient motive for murder? After all this time?

Darina thought what a pity it was she'd had to discard her theory about David Bartholomew and Shelley, it fitted all the facts so nicely. Alerted by Shelley in Italy to Bruce's Achilles' heel, buoyed by her promise to back him financially once she was in control of Yarramarra, maybe even sexually committed, David had taken the opportunity to dispatch the Australian, thus turning Shelley into a rich, available widow and maybe even removing *Table* as a competitor to his proposed food programme. It had all fitted together so neatly Darina wondered for a moment if David hadn't been killed by some pervert after all.

Then she remembered the intruder in her garden the previous night. No, almost certainly the production manager had died because he'd set up his own company to produce a rival series to *Table,* once again threatening the programme's existence. Except, it had originally been Bruce's death that had threatened the existence of *Table.* So that didn't make sense.

But David hadn't been the only member of the *Table* team to meet Shelley in Italy. Mark, too, had been there and, according to him, had been close to her. A rich widow would come in very handy for him if he really was in trouble financially. Yet David had been offering him another, much needed, career opportunity, so why kill him? Unless, perhaps, he was threatening to come between Mark and Shelley?

Jan had been in Italy as well, it wouldn't do to leave her out of the picture. Level-headed Jan, used to coping with detail, she could well be capable of planning any number of murders. Motive was a difficulty, of course. Darina could see her protecting her position as studio director of *Table* by dispatching David, but why kill Bruce? It wasn't only Jan's denial of any interest in the man, there had been no sexual spark between them, so an affair didn't seem a possibility and Jan had admitted herself the programme, so vital to her career, had needed Bruce.

Back to Shelley. She had seemed really scared this morning and surely her visit proved she hadn't had anything to do with Bruce's death, otherwise why tell Darina exactly how he could have been killed? Especially if she actually believed Darina might be able to solve the murder. Or had she learned Eileen Miller had already told Darina about Bruce's allergy?

Darina suddenly thought of all her other visitors that morning and wondered if Shelley had expected to find her on her own. And if she had, would Darina be alive now?

She shivered and pushed away the ridiculous thought. Shelley was so much smaller than herself, she couldn't possibly have overpowered her. But if the victim was unsuspecting and the attacker skilled, size needn't necessarily matter.

Shelley was a successful food journalist, could she really be as dim as she had appeared?

Darina rose. The wine had not been the best of ideas and coffee was called for. First, though, she went round the house fastening the security grilles over the windows.

THAT EVENING Darina went for a quiet supper with William's uncle and aunt in Eaton Square. She enjoyed a close relationship with them and often had a meal round there when she was in London.

It was well after eleven when Darina drove back to Chelsea. There was no parking space outside the house and she had to drive almost to the end of her road before finding one.

Someone had been waiting in a car parked almost opposite her house, waiting for a considerable time. It was with a sigh of satisfaction that Darina's arrival was noted. Quickly slipping out of the car and crossing the road, Bruce's killer, anonymous in a trench coat and flat cap, came up behind Darina. A quick glance confirmed there were only the two of them in the street. Out of a deep pocket, one hand drew a weighted sock.

Then a front door opened, warm light spilled on to the dark pavement and people were on the doorstep exchanging noisy and lengthy goodbyes.

The killer swiftly recrossed the road. Plan B would now have to go into operation. It was a nuisance but needn't be a disaster.

TWENTY-THREE

DARINA rang Shelley at her hotel in the morning. The girl sounded only half awake and Darina apologized for disturbing her.

'No problem'—a yawn came over the telephone—'I should be up anyway.'

'I just wondered if you'd spoken to the police.'

There was the slightest of pauses then Shelley said, 'I've got an appointment on Monday. The inspector type didn't seem to think it was that important and said he couldn't manage it before.'

Darina wondered. Was Shelley just spinning her a line?

On the other hand, her own experience of Gatting suggested the story could be true and it was, after all, the weekend. She made up her mind to call the chief inspector herself on the Monday, apologized again for disturbing Shelley and rang off.

ONE O'CLOCK saw Darina at the Cantlow house in Putney. Anthea greeted her pleasantly, thanked her for an offering of home-made marmalade and took her straight into lunch.

'Sorry for the rush,' Neil said. 'Have to be ready for when Mike and Jean-Pierre arrive. Now that the personalities have changed so much, I'm wondering if we shouldn't alter some of our programme ideas.'

Darina gave a mental sigh as she realized that would mean some rewriting to the book of the series, wondered if there was much point in it being produced at all, and looked at Anthea, ladling out a casserole at the sideboard. 'Once again you've got a television invasion,' she commented.

'As I told you at lunch the other day, I'm married to television rather than a husband.' Anthea looked on edge, her eyes moved restlessly, a muscle twitched constantly at the corner of her mouth. Darina thought she seemed a woman at the end of her tether. 'The number of meetings Neil feels is necessary would daunt a Methodist.'

'You're a fine one to talk,' said her husband. He turned to Darina. 'Anthea's just as bad. Half the time I come back here to find she's got some author or colleague closeted with her, or is off to some meeting of her own. There was one last night and another the night before.'

'Were you here yourself? No. So just admit that if you'd wanted an adoring little housekeeper instead of an intelligent companion, you wouldn't have married me in the first place,' Anthea said with barely controlled impatience as she sat down at the table. 'I'm sure Darina's fiancé wants more than a compliant cook, she's far too intelligent to have settled for anything less than an equal relationship.'

'When's the wedding?' Neil asked.

'Actually, that was one of the reasons I wanted a little chat before the meeting.'

'Don't want me to be bridesmaid, do you?'

'Honestly, Neil, can't you see Darina is being serious?'

'OK, so you don't want to be overshadowed at the altar by my good looks, how else can I help?'

Darina gave him a level gaze. 'Perhaps I shouldn't be asking this but it could be quite important for me. You mentioned another series of *Table* the other day and I'm wondering if you are wanting to retain me as a presenter?'

Neil's eyes were uncommonly shrewd as they regarded her. 'And this has something to do with your marriage?'

'She's obviously worried about fitting in television commitments with a brand-new husband,' Anthea said caustically.

'But you've been living with the guy for months, now, haven't you?'

'And I bet spending several days a week in London has been a severe strain, hasn't it?'

'There have been difficulties,' Darina acknowledged to Anthea.

'Are you saying you don't want to be considered for another series?' Neil asked sharply.

'Then there is definitely going to be one?'

'It's all still up in the air, we've got to see how the new team works out, but I'm optimistic.' He paused and gave Darina another sharp glance. 'I *was* hoping that you would be part of the new *Table,* are you telling me that you want to pull out?'

'I'll be completely honest with you, Neil, I'm not sure.'

'You mean you're going to sit at home and let your new husband call all the shots?' Anthea sounded shocked and something more, there was a touch of hysteria in her voice. 'You can't do that, you'll always regret it.' Darina remembered Jan saying something similar.

'No, not quite that. I just have to think about how I am going to meet my commitments and it helps to know what those commitments are likely to be.'

'So you *are* willing to take on another series?'

'I didn't say that either, Neil. Look, can I just have a few days to think about things and discuss them with William?'

'Of course,' he agreed quickly. 'But let me know your decision as soon as possible. There's a lot to get sorted out.'

'I will,' Darina promised then added, 'One of the things that's made me feel I have to think this through carefully is that I had a long talk with Shelley yesterday and I think it was her work that helped ruin her marriage with Bruce.'

'That cold little bitch,' Anthea said quickly. 'She wouldn't know how to give to a relationship if it was Christmas!'

'That's a bit strong!' Neil objected.

Anthea suddenly hurled down her napkin, whatever frail control she had been maintaining suddenly lost. 'And neither do you! I never get any consideration, any acknowledgement I have my own life to lead. You expect me to be there for you all the time. When are you there for me?'

'Well, thank you!' Neil burst out. 'Why do you think I work like a dog if not for you and the children?'

'Oh, come off it! You work for yourself. This house,' she glanced around the pleasant room, 'the children's education, our entire life style, those are just desirable by-products. If making television programmes brought in nothing, if we had to scrape along on a shoestring, you'd still do the same thing.'

Both appeared to have forgotten Darina's presence. She sat uneasily in her chair wondering if she should leave the room but hypnotized by the display of such deep emotions. No inhibitions to Anthea now as she continued to berate Neil. 'You're the victim of addiction just as surely as any coke-snorting junkie.'

Neil stared at her. 'You know you mean everything to me, you and the children. Without you I'd have nothing.'

She looked back at him fiercely. Her hands gripped the edge of the table. 'Then show it,' she whispered in a passionate undertone. 'Just for once do something that proves we mean more to you than a damned television programme.'

He opened his mouth, then closed it again and gave a tiny, hopeless shrug of his shoulders.

'You see,' Anthea shouted. 'There's no way you can show you care. Compared with your bloody programme, I'm nothing. At least Bruce was willing to talk, to take the children out from school, to listen to my problems. I tell you, I can't take any more!' In a violent movement, she pushed back her chair and rushed out, slamming the door behind her.

Silence swept the room as Neil half rose then fell back in his chair. 'It's no use going after her, it would only make things worse,' he said dejectedly.

Neil gazed miserably at the table for a moment then said: 'Anthea's an unknown quantity. She keeps everything bottled up inside her until suddenly, bang, she blows up.' He drummed impatient fingers on the polished surface. 'I never know what to do with her! I thought that trip to Australia would be an opportunity for us to get together. All it seemed

to do was make her more restless. I know she was attracted
to Bruce but he's gone now and I'm damn well going to make
sure nothing else comes between us.'

Darina could think of nothing to say.

Then he added, 'I get so involved with what I'm doing it
must be hard for Anthea.'

'Even though she's got a demanding job herself?'

In a few minutes Neil had aged several years, the teddy
bear charm had vanished leaving him drawn and weary. 'Does
work ever mean the same to a woman as it does to a man?
Sure Anthea's a great editor, sure she's become a director but,
at rock bottom, what matters to her are me and the children.'

Darina's silence must have been eloquent for Neil thrust
his plate away from him with a rough gesture. 'God damn it,
let's leave it, can we? Have some more wine.'

He reached for the decanter but Darina refused, watching
while he filled his own glass and stared moodily at the wall-
paper.

How far, she wondered, would anyone go to demonstrate
their love? Where did passion lead? Down a road to compro-
mise? How far was it possible to combine devotion to a person with devotion to a career?

She got up and cleared away their plates. On the sideboard
was a bowl of fruit salad and a jug of cream but neither Neil
nor she was in the mood for food.

'I'll make some coffee,' Neil said. 'The other two will be
here in a few minutes.'

Darina helped him take the dishes out to the kitchen, wasn't
allowed to stack the dishwasher so watched as Neil compe-
tently handled the business of making coffee. After a moment
she asked, 'By the way, Neil, that jacket of Bruce's Mary
Burgess produced after he died, was there anything in the
pockets?'

'Eh?' He paused in loading the espresso machine, his eyes
alert.

'Someone has suggested Bruce carried something against a

condition he had, something that might have saved his life if he'd transferred it to the one he wore on the programme.' Darina watched him closely.

Neil attended to his machine. 'I went through his pockets before it was delivered to his flat, there was only a wallet, no pills or anything like that.'

'Ah!' said Darina. 'Who delivered it to the flat?'

'Anthea did, she took charge of returning all his things to Australia, she offered.'

'I see,' said Darina.

'Well, I'm pretty short of time.' Neil appeared to think he had to apologize for some dereliction of duty.

Darina remained silent.

The coffee ready, Neil picked up the tray. 'Let's go through,' he suggested.

The front door bell rang as they reached the hall, Mike Darcy had arrived and Jean-Pierre Prudhomme came up as Neil was welcoming him inside.

The four of them had an interesting and fruitful discussion, with ideas flowing freely. Jean-Pierre was particularly inspired, consulting a notebook which seemed to be filled with comments and suggestions on various aspects of the series.

'Are you finding your *Table* appearances are making any impact on the sales of your wines?' Darina asked as they were wrapping up the session.

'Ooof, what a question! One does not appear on the show to sell one's wines,' he said.

'But surely it must help?' persisted Darina.

'In time, if one continues, one 'as to say one 'opes so.' He smiled at her, his mobile face wrinkling into a map of tiny lines, his brown eyes almost disappearing, like a lizard's in the sun. 'The power of television, it is enormous, no? You do not find this?'

Oh yes, Darina agreed, she certainly did. Visions of the letters she had to answer, the interest that was now being shown in her participation in any number of events and projects, rose before her. It would be quite easy to have her head turned and to consider her talents were unusual instead of realizing she had just been lucky.

'You can't manage to get back to Bordeaux all that often at the moment,' she suggested.

'Ah, no, but I 'ave a flat in Paris. Usually I fly there Thursday evenings after the recording and spend the weekend catching up on business.'

'Does your wife join you there?'

Something flickered in the dark eyes. 'I am widower.'

Darina remembered Mark's enthusiastic description of Marie Prudhomme. 'I'm so sorry, I heard she was lovely.'

He shrugged his shoulders. 'She 'ad a car crash but she was leaving me at the time. My real regret is my son was killed in the car as well.'

'No! How terrible!'

Darina could think of nothing else to say that wouldn't sound banal and trite. What a tragedy for him, a double loss, triple really, because in a way he'd lost his wife twice, once through her walking out on him and a second time through her death. And his son as well! 'Was it a long time ago?'

'Several years but you do not forget, sometimes it is as if it were yesterday.'

No wonder he preferred to spend time in Paris rather than at his château.

Darina tried to move on to more neutral ground. 'Had you planned to go back to France this weekend?'

Some of the strain left his eyes. 'I find it desirable sometimes to remain in London. This weekend it is fortunate I do so because Neil rings me yesterday and asks for this meeting.'

'Where do you stay?' Darina asked curiously.

'I 'ave good friends in the wine trade who live in London. They 'ave a room in, 'ow do you say? The under-ground floor?'

'The basement?'

'Ah, that is it, the basement. It is very comfortable, 'as its own entrance and bathroom. I am very 'appy there, it's Chelsea.'

'Chelsea, that's where I live! You must come and have a meal with me one evening.'

'That would be most delightful.' Jean-Pierre was about to add something else but Mike had got up to go and he rose too.

'Can I give you a lift back? I have my car here.'

Jean-Pierre was effusive in his thanks but, 'Alas, I 'ave another appointment elsewhere and the Métro, which you call "the Tube"'—his accent turned the word into something strange and charming—'is most convenient. Au'voir till Monday.' He kissed Darina on each cheek once and then again on the first.

Mike, too, kissed her goodbye. 'Who would have thought when we were doing my show that evening we'd end up fellow presenters?' he said with one of his easy grins.

'You never know what life will offer,' commented Neil sententiously.

Darina asked him to give Anthea her thanks for the lunch and hoped she would soon feel better then waved goodbye to the others as she got into her car.

THE TRAFFIC was troublesome. An accident had caused massive hold-ups and progress proved first slow and finally impossible. Darina switched off her engine. All around her was mayhem: cursing drivers, anxious passengers, and the noise of horns blown in a frenzy of impatience like imprecations sent to exhort the god of traffic to do something, anything, to release the net he'd snarled round so many innocent victims.

Darina watched the driver in front of her get out of his car and walk forward to assess the situation, then return. He stood for a moment between his half-open door and the body of the car, then suddenly banged the roof in fury. He looked at his watch, looked again at the traffic around him, reached into the car, retrieved a small case, shut the door and walked off in the direction of the Underground station, leaving the car unattended.

Marvellous! Now when the traffic actually started flowing again, if such a miracle was ever to occur, Darina would be caught behind the abandoned vehicle.

Darina sat back in her seat with a sigh then slowly began to realize that she was actually quite content to be sitting surrounded by this exasperated horde of travellers as darkness fell.

At least here she was anonymous, here she was secure, here no one was interested in removing her from the face of the earth. As so often in the last few days she thought of David, jogging across Wimbledon Common. Had he recognized his attacker? Had he known why death came that morning? Had he tried to defend himself or had he been caught unawares, dispatched all unknowing as well as untimely to his end?

Bruce must have known as soon as reaction to the nut oil set in what was in store for him. Darina remembered the frantic way his hand had reached into his jacket for the life-giving syringe that wasn't there. She remembered also Lynn with her bruised and battered face and Shelley, frightened and aggressive.

She thought of Anthea's explosion at lunch and Neil's exasperated helplessness. Then odd moments from the previous few weeks drifted into her mind. She made no attempt to analyse anything but after a little she was aware something was nagging at her. Somewhere along the line she had missed something important. She had all the facts, she was sure, she just hadn't realized how important some of the detail had been. If only she could identify what it was that was nagging away at her, she might be able to work out the solution to this mystery.

The traffic ahead began slowly to move.

But not the car in front of Darina and no one was giving way from the opposite direction. A little further ahead on the now clear road was a petrol station. Darina got out of her car and started to push the one in front, guiding the wheel through the window, steering it towards the garage.

A young man came up to help, enrolled another chap on to the job and relieved Darina of most of the work. In a few minutes the car was pushed on to the forecourt, clearing the road for the cars behind.

'Thanks,' said Darina to her assistant.

'You're welcome. Girls weren't made to do a job like that.' He gave her a quick salute and went back to his car. Darina thought how nice it was to be treated occasionally as a fragile female despite her size. She slipped back into her car, put the Volvo into gear and moved forward, still thinking of the young man. Usually it took the French to make you feel truly feminine, Jean-Pierre always raised her morale, why on earth would his wife have wanted to leave him? It must have been a pretty powerful attraction, the Frenchman was so chivalrous and charming. But the young Englishman had been a bit of a white knight, too. Darina wondered idly if he was married, then thought he'd probably be the type who wouldn't want a wife to have a career.

It wasn't long before the traffic ground to another halt but by then her mind had done a quick flip, rattled a couple of pieces round another way and identified what had been nagging at her. In some dismay she looked at the result. Could that really be who had killed first Bruce, then Kate Bennett and finally David Bartholomew?

TWENTY-FOUR

DARINA spent the rest of the short but tedious journey home trying to pick holes in the theory that had presented itself.

It held together. By the time she reached Chelsea, she was sure she knew who the killer was. It wasn't a pleasant identification. But motive, opportunity, means, they were all there once you had recognized them and no one connected with *Table* made an acceptable candidate for the murderer.

It also explained the intruder in her back garden on Thursday evening. But how desperate the killer must now be to go to such lengths! Darina was certain nothing like this had been envisaged when Bruce had been so neatly eliminated. Everything after that had been a policy of cover-up and extemporization.

Should she, she wondered, go immediately to the police station and make a statement, no matter how ridiculous or unprovable they thought her theory? It was possible a properly mounted investigation could unearth sufficient circumstantial evidence to make a case, at least for the murders of Kate Bennett and David Bartholomew. And once she'd been to the police, there would be no point in the murderer trying to eliminate her from the scene.

Then she shivered as she realized that others could be in danger beside herself; at least one other person was at major risk, perhaps two.

She was now almost home. It would be sensible to ring through a warning, even if it was disbelieved, before going to the police. Darina parked and looked for her key.

THE FIGURE standing behind the kitchen door had been waiting a long time.

It had been easy to con the cleaners into allowing entry to write a quick note to Darina. Easy to make them think the visitor had left instead of slamming the front door and slipping into the cupboard under the stairs.

The murderer eased muscles stiffened by the long vigil and checked, once again, that the weighted sock was ready. Such a simple weapon, so effective when wielded correctly. The cleaners would be blamed for the break-in when the house was found ransacked and Darina dead. It would be a fitting end for the interfering busybody. With her removed perhaps something could be salvaged from the wreck of what had been such a brilliantly simple plan.

There came the sound of the front door opening and the killer tensed against the wall.

DARINA CLOSED and locked the door carefully behind her, the sound of the heavy steel bolt clunking home bringing a welcome feeling of security. Before she left for the police station, she'd check Charles and his fellow worker had fastened all the grilles properly after they'd cleaned the windows. On the mat were the set of spare keys that had been posted through the letter box. She put them on the hall table and looked around her.

For a moment she stood absorbing the aroma of cleaning agent and freshly polished wood, appreciating the way everything now gleamed. She opened the drawing-room door. At last the place was looking cherished again. Was Mrs Hope having a similar effect on the Somerset cottage? All that was needed now was the smell of something cooking; until a delicious aroma wafted from the kitchen, no home was really complete.

Darina undid the buttons of her three-quarter-length military-style jacket but left it on as she walked towards the kitchen, her thoughts on coffee. She could make her telephone calls while the kettle was boiling. She felt in her bag for her organizer, into which she'd copied all the home numbers of the people connected with *Table*.

Darina pushed open the kitchen door as she had done times without number. No sixth sense alerted her to danger. She switched on the light, put the organizer by the wall telephone, picked up the electric kettle and made for the sink.

And the figure who had waited so long, so patiently, advanced to deliver the mortal blow, the weighted sock rising in a lethal arc towards the spot so conveniently exposed by the long hair being tidied away that day in a thick, looped plait.

As she reached to switch on the tap, the dark surface of the window above the sink acted as a mirror and Darina caught for one tiny moment a sight of that raised arm. Her body twisted in instant reflex as she swung out with the kettle. The movement saved her life but incredible pain ran down a nerve in her arm as the weighted sock caught her left shoulder. She reeled under the blow, her arm hanging useless, the nerve screaming its protests. The kettle bounced harmlessly on the floor.

The sock was wielded again with cruel force.

But again Darina managed to twist away, this time lashing out with a foot in imitation of martial arts glimpsed on the cinema screen. With more luck than skill, she caught her attacker in the groin and with a startled hiss of pain the killer jumped back, crouching, one hand massaging the inside thigh, the other still holding that deadly sock.

For the first time Darina had a chance to look at her attacker. It was a spectre, a faceless figure in a trench coat topped by an obscene head, the features flattened and distorted underneath a stocking mask that defied identification.

There was no hiding, though, the murderous intent in the bright eyes that shone through the nylon.

Darina's right hand reached for the strap of her handbag, dislodged by the blow to her shoulder but still hanging there, caught on the little buttoned strap that aped an epaulette. It was the work of a moment to wrench it down the useless left arm and swing the heavy leather, weighted with the impedimenta of her life, in a wide arc that kept her intruder at a respectful distance.

But only for an instant, then the sock caught the bag as the heavy weight was used as a medieval knight might have wielded a ball and chain. Darina had to let go and retreat as, with a savage curse, the black leather sack was flung aside and the killer came on.

Except by then Darina had managed to grab one-handed at the back of a kitchen chair and hold it in front of her.

Her only hope was to prevent that sock connecting with her head. Fear coursed through her body, she remembered David felled while running, Kate thrown from her hotel window. Adrenalin turned the fear into a primitive urge for preservation. Behind her was the back door, but it offered no escape, it led only to the walled garden. Anyway, before she had time to unbolt the security lock, she would be lying on the floor, unconscious or already dead. Across the kitchen was the door to the hall, if only she could reach that, she might have a chance.

The chair leg was grabbed and wrenched at as the sock was swung at her again, not near enough this time to do damage. Darina jabbed with the chair, gaining a tiny bit of ground, which she lost almost immediately as, with a sudden, two-handed effort, the chair was finally yanked from her grasp. The killer staggered, off balance for a second before the chair, like the bag, was flung aside.

Darina dodged behind the kitchen table. One-handed, she tried to push the heavy piece of pine furniture towards her attacker.

With a muttered oath and a sudden surge of strength, the killer grasped the wooden surface and flipped the table on its end, the legs grating on the tiled floor, its top catching and tossing another chair on its side. The barrier between Darina and her assailant had vanished and she was left, without a weapon, with the door to the hall as far away from her as ever.

Behind her was the hob and wall oven, flanked on either side by work surfaces. Replaced on the surfaces were all the items so painstakingly cleaned by Charles and his partner. Darina grabbed for a pottery jar and threw it as the figure swung its loaded sock once again. Wooden spoons and spatulas showered down as the jar glanced off the trench coat and crashed on the floor, pottery shards skittering across the ceramic tiles. Spice containers followed, a jar of vanilla sugar, several bottles of oil, all thrown in desperate haste and with little accuracy, doing no more than delaying the killer's fatal advance. Until a precious glass salad bowl caught the arm flung up to protect that stockinged head and her assailant cried out in sudden pain as the glass broke and blood appeared from a long cut across the back of the left hand. It dripped ever faster to the floor. The sock was lifted in the right hand with renewed vigour and Darina dodged and kicked, twisting and turning to avoid the vicious swipes of the weapon that was swung again and again. She tried unavailingly to work her way towards the door that led to the hall, at the same time searching for something else to throw.

Her hand connected with the food processor, for once not plugged into the wall ready for use, electric cord efficiently wound round its motor by the cleaners. With the strength of desperation, Darina threw the heavy gadget as she dodged another murderous lash of the sock.

The processor caught the upraised arm. There was a scream that combined anguish and outrage. The loaded sock was dropped by a hand unable any longer to grip and Darina's attacker was on the defensive.

But only for a moment. Then the killer had moved backwards with astonishing speed and agility to seize one of the set of knives Darina kept razor sharp on a long magnetic wall bar.

Even held in the left hand, the weapon was murderous.

Blood still ran from the long cut into the cuff of the trench coat, slowly turning it dark red, and more fell on the floor, joining the pools of oil and assorted culinary flavourings that turned the Provençal tiles into a grocer's nightmare.

Darina felt despair grip her; her hands turned into claws and she prepared to defend herself against the final lunge that would drive that knife deep into her vital parts; she was out of breath, felt her strength was failing. Her eyes darted from side to side, seeking something, anything, that would help save her, keep her out of the reach of that deadly blade.

With a sudden burst of energy, she flung open the fridge door, the flash of its bright, white interior halting her attacker for the briefest of moments.

It was enough for Darina to be able to fling the nearest thing to hand, a terrine of turkey breast studded with pistachio. With a breathless imprecation, the figure dodged the heavy iron dish. A pottery container of chicken and duck liver pate followed, it failed to come anywhere near Darina's killer, as did two bottles of French Maille mustard. Any moment now the knife blade was coming her way and, too late, Darina could see she had boxed herself into a corner; the open fridge door was between her and the way out of the kitchen.

There were no bottles of milk in the fridge that could be smashed into a weapon, milk came in cartons from the supermarket these days, and Darina had failed to place a bottle of wine there before she left for the meeting. She had no time to see if there was anything else useful in the bowels of the fridge, could only grab at one of the vegetable containers from the bottom and attempt to use it as a shield. The light plastic, even filled with a lettuce and half a pound of tomatoes, was unlikely to prove in any way effective.

With a cry of triumph, her assailant advanced with the knife held poised for a vicious thrust into Darina's body, then slipped on a long slick of Darina's precious green, extra-virgin, estate-bottled olive oil. With a shriek that reverberated round the room, the three-times killer slithered on the slippery floor, now more treacherous than a minefield, tried to maintain balance, failed and fell, the head striking one of the upturned chairs with a sickeningly heavy impact; the knife skittered under the dresser, well out of reach.

Darina leant against the fridge, panting heavily. The end had come with such astonishing suddenness she couldn't for the moment believe she was still alive; that the deadly blade wasn't plunged in her flesh.

The body on the floor stirred and groaned. Darina realized her danger was by no means over. Her mind started to work once again and she slipped the narrow leather belt from the loops of her trousers, knelt on her assailant's back, forced the arms behind the inert body and bound them together. She looked at the still bleeding cut on the back of the left hand, found a tea towel and wrapped it tightly round the wound. A kitchen drawer yielded twine which she used to tie together the ankles. Then she retrieved the knife from under the dresser, holding it by the blade. Finally, moving round the spilt oil with infinite care, Darina reached the telephone and called the police.

TWENTY-FIVE

DARINA'S CALL received the promise of rapid police assistance together with the assurance that Chief Inspector Gatting would be informed of the situation.

Darina rang off and sagged against the kitchen cupboards as she felt her strength finally drain away. Stumbling, she righted the kitchen table and then a chair and sank into it, her knees trembling uncontrollably. She laid her arms along the table and rested her head on them, her eyes closed, allowing delayed shock to shiver through her.

She didn't even try to think about what had happened. It was enough that she was alive and unharmed. If she sat very still and blanked out everything, just for a few minutes, perhaps she would be able to cope with what had to follow.

The kitchen was very quiet. The old clock that hung on the wall beside the window ticked peacefully away and the horror of the preceding few minutes gradually lost its crippling power. Slowly Darina began to think maybe it might not stain the walls of the kitchen indelibly and even that, after several centuries had passed, she would be able to work in this familiar room without feeling threatened.

Another groan came from the floor. Her assailant was stirring, beginning to fight against the restraining bonds.

Darina pulled herself upright and opened her eyes. The body had twisted on to its side, the bound legs were writhing, the arms jerking. Darina stooped and pulled off the stocking mask.

Jan glared at her.

There was another futile lash of the director's feet then she collapsed back on the tiles and closed her eyes.

'Do you want to talk about it?' asked Darina.

There was no response.

'Shelley and you got together in Italy, didn't you? That was when you learned about Bruce's allergy.'

Jan's eyes remained closed.

'Did you discuss the sins of men, exchange experiences of your ill treatment at their hands?'

Jan started wriggling again. For a moment Darina thought she was trying to launch another attack but almost immediately realized that the director was attempting to sit herself up. All around the floor were fragments of broken pottery and glass and the slippery oil had mixed with spilt spices and herbs into a gunge that released a complex aroma, summoning up Mediterranean and Oriental memories.

Darina found a broom and swept up the worst of the mess. The police forensic team could curse as much as they liked, she wasn't leaving those dangerously sharp shards within reach of her prisoner.

Jan had now managed to twist herself until she was sitting upright, hands still secured behind her, her back leaning against the cupboard under the wall oven. She watched, expressionless, as Darina completed her rough clean-up operation and sank once again on to the kitchen chair.

'Shelley wanted to be free of Bruce but divorce wouldn't have given her control of Yarramarra. Of course, at that time neither of you knew that Bruce was to invest in Neil's company and join *Table for Four*. Did Shelley contact you when she heard? Or did you get in touch with her? Which of you, in fact, suggested your deadly pact? And how were you going to split the proceeds?'

At last she stimulated a response from her assailant. 'Shelley knew nothing!' Jan's voice grated like a mincer asked to deal with too much gristle.

'Come off it, you can't expect me to believe that!'

'Believe it or not, it's true.' Jan's head was up and her eyes were blazing with aggression, her hands wriggling behind her back, attempting to free themselves from the confining belt. Already the tea towel had been discarded.

'Why are you protecting her? Has she paid you off already? If so, you must have murdered for very small gain.'

Extreme pain passed across Jan's face. Suddenly the fight went out of her and she slumped lower on the floor. 'You wouldn't understand,' she muttered. 'Shelley and I...' Her voice trailed off, her eyes closed and she seemed to retreat within herself, become again the reserved, contained director Darina had thought she knew.

Darina looked at the trussed figure, the once immaculate slacks now smeared and crumpled, the trench coat stained with culinary aromatics and streaked with oil. A short while ago she had been filled with murderous intent. 'Shelley told me she was frightened. I thought she must be acting, trying to put me off the scent, but now I believe she was genuine. She knew you were behind the deaths and feared she was next.'

Jan's eyes flew open, once again there was that sense of incredible pain passing over her face. 'She's a stupid cow! I thought in Italy that she was everything I'd ever wanted. For a few short nights...I thought she felt the same, that we could laugh at men and plan a future together. When Bruce joined *Table* I thought it was fate. It made everything possible. After I'd removed him, she could provide the money and I the expertise; I'd be able to produce my own programmes at last and she would be the star. Together we could reach the top.'

'So what went wrong?'

'She gets together with David bloody Bartholomew, that's what went wrong!' Again that gristle-grinding scrape in her voice. 'As if I hadn't shown her we don't need men. God, she was keen enough to find an alternative when we met in Italy. All over me and pathetically grateful for what I could give her. Had me dancing on the end of her string!'

'So she did give you the idea of murdering Bruce?'

'She told me about Bruce's nut allergy apropos of nothing

at all. God she was clever! Told me in her sweet little voice
how close he'd come to death without actually suggesting a
thing!'

'But she didn't know then that Bruce was going to join
Table, that you'd have the opportunity to lace his drink with
almond oil,' protested Darina.

'Hazelnut oil,' Jan corrected her, satisfaction darkening her
tone. 'I thought it would blend well with the apricots. Three
drops in the jug, whisked in after I'd left the hospitality room
for a pee during lunch. I was afraid it wouldn't be enough,
that I might have to try again, but Shelley had said it wouldn't
take much and when I saw him collapse like that on camera,
I knew he was dying, that without his anti-histamine he was
finished.'

'Did you remove the syringe from his other jacket later?'

Jan nodded. 'As long as no one suspected he might have
an allergy, I was safe. I removed it while the jacket was sitting
in the hospitality waiting room. No one noticed; everyone in
television is too concerned with their own little ploys.'

'And so because no one else knew about his allergy, he
died his so-called "natural" death.' Darina could hear the
horror in her voice. Horror not only at Bruce's death but her
own inability for such a long time to recognize the cold-
blooded ruthlessness that lay beneath the director's controlled
surface.

Control had been lost now. Jan's eyes were passionate and
wild as she spat out, 'He deserved to die! Look what he did
to Lynn and look how he treated Shelley. You wouldn't believe the stories she told me of his behaviour. And then when
she comes over here, she won't have anything to do with me!
After I made sure she had Yarramarra, even got rid of that
interfering bitch of a sister-in-law!'

'But she didn't have Yarramarra,' Darina said quietly,
'Bruce left most of it to Kate, who willed it to Bruce's
mother.'

'But Shelley was backing David! She has to have money!'

'It was what Bruce invested in Cantlow Productions, enough to have got David's company off the ground, nothing more.'

'She still gave it to him, not to me!'

'So that's why he had to die?'

Jan said nothing, the look in her eyes was once again wild and uncontrolled.

'And no doubt Mark would have been next. He mightn't be able to mount a rival television programme but Shelley had clearly identified him as another possible partner. Would that have been after dispatching me?'

'You? You've been nothing but a nuisance from the start. If it hadn't been for that Mike Darcy show, Kate Bennett would never have come over here. Then you started interfering, asking questions. Did you think when you enquired if the tape taken when Bruce died was around anywhere that I wouldn't guess what you were up to? It was only going to take someone to alert you to what a food allergy could mean and you'd be there! That bloody professor was leading up to it, I could tell. I had to stop him, tell Neil it was all too complicated to go into.'

'Just as you stopped the health farm chef pursuing the same line,' Darina told her. 'When I finally realized that I could substitute you for David Bartholomew as chief murder suspect for nearly all the same reasons, I remembered that and the professor. That was when I was certain you were the killer. It took me so long because, stupidly, I didn't think of you as a natural partner for Shelley. But you had all the necessary attributes and you're trained in the martial arts; patient, cunning, passionate, dedicated, you are far better equipped to be a killer than poor David ever was.'

'Shelley told me you would find me out. She invited me round to her nicely public hotel lounge yesterday afternoon and said she was sure I was the one who'd killed Bruce. She announced she'd told you all about Bruce's allergy so it was no use killing her the way I had her sister-in-law.' Jan's voice became contemptuous. 'She's not only a bitch, she's stupid as well. It wasn't difficult to suggest that, for her sake'—the voice became a parody of loving concern—'I'd lay off, that she was safe, Mark was safe, you were safe, everyone was safe. After that it was easy. She wouldn't let me up to her room but she was happy to talk. My God, how she talked. All about her visit to you. All about your house. Did you know it really impressed her? She said it wasn't like Australia.' She mimicked bitterly Shelley's low, slow voice. 'That's all she could say about Italy, it was so different from Australia.' The mimicry was even harsher. 'That girl is totally uneducated—except about food. Food is the only thing in her whole life she has ever cared about.'

'So you heard about my meeting with Neil today and the fact that the cleaners would be working in the house. How did you manage to get them to leave you here? I thought they were reliable.'

'They thought I'd left after writing you a message. Men are so stupid, they think women are harmless. If I'd been a man, no doubt they'd have been more careful.'

Jan was silent for a moment. When she spoke again an unexpectedly hopeless quality had entered her voice. 'It's all been for nothing, that's what I can't stand. Even if it had all worked, I could never have taken Shelley where I'd hoped. She hasn't the potential. How could *I* have been so stupid? I was taken in by a pretty face, I had no more sense than bloody Bruce Bennett. How could either of us have thought she was worth it all?'

For a moment Darina thought the question might not be rhetorical, that Jan actually expected an answer from her. But the door bell was ringing. The police had arrived.

MANY HOURS LATER a very weary Darina was driven back to her Chelsea house and dragged herself out of the squad car, assuring the driver she was all right. She opened the front door, waved him off and went inside, once again locking and bolting the door behind her. She turned and saw a figure standing in the kitchen doorway. Fear flushed through her and the keys dropped from her hand.

Then the figure walked towards her and she saw who it was.

'William, darling!' In a moment she was in his arms.

'The case wound itself up much more quickly than we expected so I thought I would come up and join you. At least we could have Sunday together,' he explained, still holding her close. 'I arrived a little while ago to find the kitchen looking like a lion's cage that had lost its cleaner and no you. I can't tell you how worried I was. I rang the police immediately and eventually managed to find out something of what had happened. I said I'd come and collect you only to be told you'd just left.'

'Oh, I've never been so pleased to see anyone in my life,' she said, smiling at him, feeling her exhaustion begin to lift.

'Why on earth didn't you tell me about David Bartholomew's murder? I'd never have let you be alone this weekend if I'd known.' His hands roved round her body as though he had to convince himself she was still in one piece.

'Hush, it's all right, I'm fine. Did you have anything to eat before you left? No? You must be starving!'

She led the way into the kitchen, treading gingerly over the badly smeared and stained tiles, and started searching through what remained in the fridge. 'A few hours ago this was loaded with the results of a pâté-testing session. But a terrine and a liver pâté turned into substitute grenades. Pity, they came out rather well as pâtés and as grenades they were a dead loss. But there's hummus here and an aubergine caviare. Oh, and there's some nice Cheddar I brought up with me last Monday. We'll have to be vegetarian tonight.' She couldn't stop herself talking as she rescued dishes from the far reaches of the shelves, trying to stop her hands trembling. 'Would you like something hot? I've got some leek and potato soup somewhere, it wouldn't take long to heat through.' Darina opened the small deep-freeze section and started to rummage through that as well.

William gently pulled her away. 'This will do fine.' He piled her gleanings on to a tray. 'Let's take it through and leave this appalling mess. And I think both of us could do with a whisky.'

Darina glanced around the disordered room and shivered. 'I can't clear anything up, a forensic team is supposed to be coming round in the morning. God knows what they expect to find.' She opened a cupboard, took out a packet of the Prince of Wales's Duchy Biscuits, added plates and knives to the tray and followed William as he carried it through to the drawing room.

He placed the tray on the low table in front of the sofa, switched on the fire and poured them both whiskies. Darina stood watching him. She didn't feel able to decide how to sit down or where. He placed a glass in her hand and gently pressed her into a corner of the sofa, then sat down beside her.

'Now for God's sake tell me exactly what's been going on.'

Darina looked at his worried and concerned face and noted that the dark curly hair needed cutting. And the top button of his shirt was missing, at some stage he'd loosened his tie, the collar was adrift and she could see tiny holes where the threads had been. Had the button been missing the last time she washed the shirt?

'You say your case is wrapped up?'

He nodded. 'We've got enough evidence to put both suspects on the scene, the victim has picked out their photographs and I've no doubt she'll identify them when she's well enough. She's a very gutsy old girl. She keeps on saying she hopes she can prevent them victimizing anybody else. Oh, and the con merchant has slipped up at last. You remember that figurine? Well, we circulated a description on the stolen list and a very astute antiques dealer recognized it when it was offered to him, said he needed to consult his partner and got the man to come back later, by which time my London colleagues were waiting for him. All very satisfactory. But I want to hear about you. Can you bear to talk about it or would you rather just go to bed? You must have had a hell of a time. See what happens when I let you go off to London on your own?'

Gradually the warmth of the fire and the strength of the alcohol were reviving Darina. That and the carefully level tones of William's familiar voice. Slowly she started to tell him what had happened.

'Gatting got Shelley Bennett round to the station and is talking to her now,' she said finally. 'Jan has now changed her story and alleges that Shelley incited her to murder Bruce.'

'Do you think that's true?' William had listened quietly, asking the odd question every now and then to make sure he had the story straight.

'I think if so they are going to have a hard time proving it. Jan is very bitter at what she sees as Shelley's betrayal but Shelley is obviously going to stick to her story that she had no idea telling Jan about Bruce's allergy would prompt her to murder him. And at that stage Bruce was in Australia with neither of them aware of his plans to invest in Cantlow Productions so it's hard to see any lethal purpose in her betraying his Achilles' heel.'

'But surely Bruce would at least have mentioned his ambitions concerning British television? Shelley must have known about Neil's visit to Yarramarra, even if she wasn't there, so he would have been the obvious UK contact,' suggested William, leaning back in the sofa, cradling his whisky glass in his hands.

'But at the time Jan and Shelley were together in Italy, *Table* had a full team of presenters, the new series hadn't started and all the omens must have looked good. Even if Bruce had Neil in mind, there was little to suggest he would become part of the programme. It does seem more likely that, when Bruce suddenly appeared on the scene, Jan conceived the whole idea herself.'

'Based on what Shelley had told her.' It wasn't a question.

'I think Jan had built up the little relationship that had flowered in Italy into a major romance. She'd caught Shelley at a time when she was sexually vulnerable after suffering from Bruce's abuse. A loving relationship with Jan might have been just what she needed.'

'It sounds as though it was pretty shallow on her side.'

Darina shrugged. 'I think she's a pretty shallow girl. Bruce was a very attractive man but I don't suppose she would have married him if he hadn't owned Yarramarra. She's been out for herself ever since she arrived in England. Even if she isn't directly guilty of Bruce's death, I think she knew exactly what she was doing when she told Jan about his allergy. She recognized Jan's obsession with her and her driving ambition. I'm sure there were phrases used such as, "If only I had Yarramarra behind me, I could back you, together we could do such things. Maybe one day…" then leaving it to Jan to fill in the gaps. All on the off-chance it might just one day bear fruit. Jan may not have been the first she'd tried it with.'

'And if it hadn't been for that letter you received from Kate Bennett, it all might have worked out.'

Darina nodded. 'Jan must have seen it, guessed why she wanted to meet me and went round that night to get rid of her. A quick karate punch behind the ear, open the window and pitch out the body. To someone athletic and skilled in martial arts like Jan, it would have been too easy.

'Then when David got Shelley to back him, he wrote his death warrant.' Darina put down her drink. 'William, that's enough of murder, we have to talk. Was it really Bruce you were jealous of or my involvement in this television programme?'

His eyes were as watchful as hers. He picked up her hand, holding it in his, using his thumb to caress the back as he sighed deeply. 'Are you continuing with it? Will there be another series?' he asked, his voice carefully expressionless.

Darina's gaze dropped and she looked at her hand in his, feeling the touch of his thumb running over her skin and over the bones underneath the skin. She realized she didn't really know the back of her hand at all, what nonsense some sayings were. She forced herself to look at him again. 'I don't know. Neil's talking of another series and he wants me in it but, as things stand at the moment, I have no idea if it can survive this latest blow. But *Table*'s irrelevant, really. If another series doesn't come along, something else will. What I have to know is what you really feel about my career. Up until recently you've been supportive of all I've done but when *Table* came on the scene, everything changed.'

His mouth twisted in a small, rueful gesture that wasn't quite a smile. 'An empty house isn't much fun to come home to at the end of the day, I hadn't realized how much I was taking for granted.' His thumb stopped its caressing movement and he grasped her hand more tightly. 'But then neither is it much fun to sit evening after evening waiting for a husband who doesn't come home because he's caught up with a case, I do realize that.' He looked straight at her, appeal in his eyes. 'I don't want to lose you.'

'But you'd rather I wasn't spending so much time away.'

'Do you blame me?'

Darina shook her head.

William leaned closer towards her. 'Look, sweetheart, I want you, the whole of you, not someone bleeding because they've been asked to cut out part of themselves. I just want to know that you are equally committed to me. That I'm not going to lose you to the excitement of television or some hunk of an Aussie.'

Darina gave a snort that just avoided tears. 'Excitement of television, my foot! It's harder work than anything else I've ever done, including catering.'

'But you do get a buzz from it.'

'Yes,' she acknowledged slowly. 'I have to admit I do.'
Then she smiled at him, with warmth, intimacy. 'But not
nearly as much of a buzz as I get from you. And hunky Australians don't come into it at all!'

'As long as I know that, I don't mind anything else.'

A NEW YORK
STATE OF
CRIME

MICHAEL **JAHN**

DORIAN **YEAGER**

BARBARA **PAUL**

Three Tales of Murder Most Manhattan

MURDER ON FIFTH AVENUE by Michael Jahn

A killer is stalking the elegant stores on Fifth Avenue in a wave of murder that puts Captain Bill Donovan on the most perplexing case of his career.

LIBATION BY DEATH by Dorian Yeager

Vic Bowering is back, looking for an acting job, but she lands another mystery when she's hired as a bartender after the regular loses the gig to his own untimely death.

CLEAN SWEEP by Barbara Paul

This original short story spotlights Marian Larch's companion, Curt Holland. His effective—if not always exactly legal—computer investigation firm and team of brilliant hackers uncover a sweepstakes scam that's murder for the unlucky winners.

Available August 1999 at your favorite retail outlet.

Look us up on-line at: http://www.worldwidemystery.com   WNY317

GO CLOSE AGAINST THE
ENEMY
Takis & Judy Iakovou

A tragedy finds Nick and Julia Lambros, owners of the
Oracle Cafe in Delphi, Georgia, coming to the aid of April and
Davon Folsom, an interracial couple who want their stillborn
child buried in the church cemetery. But the predominantly
white congregation, led by Deacon Fry, stages a protest. Days
later, the deacon is found dead and April is accused of murder.

Thugs, threats and dark secrets get more dangerous by the
moment as Nick and Julia tackle a mystery that makes running a
restaurant seem like vacation.

Available July 1999 at your favorite retail outlet.

Look us up on-line at: http://www.worldwidemystery.com   WTJI314

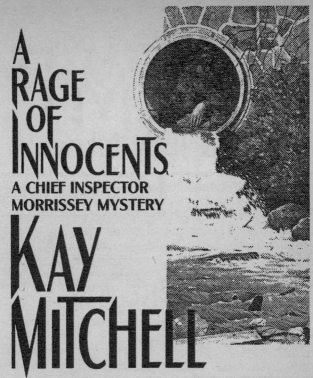

A RAGE OF INNOCENTS

A CHIEF INSPECTOR MORRISSEY MYSTERY

KAY MITCHELL

A MATTER OF LIFE AND DEATH

An alarming rise in violent crime puts Malminster's Chief Inspector Morrissey on the path to a conspiracy driven by the most passionate of motives—the desire for a baby.

Desperate individuals will go to any lengths to have one, while others will go to any lengths—including cold-blooded murder—to profit on those desires.

Available August 1999 at your favorite retail outlet.

Look us up on-line at: http://www.worldwidemystery.com

WKM318

FIXED
in his
FOLLY

David J. Walker

A MALACHY FOLEY MYSTERY

When high-powered attorney Harriet Mallory develops maternal instincts for the child she gave up for adoption thirty-one years ago, it's Mal Foley's reputation for discretion that lands him in her plush ofice.

But when he locates Harriet's son, now an alcoholic priest on a downward spiral, Foley discovers a man trapped in a maelstrom of vengeance and death. Threats targeting all of the priest's "family, friends and fools" are being systematically carried out. Foley's not sure if he's a friend or a fool, but he just may be the next to die.

Avaiable July 1999 at your favorite retail outlet.

Look us up on-line at: http://www.worldwidemystery.com   WDW315

SOUR GRAPES

NATASHA COOPER

A WILLOW KING MYSTERY

Now a full-time mother and bestselling writer, Willow King is content to leave crime solving to her police chief husband. But she can't resist a case involving Andrew Lutterworth, accused of a fatal hit-and-run that landed him in prison for manslaughter.

But what could motivate a man to admit to a crime he did not commit and willingly go to jail because of it? The truth behind the puzzle is as dark and perplexing as the human psyche.

Available August 1999 at your favorite retail outlet.

Look us up on-line at: http://www.worldwidemystery.com   WNC319